DARE

BROTHERS OF INK AND STEEL
BOOK ONE

AURORA WILDING

DARE
BROTHERS OF INK AND STEEL BOOK ONE

Previously written under the pen name: Allie Juliette
Mousseau

Published by Wilding Love Publishing, Inc.
Edited by Nicole Hewitt and Maria Vickers
Cover by Epic Daydreamer Designs

CONTENTS

Author's Note   v
DARE CHAPTER PLAYLIST   vii

Prologue   1
Chapter 1   11
Chapter 2   24
Chapter 3   35
Chapter 4   48
Chapter 5   59
Chapter 6   75
Chapter 7   96
Chapter 8   112
Chapter 9   128
Chapter 10   139
Chapter 11   155
Chapter 12   181
Chapter 13   200
Chapter 14   214
Chapter 15   242
Chapter 16   267
Chapter 17   279
Chapter 18   301
Chapter 19   322
Chapter 20   337
Chapter 21   350
Chapter 22   359
Chapter 23   377
Epilogue   382

A Final Note From The Author   385

About the Author   387

Also by Aurora Wilding   389

AUTHOR'S NOTE

Although fiction, this novel is based on true and
actual events.

DARE CHAPTER PLAYLIST

Prologue: "Face Down" The Red
  Jumpsuit Apparatus
Chapter One: "Savin' Me" Nickel-
  back & "We Own It" 2 Chainz
  with Wiz Khalifa
Chapter Two: "Glad You Came"
  The Wanted
Chapter Three: "Wonderwall"
  Oasis
Chapter Four: "Till I Collapse"
  Eminem
Chapter Five: "Contagious" Trapt
Chapter Six: "Down" Jason
  Walker
Chapter Seven: "Hysteria" Def
  Leppard
Chapter Eight: "Show Me What

I'm Looking For" Carolina
Liar
Chapter Nine: "Why Don't You &
I" Santana with Alex Band
Chapter Ten: "E.T." Katy Perry
Chapter Eleven: "The Other Side"
Jason Derulo
Chapter Twelve: "Stronger (What
Doesn't Kill You)" Kelly
Clarkson
Chapter Thirteen: "The River"
Good Charlotte with M.
Shadows
Chapter Fourteen: "Can't Help
Falling in Love (Fools Rush In)"
Michael Buble
Chapter Fifteen: "Survival"
Eminem
Chapter Sixteen: "Beautiful Pain"
Eminem
Chapter Seventeen: "The Fighter"
Gym Class Heroes
Chapter Eighteen: "Strong
Enough" Sheryl Crowe
Chapter Nineteen: "Are You with
Me" Trapt
Chapter Twenty: "Empire"
Shakira

Chapter Twenty-one: "You're
    Going Down" Sick Puppies
Chapter Twenty-two: "Safe &
    Sound" Taylor Swift with The
    Civil Wars
Chapter Twenty-three: "Unpack
    Your Heart" Phillip Phillips

DEDICATION

For the girls and women who deserve better.

DARE

PROLOGUE
BELLA

THREE YEARS AGO

I hear his car pull into the parking lot of my apartment building. I know it's his car because of the angry, violent screech of the tires. My body begins to shake from an adrenaline spike as I race to the window to confirm it—I've been on high alert since I'd moved into my own place two months ago after Emma was born.

The car is bathed in the glow of the streetlight, and I watch as his silhouette rises out of it—hulking, imposing. He leans into the back seat for a moment and pulls something out before he slams the driver's door shut, making me jump. That all-too-familiar pounding of my heart kicks into high gear. Thank God Emma is sleeping.

Quickly, I dial 911 and position the phone

into the crook of my shoulder to hold it against my ear. The operator answers.

I almost whisper in an attempt to keep Emma asleep and control my breathing, but the blood is rushing through my ears, making my heartbeat sound louder and louder.

"I'm at 511 Blue Grass Apartments, and my husband, who has a restraining order against him, is coming up the stairs, and he has a weapon."

The operator says something in an attempt to comfort me and begins peppering me with stupid questions that are just a waste of time, and even worse, a distraction. I reach into the kitchen drawer while grunting yes and no into the receiver until my fingers find the cold metal I've been looking for.

Holding the pistol carefully, I check the clip, load the chamber and remove the safety. Cupping my left palm under the hilt to steady my grip, I move soft-footedly toward the front door and peer out the peephole. He comes up the stairs noiselessly. Bile comes into my throat when I see that his right hand stays hidden behind his back while his left hand wraps around the doorknob as he tests the lock. The bolt holds fast.

Horror washes over me. He would have broken in if he could have. I swallow and try to force the image of what *would have* happened if that door hadn't been locked and I hadn't been ready out of my mind.

He swears under his breath before knocking on the door. "Hey, Bella, are you home? I need to talk to you." His voice is sickeningly sweet.

His right arm is still tucked up behind his back, and I wonder what he's hiding.

When I don't answer, he knocks harder and repeats himself louder.

I bend at the knees and set the phone down on the carpet in front of the door. I'm waiting— for his next move, for my own courage, for the police to show up. He's quiet for a moment. Slowly, I come back up to look out the peephole again. At that moment, he pounds on the door with the full force of his fist.

Startled, my breath hitches, and I jump back and aim the pistol at the door.

I wonder if all of this would end if I sent a bullet sailing into the dark grain of the wood. It's not that thick of a door, so the bullet would go through. It would prove to him I mean business. If I got lucky, it would kill him.

Is there a law about self-defense and shooting your attacker through a door? Probably, but we both know he exists above the law.

"LET ME THE FUCK IN, BELLA!" he shouts.

When it was only me, he could make me

quake and beg for mercy, but Emma has given me a new will, a new strength and a new sense of power I won't let him strip me of. For the past year, I've tried to protect myself from him, but I've failed. I *will* protect *her* from him with my very life.

My index finger curls around the trigger. I feel the give of the weapon as I press my flesh against the crescent-shaped steel. He shouts obscenities at me, every vile word he can probably think of. If the police won't come for me, they'll certainly come for my neighbors, who I'm sure have called them. Of course, not one will open their door to confront him, but I don't really blame them. We live in low-income housing, and the other three apartments in the building are occupied by a disabled man and his family and single moms and their kids.

"Hey, what's going on?" I hear a male voice ask.

I freeze, the pistol still aimed. *Who the hell is it?*

"Nothing. Just trying to get *my wife* to open the door so I can see my kid!" he roars scathingly.

"Why do you have the butt end of a pool stick behind your back?" another man's voice questions.

So that's what he was hiding, the thick half of his pool stick. I shudder, realizing what it must have been intended for—beating me.

"How about you hand it to me, Jim? I don't want any trouble."

The man calls my husband by name. I bring the gun to my side and look out the peephole again. Three police officers have him surrounded and seem to be trying to talk him down. I know these officers—they're Jim's coworkers and friends.

"Let me talk to you for just a minute," Jim says more softly, and I realize he's slurring his words.

Two of the officers, one named Chris and another guy whose name I can't remember, move away from the door with him to talk by the stairs.

Arrest him! I breathe out, silently screaming.

A moment passes, and Chris nods as if he understands whatever Jim is saying. He then knocks with an air of authority against my door.

I quietly step back into the kitchen, hide the pistol in the drawer and speak against the only barrier between Jim and myself and my daughter —the door.

"What do you want, Chris?" I'm incredulous. "Why isn't he being hauled off in cuffs?"

"Bella, I need you to open the door," Chris says, semi-ordering.

"I can't open that door," I respond firmly.

"Bella, he only wants to see the baby," Chris urges. "And we're right here, so nothing's going to happen. But he won't leave until you let him make sure Emma is all right."

"She's fine," I hiss through my teeth. "It's after midnight, so she's obviously sleeping."

"We're going to have a problem if you don't open the door," Chris warns. "I don't want to have to get a warrant to search the premises."

And there it is. They'll side with him. Again. They'll make up some bogus reason to get a search warrant, and they'll bring Jim in with them, restraining order be damned.

The anger rises volcanically within me as I let my fingers twist the locks and turn the knob. I throw open the door. Chris enters first, his blue police uniform betraying his true loyalties. Jim follows him and glares at me threateningly while the other uniformed officers bring up the rear.

"She's sleeping," I remind them.

Jim doesn't care. He takes long strides into Emma's room, escorted by his own parade. Officer Chris Blakely looks down at his shoes. I think he must have had a mother to teach him right from wrong, and he knows what he's doing right now is not only wrong but illegal.

"Just because he's your friend doesn't change what he's doing," I say, folding my arms over my chest furiously.

"He didn't hurt you; he just wants to see the

baby," Chris deflects, picking his arrogance back up like a shield.

"You're breaking the law! You know I have a restraining order against him," I retort. "He doesn't even have visitation rights—they were revoked!"

He winces a little. "We'll make sure we escort him off the property as soon as he's satisfied."

"You're kidding, right!?" I keep my voice down for Emma's sake. "What do you think he was going to do with the butt end of his pool stick? Do you see a pool table in here?" My tone is sarcastic.

"He stated that you had the other half."

"I don't have anything!" I snap. I can see I'm not getting anywhere, so I try reasoning with him "Do you know how he came up here? He tried to break in silently, working the door until he realized he couldn't get through the bolt. He was going to beat the shit out of me—either that or kill me. *How could you let him in?*" I feel the heat of my rage rise into my cheeks, reddening them. I pull my fingers through my hair and feel my hands shaking.

"He's a good cop, Bella."

"Right, and so are you," I say cuttingly.

I watch my soon-to-be ex-husband walk back out into the living room. He makes himself at home and sits on my sofa, holding Emma's sleeping form.

A cop I don't know stands over him like a babysitter. Jim doesn't even care; he knows he has the department wrapped around his finger. He grew up with these guys and went to school with these guys; they have a history together. They've all been friends for years. In this town, I don't stand a chance. It's his town.

"Bella, you know he's an ingrained part of our force. He had a little too much to drink, but he didn't see it through," Chris continues. "No harm, no foul."

I want to spit on him. "Have you forgotten he pointed his shotgun at my head and threatened to kill me? Or that when I tried to leave him, he told me if I didn't stay, he'd make me a paraplegic?"

Shame passes over Chris's features.

"Can I talk to you in the other room?" Lee, Chris's partner, asks me.

When I look back toward Emma and Jim, Chris assures me, "I've got this. He's not going anywhere with us here."

Even though I don't like it, I follow Lee into the nursery. He checks over his shoulder, and when he feels confident we're alone, he turns to me and quickly says, "Watch your back, Bella. He's out for blood. He says the first chance he gets, he's going to take the baby and run."

I let my mouth form the word, "Kidnap?"

Lee nods his head. "He said he'll kill you if he has to, but he's going to get Emma one way or the other."

My breath rattles in my lungs. "Arrest him! I have a restraining order; he broke it tonight and confessed to *you* what he's planning on doing next."

Lee's eyes trail away from mine to graze over the large, colorful alphabet I made that hangs on the wall in Emma's nursery. "He plays golf with the police chief. And the judge you got to give you that order moved back to the city last month. None of the judges here now will hold him in contempt."

I can't believe what he's saying. Is he actually saying I have no protection?

Lee's gaze meets my eyes. "He's insulated here, Bella."

"What am I supposed to do?" I whisper as the feeling of desperation wraps itself around my mind.

CHAPTER ONE

JOSH

PAST

*A*ll *my shit is packed and ready to go for me,* I think with sarcastic malice, seeing the two fucking suitcases at the bottom of the stairs right by the door.

You're welcome to get the fuck out.

I'm furious with my parents. "How could you do it? How could you send me away?"

"Because you're in trouble, son … and it's a kind of trouble even our love ain't fixing. Cade is family, and he deals with this kind of thing every day. He'll be able to help you through this pain, Josh."

Fuck my pain! Fuck Uncle Cade. "It looks like you're giving up on me; that's what it looks like! I've heard of the kids who get sent to those places

—no parents, no families who care about them— they get dumped! Because their parents don't want them anymore! And why would they, after they fucked up so bad they can't be forgiven!" A tornado of fury tears me apart from the inside out.

My dad firmly holds my shoulders straight and makes me look at him. "Joshua Levi North, we are family. There is no stronger bond than that. We love you and want you more than our own lives, boy! This is temporary, so you don't have to be surrounded by it *every day*—it's here at home, at school, the arcade, the skateboard park, every street you walk on in this town— the memories are only making you angrier." My dad's eyes soften. "It wasn't your fault, Josh."

"I wasn't there when he needed me! If I'd been there, he would've talked to *me*; he would have let me know what happened. HE WOULDN'T HAVE DONE IT!" Rage I have no control over and can't stop pours out of me. "IT WAS MY FAULT!"

My dad looks calm and sad. I hate that I'm putting him through this, and my mom and everybody else in my family. It makes me hate myself more.

He *doesn't* stop the discussion. "We all have our own choices in this life. He chose a direction—you had nothing to do with that decision, and you couldn't have stopped it once he decided it."

I don't buy it. It's too fucked up! He was my best friend. I could have stopped him. I could have changed it. I could have made it right! I could have reminded him what he meant to me.

"Fuck this shit!" I hate my dad for doing this to me. "I'll just be like the bastard son you all don't talk about."

Dad grabs my chin in his big hand—it's a strong hand, powerful, just like the man it's attached to. I'm being a mouthy, sixteen-year-old asshole, and I know it; this isn't how I speak to my father.

But I'm not me anymore, am I? Isn't that what this is all about, after all?

"We love you, Josh," he assures me.

It's true; love radiates from his eyes. But I can't *feel* it. It doesn't touch me.

"But I'm trash now," I say. "The kind you take out to the curb on a Sunday night and never see again."

"Colt, maybe this isn't the best idea." My mom has been listening. She comes around the threshold and stands to the side between us. She's looking at me—her face is tear-streaked, and her hand shakes next to her mouth.

I'm hurting my mom. I'm. Hurting. My. Mom! I might be sixteen years old and have already had a string of girlfriends, but I don't love anyone as much as my mom. I'm hurting too many people. Me. I am. I don't know how to stop!

And that brings out the son-of-a-bitch kid. "And what about the other kid, Dad?" I ask quietly. "Is there forgiveness for *that*, Dad? 'Cause I don't think God forgives for *that*! *That* I did on purpose. I threw the punch, and I can't go back and undo what I did." I laugh, and it's maniacal. "I can't even feel sorry about it! How fucked up is that? And don't you lie to me! I hear people talking. I'm a big, ugly stain on the North name and reputation in this town … maybe that's the real reason you want to get rid of me."

Mom breaks down crying. My dad's eyebrows press down—they always do when he's thinking hard. He nods and then says slowly, "People talk. They can be ugly, judgmental, and just plain hypocritical. Truth is, we've all had our struggles, son. Them, me, your mom. And your struggles, for a young man of your age … not one of those people can talk because I'm sure none of them has dealt with what you've had to. If they'd shut their mouths and understand …" My dad puts his hand on the nape of my neck—it's loving and affectionate. "I can understand a portion of your struggle, but I dealt with mine differently. Uncle Cade, on the other hand, dealt with it just like you are."

I have to admit, my uncle is fucking awesome for a guy almost as old as my dad. He owns a mixed martial arts gym and training center in Minnesota—where he and my dad are from. His house is a place for fucked up kids to go, who, now like me, can't get their shit together.

"What are you going to tell people when they ask where I am?" My tone tells them that I've surrendered as I stare down blankly at my black Chucks and Van Halen t-shirt.

"Boarding school in Vancouver that specializes in kids readying themselves for professional athletics." My dad forces a grin. He thinks he's crafty.

I'll admit it. He is.

"I'm sorry for my foul language, Mom."

"I understand, baby. I love you so much." She suffocates me in her version of a goodbye hug.

I hug her back, and then my dad walks me out to the driveway where my Uncle Cade is waiting for me in his black, classic '74 Camaro.

"I'm scared, Dad," I confess before I get into that car to leave the only home I know. "What if I'm so lost, I can't find myself ever again?"

He puts an arm around my shoulders and moves in close. "Don't let the fear defeat you, Josh. We all fall apart, and we all lose ourselves in this life. You've got to dare to push through the fear. You've got to dare to find the broken pieces and put yourself back together. And when you can't find all the pieces, you have to dare to be stronger so new ones can grow in their place. That's when you'll find your true self and be whole again."

JOSH
PRESENT

I WATCH AS THE BRIGHT ORANGE AND YELLOW flames consume the house. It's mesmerizing, really, the way fire destroys. Each lick of flame devours whatever's in its path. The guys and I are working to keep the fiery hell contained. The house is old and situated close to a tent camp, one of the temporary residences for the nine thousand oil rig workers here in Williston, North Dakota, who are working to get a piece of the fortune that can be made from the oil boom. Don't blame them, really—Walmart's starting salary is at seventeen bucks an hour while rig workers are pocketing triple digits per hour—but they're all packed in here like fucking sardines. If one of those makeshift huts catches, they'll all catch, and wouldn't you fucking know it, the wind is pick-ing up.

The downstairs windows blow out, sending shards of glass onto the porch. Lace curtains flutter out of the window as they're ravaged by the fire. The chief yells instructions to the men working the hoses when something in the upstairs window catches my eye.

The guy who got out of the house right before we arrived is standing about twenty feet away from me, choking his ass off. He told us he'd been the only one inside.

"Are you sure no one else was in the house with you?" I shout over the chaos.

"No, man," he coughs out, but he looks to the ground like he has something to hide.

And there it is again. The shadow of a small child passes by the window; there is no mistaking it.

"YOU LEFT A KID IN THERE?!" I yell at him.

Asshole buckles to the ground in a coughing fit, tears streaming from his eyes and nods.

I hate assholes!

I run full-out to the house, or what's left of it, and take the porch steps two at a time.

"NORTH!" the chief yells.

"KID!" I shout as I point up to the window.

I kick open the door and push myself inside. To the right of me is what used to be the living room. I can see a sofa and coffee table that are

17

now nearly unrecognizable. To my left are the stairs to the second floor, or what's left of them.

Fuck me.

The staircase collapses under my weight when I'm about halfway up. As I feel it give way, I push off, reaching for the landing above me. My gloved hands catch, but I don't find enough purchase. The railing on the wall saves me from a nasty fall, and I pull myself up the rest of the way.

Finding young kids in fires sucks, and that shadow was small. Kids are usually so afraid they hide. The air is almost gone in here, and I'm praying the kid is close to the floor. Usually, they hide under a bed or in a closet.

I take a deep breath before I pull down my oxygen mask. "HEY, LITTLE BUDDY!" I shout out. "WHERE ARE YOU?"

No one responds. "I'M A FIREMAN. I'M HERE TO HELP YOU!"

A weak and faint "Over here" reaches my ears.

It's coming from my right—down the hall. There are three rooms on that side. Time is of the essence if we're both going to make it out of here alive. I've thrown my lot in with this kid—if he dies, I die, 'cause I'm not leaving without him.

"I KNOW YOU'RE SCARED, BUT I'M GOING TO GET YOU OUT OF HERE, OKAY?"

"Okay."

I move toward the small voice. "WHAT'S YOUR NAME?"

"Henry." He doesn't sound much older than six or seven.

Now, I'm in his room. I can still see the blue of the wall paint behind the fire and a toy box with strewn toys in the corner, but I can't see much else. The room is filling with smoke fast.

"I need to find you, Henry," I urgently say while trying to make my voice confident. But time is running short.

He doesn't answer. I quickly check under the bed. Nope.

"I have a puppy outside—a black and white spotted Dalmatian, just like in *101 Dalmatians*." The closet door is on fire. I open it wide as it literally deteriorates in my hand. I don't see him. I push through the smoke and the clothes. "Do you want to go see him?"

"Yes." The voice comes from behind me.

"Buddy, you've got to tell me where you are."

The heat is unbearable. I'm using my helmet's light, but the smoke is so thick now I can only faintly make out where the window is because of the fire trucks' lights bouncing off the walls.

"I … I'm s-s-scared," his voice stutters.

I rush in the direction of the sound, and there

he is, lying at the bottom of the empty toy box, clutching a teddy bear.

"Hey, Henry." I smile. "Don't be scared, I know the way out."

Lifting him out of the toy box, I hug him close to me before I put my boot through the window and begin kicking as much glass out of the frame as I can. A moment later, a fireman's hands reaches through. I hear the floor beneath me groan in protest as if it's demanding a sacrifice. I shove the boy into the safety of waiting arms, but before I can see the other firefighter's face clearly, I feel my body break through the floor as it plummets into the hungry fire below.

I HATE HOSPITALS MORE THAN MOST PEOPLE DO, but I try hard not to think of the reason for that; it won't help my situation.

My chief is pissed. My trainers are pissed. My brothers are pissed. The only reason my parents aren't pissed is because they're in Europe, and I swore my brothers, Caleb and Jake, along with my brother-in-law Nate to secrecy. That included not sharing the news with their significant others. I don't need more people in here telling me what I did was stupid or heroic or asking me what the fuck I was thinking.

My actions had been neither stupid nor heroic; I had simply been doing my job. I found out later that the "asshole" had been staying with the little boy while his mother was at work—they'd been dating for a couple of weeks. Douchebag had been wasted on God knows what when he fell asleep with a lit cigarette. Apparently, he didn't want to admit that he'd gotten himself out and left the kid, so he thought it'd be better just not to mention him—the kind of logic that only makes sense to someone who's wasted.

I've been positioned onto my stomach for the past few days as my back heals. I get to watch what's going on around me through a mirror placed under my face. I can still see my chief perfectly as he's standing next to me, reaming me a new one, though.

When he's finished, I say, "Just make sure the kid gets to see the puppies at the firehouse." I wheeze in a breath. "Better yet, give him one."

"Josh, you make me a fucking lunatic!" The chief leans down close my ear. "You came too close to dying. Maybe you can exhibit a little more self-control next time."

"Did the kid live?" I rasp out.

"Yeah, the kid lived, smartass," the chief concedes. "Get better, son."

The fall had given me a couple of hairline

fractures in my spine, and I had pulled muscles in my right leg and arm.

After the chief leaves, I have to deal with the real heavy hitters, my training team. I hear them walk into the room and wait for a new round of lectures. In three months, I have a main card fight to defend my title against Patrick Dalloway.

"Good thing you're in such great shape, North. The doctor said it'll only take a few weeks to recover from the muscle strains. Same with your back, but you're going to have to take it easy and won't be able to start heavy training again until next month," Coach grits through his teeth in frustration.

I groan. No training for a month sounds ridiculous. I'm sure I can push up that date.

"Don't even think about pushing up that date or trying to help speed things along," he barks, reading my mind. "You're still a man made of flesh and bone like the rest of us."

"Yeah, but unlike the rest of you, I have a whole lot of muscle," I jeer before I break into a coughing fit. *Fucking smoke inhalation.*

"Save your strength, pretty boy," I hear McGee, my third coach in command, instruct.

I have three main coaches who arrange my training, accompany me to fights and make sure I'm on track at all times. They're pretty much my caretakers. Silva, Caruso and McGee.

"The hospital hired a massage therapist a couple months ago. They say she can work wonders, and she'll be here to work on you in just a few minutes," McGee says as a nurse comes by and shoots a syringe of clear liquid into my IV drip.

I watch through my mirror as Caruso walks slowly past me, examining me.

"Don't be your normal self and hit on her first thing," he says gruffly. "If she's really as good as her recommendations say, she could be a good addition to your training entourage, keeping you limber for your fights."

"So, what then? No happy ending?" I joke. I'm not going to be able to stay awake much longer; whatever the nurse put in my IV is taking me down fast.

"Exactly that!" Silva snaps.

Someone taps on the door, and I hear a feminine voice call into the room, "Hello, I'm Sophie."

CHAPTER TWO

SOPHIE

C lutching my clipboard as if it could shield me from these three hulking men whose physical presence exudes danger and authority, I step into the room. I can't quite conjure a smile, but I can project a businesslike attitude and focus on the patient.

"Hello, Sophie." One of the men leans in and offers his beefy hand for me to shake. "I'm Carlo Silva. The hospital staff can't say enough good things about you."

"Thank you. But I'm definitely not the town hero like our patient here." I look toward the man who is lying face down on the hospital bed.

"I'm not a hero," I hear the softly muffled voice speak self-deprecatingly toward the floor.

"Just remember," another man comes closer,

"his bark is worse than his bite." He smiles disarmingly, and I can't help but smile back. The patient had just been given a dose of morphine; he wasn't going to have much bark or bite.

The three men exit the room and leave me to my work. "Talk is, you saved a little boy from a house fire."

"You can't believe everything you hear." His voice is ragged from too much smoke inhalation.

I wonder how true that is. The talk of the hospital for the past week has been all about Josh "The Jackhammer" North—city firefighter and national Mixed Martial Arts title holder—especially from the female staff. Apparently, he's a serious hottie with commitment issues who has a rep for being a man-whore, but not a womanizer. Perfect weekend fling material, I've heard. He'll treat you very right; just remember, it's not forever. I've never been into guy sharing that way, but I have to admit his celebrity has made me curious.

"Well, how about that Josh North took a nasty fall during a house fire and sustained muscle damage and a fractured spine."

"Sounds about right." He groans. "Come closer to the mirror. I want to see who that pretty voice belongs to."

"Maybe next time, Romeo. I have work to

do," I quip lightheartedly. "You may have noticed I turned up the heat in the room. I'll keep your back and arms covered for now, but I'm going to lower your sheet and start with your legs."

"Perfect place to start." He coughs a little but sounds as if he's ready to fall asleep.

I fold the sheet down and can't help but let my eyes rake over his perfectly sculpted legs. Each muscle is ridged and defined. Intricate, black-inked mandala designs highlighted with tribal art adorn each calf muscle and trail onto his upper legs. Feeling like a child about to dig into a rich dessert, I can't wait to sink my fingers into his muscles.

Pouring the almond oil into my palm, I work my hands together to heat the oil before I touch it to his skin. I begin on his right calf, gently warming the muscle so I can begin kneading it. On the outside right calf, he has a black script tat that reads, *He who is not every day conquering some fear has not learned the secret of life.*

"Are you an Emerson fan?"

"Yeah, I am." He sounds half asleep.

"Nice." I slide my hands from his ankle, up his calf to his upper thighs, and sink my fingers into the muscles that are waiting for me there. He moans, and I can't pretend I'm not affected. After I clear my throat, I continue, "Look fear in the face. We must do that which we think we cannot."

I can hear the smile in his voice. "Eleanor Roosevelt."

"You seem pretty smart for a guy who likes to get wrecked for a living."

"Come closer so I can see you." His words run together. "There could be a happy ending after all."

"A what?"

The next sound I hear is Josh snoring. He's out like a light.

"So it *is* true! Tell me, are the rumors true?" Ayana, my roommate, grills me before I even get through the front door.

"Do you mind if I put my bags down before we leap into your *please give me the R rated version of your day* moment?" I laugh.

"Fine," she concedes. "Hello, Miss Charlie!"

Charlotte lets go of my hand and runs into Ayana's embrace.

"I made your favorite—fish sticks and French fries," Ayana coos into Charlie's ear, making her giggle.

I laugh at them as I wriggle out of my jacket and hang it in the closet. Pulling Charlie back to me, I work her coat off as she dances and spins around. "Go get washed up for dinner, sassy-pants." Playfully, I give her little bottom a tap, and she runs off into the bedroom we share.

"Honestly, Sophie, these are the bragging rights you've earned and deserve when you put that sparkly new graduation certificate to use," Ayana sing-songs as she moves back toward the small kitchen table she was situating with plates. "Is Josh North as hot in real life as he is on the magazine covers?"

I roll my eyes. "I've never seen any of the magazines he's been on."

"Of course you haven't! I knew you were going to say that." She's mockingly disgusted. "That is why I, your smartest friend, went to the library this afternoon and got these!" she squeals as she litters the center of the table with popular, glossy photo magazines.

I look over the covers. The word "hot" doesn't do Josh North descriptive justice. Scorching? Volcanic? Meteoric?

"Is he really that gorgeous?" She gets into my face, demanding the truth.

"Um …" Shit, I know I'm blushing. "He's lying face down on a hospital bed; I didn't get to see his face."

"Yeah, you just got to see his ass!" she says, calling me out.

"Oh my God—yes, I did!" Her enthusiasm extracts the truth. "And I've never seen legs so cut." I snatch up the *Sports Illustrated* that he adorns the cover of. He's in a fighter's stance.

"Did he make a pass at you?" I can tell she's expecting a juicy answer.

I bark out a laugh. "He *passed* out."

Ayana laughs. "Ah, meds." Ay is a nurse at the hospital on the night shift. "Well, I wonder about Josh's *other* jackhammer."

"AY!" I slap her arm.

"What's a jackhammer, Auntie Ay?" Charlie's innocent little voice questions from behind us.

"He's a patient and athlete Mommy is working with," I answer as she climbs into my lap.

"Is this him?" She points to a Josh North I've never seen before—he stands on the cover of *GQ* in a crisp, black tux.

"Yes, that's him, but to me, he looks more like …" I flip the magazine backside up on the table, "that."

"You're silly," Charlie decides of me. She slides from my lap and squiggles into her seat.

Ay puts food on each of our plates. When she sits, she says, "When do you work his torso?"

I smile in spite of myself. "Tomorrow."

"THAT WAS NOT THE WAY I WANTED OUR introductory conversation to end," Josh explains the next day. He's alone in his room this time, still face down in the bed, his voice still raspy.

"Don't worry about it. Heavy pain meds do that for a reason. The more you let your body rest, the sooner it heals."

"Holy shit! How did my coach just throw his voice into your mouth?" he quips good-naturedly.

"I'm going to fold your top blanket down to work on your arms and back." I bring the covers over the lower half of his body.

His back, arms and shoulders are as perfect as his legs and ass. His muscles, even relaxed, bulge. I slide my hands over the planes of his back, from ass to neck, very gently, on either side of his spine. He has a black and white yin and yang tattooed between his shoulder blades over his spine. It's surrounded by twelve oriental symbols or letters.

My hands glide over the art of his muscle and ink, and I feel like I'm making love to him. I pride myself on melding my body with my client's when I work, but this is entirely different. I feel the difference in my heartbeat, my quickening breath and the sweet, familiar ache between my thighs.

Smoothly, my hands and fingers work over the black tribal tattoos inked on both of his highly defined arms. His biceps clench as I reach them.

"Relax …" I barely get the word out.

"I can't," he says breathily. Sexily.

His forearms are beautiful and thick with

corded muscle. I've always been an arm girl. I don't know what it is about arms, but they turn me on more than any other body part—except for maybe eyes—and these are the finest arms I've ever touched.

The tats continue over both his hands, and I follow them to the ends of his strong fingers. I rub each one before I flow back up to his swollen shoulders.

As I knead down and into his left ribs, I trail over the quote etched in ink there: *I Am My Brother's Keeper.* I wonder at the meaning behind it.

On his right side, in cursive script, is the quote, "Do the thing you fear the most." I read it out loud.

"Mark Twain," he informs me.

I consider the script on his leg about fear, and I wonder what he's striving to conquer. And if he's beaten it yet.

Moving down, my hands cup his hip. His body now glistens with the sheen of the sweet almond oil I've rubbed into him. I consider myself a medical paraprofessional, but my next move doesn't feel professional at all. It feels animal and hungry. My fingertips dig into the muscles of his ass.

He moans, and my eyes fall closed. I don't speak, and I try desperately not to think as I knead and press and push. I fail. The slickness growing between my legs reminds me that I'm human and I'm a woman. I've never had this reaction with a client before. But I've never had Josh North as a client before.

"Sweetheart, you're killing me," he exclaims, and I feel his hips pushing against the mattress. That can't be easy with the fractures in his back.

I'm sure he has a hard-on, and I feel a small smile tug at the corners of my lips in satisfaction over the fact that I'm the one who gave it to him.

"I apologize," he says. "I was given strict orders to be on my best behavior with you, but you rubbing *there* is *not* going to be conducive to that end result."

"Your gluteus maximus is a connective muscle that needs to be included in your healing." *Oh my God, I'm dying!*

The oxygen empties from his body as he strives to relax into my grip. The words that he just said finally seem to make it to the language sensors in my brain.

"Best behavior?" I pull down the curve of his ass to drift down his legs.

I love your artwork, Josh, I think in my head as if I spoke the words out loud and as if he and I were close, intimate friends. I wonder how many of the stories in the articles about him that I devoured last night in those magazines Ay brought home are fiction. They made him out to be an indifferent, unattached and unapologetic bachelor who's been seen in the most exclusive venues with the most popular starlets and models.

"Yeah, I … um …" he starts to say before switching gears. "Wait a minute, you said something yesterday about Emerson and Eleanor Roosevelt when I rudely checked out on you."

"Nothing rude about it. I'm glad to have relaxed you so much."

"Yeah, well, you're doing anything *but* now."

"Excuse me?"

"Nothing. Did you study philosophy?" he attempts to recover.

"Only a little, but I really enjoyed it," I confess. "Did you?"

"I majored in philosophy," he says matter-of-factly.

My hands stop as I try to compute that one.

"University of Minnesota." He chuckles at my mute response. "No one ever believes me."

"I believe you. I'm just surprised," I admit.

"Did you study philosophy?" he asks again.

"I probably would've taken more classes on it if I'd gone to a four-year university. Taking care of Charlie and studying was a real strain on both of us. Massage in the medical community has strong career potential and didn't take four years." I pause to think for just a second. "You've made some interesting career choices for a philosopher."

"I guess I have," he says lightly.

Fighting, fear, philosophy, I muse to myself. And just like that, Josh becomes a puzzle I'd like to solve.

CHAPTER THREE
JOSH

PAST

"I'm not sharing my room with this motherfucker for anything!" Liam shouts, pointing at me. "I don't care if he is your blood! He's a douchebag!"

"Look who's calling who a douchebag!" I lunge at him, and we roll across the floor in the bedroom that we're forced to co-exist in.

Liam gets the upper hand. He's got me by at least fifteen pounds. He pins me and punches me twice across the jaw. The pain is refreshing. It makes me smile manically. I needed this. I'd been trying to be the "perfect" North to save face for my family since I got to Cade's hell house a week ago.

Most of the kids here hate each other vehemently. Some of them are from rival inner-city gangs; others are just passing through until they're assigned to the next foster home; some are runaways, others are unwanted, homeless delinquents, and a few others are "weekenders" —kids who are kicked out of their homes when Mommy wants to bring home a boyfriend for the weekend and doesn't want her baggage to be seen.

It fucking sucks for all of us, but I don't give a shit about their problems, I've got my own.

Liam, my roommate, is all into this girl who's been here for a while, and he didn't like that I was talking to her. He warned me, but that only made me laugh as I put my arm around her to get him more worked up. And now, here we are.

I can taste the blood and salt from my lip, and it feeds my frenzy like a shark. I punch Liam in the ribs and throw him off of me. I turn, get to my feet and swing at him hard and fast, so many times that I lose count.

Cade pulls me off of him. Wrong move. I turn my fury against my uncle.

I don't connect once; he blocks my every swing. The frustration makes me see red.

"When you fight angry, boy, you'll lose every time," he calmly instructs like he isn't involved in an all-out fistfight with someone way younger than he is.

Out of my peripheral, I see Liam kneeling on the floor next to the wall, trying to get back up.

"Fuck you!" I rage at my uncle.

"You could put all of this energy into the bags," he reminds me.

"I'm not going to your fucking gym! I'm leaving! I hate it here!" His stupid training center is set up to *help* troubled teens like me "release the negative energy they're holding and channel it positively." Fuck that! Makes me want to puke! I'd heard the lecture all week from him, his wife and his crony followers like Liam here, for whom the training center is the sun of the freaking universe.

We're still in the bedroom, but the other kids are trying to jam themselves in to watch us. Fucking perfect! I can't get a punch in, and all of them are going to see it. I'll lose the little clout I've built and will get treated like a fucking pariah.

In an instant, my uncle wheels me around and twists my arm behind my back. The pain is unbearable. "That's enough of that."

"Oh, come on!" some kids protest.

"They were pretty equally matched," my uncle states.

"Bullshit," I bark.

Liam spits a mouthful of blood at me. "Fuck you!"

"If either of you want a rematch, it'll have to be in the ring." Cade walks me out of the room.

I'm at his mercy as he puts me in the isolation room for the night. It's the only room in the house with a lock on the outside of the door and bars on the triple-pane window. "Cool off, Josh."

PRESENT

"Does Sophie wear a ring?" I ask.

McGee takes one stern look at me. "Don't even think about it!"

"That's rich," Caruso chuckles from the other side of the room over his *Fight* mag.

"I didn't mean it like that," I lie. "If Silva's having a meeting with her to see if she'll come on as a full-time member of the training team, I'm just wondering if she has a significant other to consider in her decision." I have to figure out who this guy named Charlie is.

"Bullshit some other bullshitter." McGee is emptying a gym bag of my clothes into the hospital drawers.

"I've hardly even seen her face." I've seen her plenty in my little mirror.

"Doesn't matter, asshat, she's had her hands all over you," Caruso laughs.

"Now, that's true." I smile at the recollection of those soft, adept hands.

"Okay, Mr. North." Two nurses and the doctor file into the room. "We're going to get you up today and turn you over." The lead nurse smiles kindly as she tugs at the sheets over me. "Won't that be a relief to get back to normal again?"

Only if Sophie accepts Silva's offer.

I'm poked, prodded and mucked with for an hour before the staff feels confident in my progress. After turning me over onto my back and letting me recline naturally in the bed, they bombard me with warnings and cautions to not be so reckless and to be careful 'cause another bad injury could end both of my careers.

I get it. Christ! Enough already.

Just as they're walking out, Silva comes walking in.

"How did the meeting go?" I ask too eagerly. In the past week, I've been trying to analyze my affections toward Sophie. I won't deny that part of (okay, a lot of) the energy is carnal. I want to be inside her in a very, very bad way. Caruso's absolutely correct in his assessment; Sophie's hands *have* been over *every* inch of me—except for the screaming, growling, growing inches between my legs. Not to mention the fact that I haven't even been able to relieve myself at all! Talk about agony.

"Are you listening to me, North?" Silva's gruff, impatient voice breaks through my thoughts.

"Sure."

"Brilliant," he chides. "Try again. Focus this time. Sophie won't accept the position."

Disappointment floods my veins. *Shit.* "Why not?"

"She doesn't want to lose her new position at the hospital."

"Why would she have to choose between the two?" I try.

"She'd be able to stay on here when you're training here in Williston, but when we're out of town, she'd be required to come with us, and she doesn't want to get replaced," Silva explains.

"She's probably read up on you," McGee jokes, but it rubs me the wrong way.

"Did she talk about her husband?" I growl more than I mean to.

"No. She didn't even mention being married." My statement appears to make Silva think. "You know, we can easily find another massage therapist who'd take the ridiculous salary I offered."

As if on cue, Sophie comes striding in. I can't stop the smile that spreads wide over my face. I've only ever seen her in a 5x5-inch mirror, upside down. She's more than beautiful; she's gorgeous.

Her dark brown hair is pulled back into a long ponytail that bounces as she walks. Her soft curves are masked by the light pink hospital scrubs she's wearing, and I wonder what she'd look like naked. She has a look of steel in her eyes, but her face softens when she sees me sitting up in the bed. I can't help but smile more at the idea that maybe I've got some pull on her, too.

"I'm glad to see you sitting up." Her hand gestures toward me.

"What do you think of that?" I say. "Doc says I'll be walking and fighting in no time." I jab soft fists into the air.

"I'm sure you're aware of the offer Mr. Silva presented me with." It's not a question, as she moves right to business.

"We have discussed it," I concede. "Didn't you approve of the salary that was offered?"

"I can't jeopardize my position here at the hospital. I have school loans to pay off and a family to support," she says, looking resolved.

"I can understand that," I say before hitting the subject head-on. "I'm sure your husband doesn't want you to travel around with The Jackhammer either."

"What?" Her eyes are instantly on alert.

"Husband?" I reiterate.

"Who mentioned a husband?" Her back straightens as she bristles.

"I just figured …" Her stance is throwing me off. "You said you take care of Charlie."

"Charlie?" At this, she throws her head back and lets out a long laugh.

She's so damn cute; I don't care that she's laughing at me. In fact, I'm thinking of how I can make her laugh again—husband or not.

"Charlie is my daughter," she says. "I'm not married. I don't even have a boyfriend."

Sophie's cheeks are a pretty shade of red from laughing, and she seems to blush even further after offering me that extra information about not having a boyfriend. And now I have my answer— she's fair game.

"Listen, a woman who's part of your entourage would certainly gain a *reputation* …" She hesitates. "A reputation just like yours." She lets each word hang in the air before saying the next.

Interesting how I've always worn that reputation like a badge of honor—except, maybe in front of my mother—and now this woman I hardly know has me wanting to erase it and render my slate clean.

"Whatever Silva offered you, I'll double it."

Silva's mouth hits the floor, and Sophie's eyes widen.

"I would have strict conditions," Sophie says

slowly, and I think the hope must be visible in my eyes.

"What are your conditions?" I wager cockily, knowing I'll meet them, whatever they are.

She looks between me and Silva, then to McGee and Caruso, and back to me again.

"Hey, guys, could you give us a few minutes of privacy?" I ask. I can tell they don't like the request, but I don't give a shit.

"Please, go ahead," I tell her once we're alone. I'm enjoying her game.

She steps closer to me and shores up the distance between us. She opens her sweet mouth to say something, closes it again, rethinks, and then finally says, "I always have my own hotel room on overnights."

"Done," I say.

"Not finished. I stay out of the press. I don't want mine or Charlie's names mentioned, and no photos can be leaked to the public. Ever," she says with steel in her voice and fire in her eyes. Apparently, she's serious about her privacy. That or *very* camera shy. "And I'll never be ringside," she demands.

"All right, no special features, no photos or press conferences, no ringside. We can easily cover you up with a sports cap, big sunglasses and a scarf if we have to. No problem."

She studies me warily. "Double his original salary offer?"

"Absolutely."

"Mr. Silva said the duration of the commitment would be three months."

I nod. I'd take three months.

"And I have the right to terminate, with full pay for the time I've worked, for any reason."

"Definitely."

Suspiciously, she adds, "And you'll continue to provide Charlie's health insurance."

"Of course," I say seriously. "Yours too."

I can see the cogs coming together and the wheels turning in her mind. I've got her right where I want her. I *know* she's about to say yes!

"No." She shakes her head. "I can't take the position."

"Why?" I ask, incredulous.

"I can't leave Charlie for all the overnights this is going to require. She's only three years old. I'd need a nanny to come with us."

"Is that all?" I let out a sigh of relief. "I'll even cover the nanny's expenses as part of your employee package."

"Yeah,"—she laughs a little—"about your *package* … having a young, impressionable little girl on board with a bunch of men means she's going to require some sheltering. And that would mean you'd have to tone down your *friendships*. No stewardess-pole-dancing-sex-scenes on the plane like in *Iron Man*."

I had been taking a sip of water. It came spitting out from between my lips. "You think I do that?" I wipe my chin.

"I know you do that," she accuses confidently. "I read all about it in *Sports Illustrated*."

Fucking magazine articles. "I guarantee that won't happen while the two of you are part of my team."

Sophie nods slowly. "I know this is probably very forward of me, and you're probably wishing you hadn't offered me the position by now ..."

She has no idea how many *positions* I'd like to offer her.

"There can't be ... any kind of ... sexual interplay ... between you and me."

Hell, maybe she does.

She continues, "I know we've had some sexual tension between us, but we can't act on it. I need to give Charlie stability and live the right example. I don't want to have to explain why Mommy and her boss sleep in the same bed."

I feel my eyebrows lift. "Do you think I'm only offering you this job because I want to get into your pants?"

Her warm, soft mouth unhinges, but she doesn't say anything.

I go on, "You can bet your magic hands I've

thought about it, about you, especially when those magic hands are squeezing my ass like you might never let go. Trust me, that was almost as good as amazing sex, and I'd be a damn liar if I said I didn't want to take it the rest of the way and finish that scorching foreplay."

Her mouth drops further with my words before she realizes it and snaps it closed.

"But I swear to you, on my honor and my name, that I will not make a move if you don't want me to. Now, if *you* make a move on *me* because *you* can't take the crackling, electric tension that's obviously between us—well, that won't be my responsibility."

She smiles, and her eyes glow. "You don't think I could resist you?"

"I think it'll be pretty damn hard."

She laughs. I hadn't meant the pun, but it fit.

"You may have met your match, Mr. Jack-hammer." She folds her arms across her chest. I wonder if she realizes how it just pushed up her round, swollen breasts.

"Oh yeah, scrapper? Do you want to put a price on that statement?" I love the game she's playing.

"What do you suggest?" She tilts her head.

"How much did Silva offer you?"

"Thirty-five *thousand* dollars," she says. "And

you just doubled that salary for three months of work."

I crook my finger, beckoning her to come closer. She takes a few steps. I shake my head. "Closer."

She sighs with a resolved smile but moves closer.

"Just a little more." I urge her until we're breathing the same oxygen. One slip, and I could be kissing her. "If I make the first move, I'll make it an even one hundred thousand."

"Are you serious?" she whispers almost against my lips.

"Completely." I let the idea of one hundred thousand dollars sink in before I add, "However if *you* make the first move, you'll owe me one night of unbridled passion."

CHAPTER FOUR

SOPHIE

"*One hundred thousand?!*" Ayana doesn't believe me. "I mean, I know you're a good massage therapist and all, but *one hundred thousand dollars? Really*??"

"That's what he said. I even signed the three-month contract."

I take the Stouffer's lasagna out of the oven and carry it to the table. It's not homemade, but it smells pretty good. Ayana sets a green salad next to it.

"Charlie, please put plates and forks on the table."

"How many plates?" Charlie asks as she climbs the "Mommy's Little Helper" step stool.

"Count," I remind her.

"I mean, I guess when you're a North and you have that kind of money, you can afford to do anything on a whim," Ay deduces while she takes two wine glasses and a plastic Cinderella cup from the cabinet.

"How could I say no?" I lower my voice to talk to Ay. "That amount of money would be a huge safety net for me and Charlie."

"Are you eating, Ay?" Charlie interrupts.

"Yes, silly goose!" Ay says.

I swipe Charlie off the stool and tickle her as I set her down. "How about I do your chores tonight, and you can go back to playing dollies?"

"Really?" Charlie squeals with rebellious delight. I nod, and Charlie races out of the kitchen.

I continue, "This is a real opportunity for Charlie and me. With a solid sports reference, I could go on to work with other pro athletes or get a position at my choice of hospitals. I'm tired, Ayana. I'm tired of scraping by, making just a little too much for food stamps and way too little for the things we really need—like a dependable car, the clothes I'd really love to see Charlie wear or a new toy she asks for," I muse. "I could afford a better daycare. And, most importantly, when it's time to move on again, I'll have money in the bank instead of being penniless and at the mercy of others or just barely surviving hand-to-mouth." I look at Charlie in the living room, dressing her Goodwill dolls. "She deserves better."

"You deserve better." Ayana pours sweet red wine into my glass. "And who knows? I mean, really, this is fucking Nowhereland, North Dakota. You're a well-hidden needle in a big ass haystack."

Is she right? Am I really so well-hidden? And if I am, why is it that I still don't *feel* safe? Will I ever feel safe? Will Charlie and I *ever be* safe?

Charlie is my life. I'd do or give her anything, and the most important thing she needs is a safe life, a safe mom and a safe place to live and play, but I can't give her any of those things. I still live my life plagued by fear.

At any moment, he could find us.

THE BELT IS WILLISTON'S PREMIERE MMA GYM. Sparring bags, floor and wall mats, a center ring, jumbo bulldozer tires, weights and weight machines, padding … It's one hell of a place for training. A mural showing a side-view of Josh jabbing a right hook is painted on the wall, larger than life. Famous quotes about fear, courage, strength and giving your all are also painted on every wall in a black tattoo-like graffiti script.

"Do you own it?" I ask Josh as he, Silva, Caruso and McGee lead me through the place.

"Part. The four of us are joint owners," Josh explains. I co-own each of my training facilities.

The place is buzzing with activity. Everyone stops what they're doing to greet Josh and congratulate him on a speedy recovery. They shake his hand, give him the masculine nod, or do the one-armed man hug thing. Everyone is talking to everyone at once, and the place seems like it's turned into a party zone.

The crowd comes between me and the team, and I find myself moving toward the outer circle, which is okay by me—I don't need to be a testosterone sandwich.

"You don't look like no fighter," I hear a deep voice say behind me. "Sweet thing."

"Well, you know what they say, looks can be deceiving," I retort as I turn.

He nods. He's huge, and he exudes an air of arrogance that I'd much rather avoid.

"So, which one of these chumps is your boyfriend?" He leans into my personal space.

Oh God! Why is it that some men can be so full of themselves that they think this kind of violation is okay?

When I ignore him and turn away, he sets a demanding hand on my shoulder.

Fuck. "Don't touch me," I hear my own voice say. It's small and shaky. I remember how physically vulnerable to this monstrosity of a fighter I am. I straighten my back, pull my shoulder from his grasp, take a strong stance and meet his eyes. "I said, don't touch me."

"When most girls say, 'Don't touch me,' they usually don't mean it."

I have mace in my hip bag, and I think to myself, *What an amazing first day at work! In the first five minutes, I pepper-sprayed some douchebag in the face! And how was your day?*

"How'd you fit all them curves up in that shirt?" he says, leering down at my breasts.

That's it! "What the hell is wrong with you? Are you a Neanderthal? Did you just come lumbering out from a cave? Who the hell talks like that? Don't speak to me again."

I take a long step away from him and feel his fingers clasp around my arm.

"Sexy bitch, you must have a stick up your pretty ass—let me help you get it out."

A fraction of a second later, an expression of severe pain rips over his face as he drops to one knee. Josh is holding his other hand—no, just his thumb—pulling it backward into a position that makes it look like Josh could detach it clean away from his hand.

"The nice lady asked you politely not to touch her, so what the fuck is your hand doing on her arm?" Josh's voice is low and threatening.

"I'm sorry, man. I didn't know she was with you," Neanderthal responds in apparent agony.

"She is," Josh growls before getting his face in the other guy's face. "But even if she wasn't, that's no way to speak to a woman. Didn't your mama teach you any better?" At that, Josh straightens his posture a bit and looks completely natural as he faces the enormous crowd around us.

Everyone—a good fifty bodies strong—is staring at the three of us.

"This seems as good a time as any for introductions," Josh waxes, friendly and upbeat, but still holding onto the guy's thumb. "This is Sophie Garner. She's the newest member of my fight team."

I hear Neanderthal groan.

Most everyone in arm's reach of me begins shaking my hand and welcoming me to the club. Almost the entire group is men, save two women who step forward to shake my hand.

After a moment, Josh continues, "Now that Sheen here has had the chance to see how people with manners meet new people, I'm sure he'll have learned the correct way to greet strangers." He looks back down at "Sheen," whose face is blotched red and white. "I'm going to let you go. When I do, get your ass back to the lockers, get your shit and don't let me see your fucking face here for the next two weeks. Understood?"

Sheen nods, and Josh lets him go. Sheen cradles his hand and quickly makes his way to the back of the gym.

"Are you alright?" Josh searches my eyes.

No. I'm shaking like a freaking leaf in a hurricane. No, I am NOT okay! I'm tired of MEN!

I find my voice. "I'll be fine."

You know, it's not even the asshole Neanderthal that makes me so furious. It's that men can somehow not care or think that these actions don't have a consequence, and that's frightening. What's he going to do to the next girl he finds attractive?

And why am I an asshole magnet?

I want to say thank you, but I can't because it gets caught in my throat. I realize the adrenaline that surged through me is now making me shake visibly, and I have to get out of here. At least away from all of these people.

"Do you have an office?" I ask under my breath.

"Of course." Josh leads me to a door on the side wall. It's painted deep red. He unlocks it and ushers me inside. After Josh turns on the light, he flips a *Do Not Disturb* sign on the outside of the door and then shuts it. "I'm sorry that was your first experience here."

"I hate men who are strong and use it to hurt others." I'm pacing, trying to expend this adrenaline.

Josh moves to his water cooler and, a second later, puts a cold paper cup of water in my hand. "Drink it."

I do. The action forces me to take a deep breath and then center myself again.

"Sheen's an asshole. Always has been." Josh strides behind his desk.

As I calm down, I notice that this is not a stereotypical, rough gym office. Instead, it's refined. A large, polished, rectangular mahogany desk with a black fitness ball as the "chair" is neat and orderly. An overhead track of lights makes the room bright and shines over the darkly stained hardwood flooring. A laptop and a laser printer sit on the desk. A black leather sofa sits against one wall, facing the other, which holds a nearly cinema-sized flat screen.

"He's fortunate I didn't pound him into a near-death experience," Josh states before handing me a set of keys. "If anyone, I mean *anyone*, acts in any way toward you that isn't more than honorable, you tell me immediately. I won't have that going on in my gym." He lowers his voice a little when he adds, "Especially with you."

Josh immediately begins showing me what each key is for—the gym, his office, and my own company car. "It's the Volvo S60 parked in the back. I even had them install a big-kid, high-back booster seat for Charlie."

I am stunned.

"I don't know what you drive now, but the Volvo is one of the safest structurally, and don't worry about using it full-time. It's yours while you have the job—with fuel costs covered.

"Josh, I don't think—" I begin.

"Yeah, you do, Sophie. You think too much," he says seriously, like he can somehow read my thoughts. "It's your job to keep my body limber and unstressed." I now notice his hand is underneath mine, and it is as if he has to hold it up to keep the keys steady. *Is he doing it on purpose?* "It's my job to make you the happiest employee there is." He squeezes my hand and then lets go. "Now for my favorite part." He smiles, and for a moment, he looks like a happy kid on a holiday, not like the rough fighter who usually looks like he's going to rip someone's head off.

He beckons me to follow him down the hallway and stops at a yellow-painted door. "This is your office."

Josh opens the door. "You can decorate it however it suits you."

Looking around, I quickly take in that despite the bold, bright colors in the gym, the walls here are subdued in a nice, creamy coffee color. The walls are bare. There is a massage table and massage chair, my own dark, polished desk, a comfortable-looking, brown eggshell-colored sofa, and, to my utter shock and surprise, a corner of the office is dedicated to Charlie. A beautiful tea set is set up on a child-sized table for easy play, and there's a play kitchen with all the accessories, a pink, fuzzy, overstuffed chair, shelves stocked with children's books, puzzles and games, and a hammock filled with stuffed animals and baby dolls.

I'm about to have an unwanted moment. I feel tears well up in my eyes. I try to push them back down, but they're rebellious and slide down my cheeks anyway. I attempt to turn away, but I'm not fast enough.

"What's wrong?" Josh is quickly concerned by my reaction. "If you don't want them here, I'll get rid of them. I just figured some days you might want to bring Charlie with you."

No one has ever bought anything for Charlie besides me. Even Jim never gave her anything after she was born—not a toy, not a blanket, not diapers, nothing.

"It's perfect," I work to reassure him. "Just an unexpected but beautiful surprise. She'll love them."

He looks like he's judging my expression … as if he isn't sure what to think. I don't blame him, and I quickly wipe the stray tears and straighten my back. I have a feeling he wants to pry, but he doesn't. Instead, he changes the subject.

"We'll have a lot of work, but you'll also have a lot of downtime. You won't want to bring her every day, but once you get the groove of the schedule, you'll find a rhythm. And don't worry about anything—don't stress if you're going to be running a little late or if she's sick and you need a day off—just let me know."

As he speaks, I realize just how amazing this job could be. I'm completely elated, but another part of me works to keep my feet planted firmly on earth. Our business partnership could easily spiral into a sexual relationship. Josh is the most gorgeous man I've ever laid eyes on. His hands are rough, manly and so sexy. His muscles ripple underneath his shirt, making me thankful to the highest heavens that my job is literally to touch them every day. However, along with that "legal" touching comes a price—I want to lick them; I fantasize about running the tip of my tongue through the ridges of his abs and tracing the lines down to his ...

His voice snaps me back. "Silva has his own office at the end of the hall, and McGee and Caruso share an office across from it."

Thank you for the wake-up call. Josh is my boss. And there is no way I can jeopardize that. And even though I've only been with one other guy since Charlie was born and am in some *serious need* of servicing ...

I. Must. Play. This. Smart.

CHAPTER FIVE

JOSH

Infatuation … according to Webster's it means, "an intense but short-lived passion or admiration for someone or something."

Infatuation? I watch Sophie as she opens the staff fridge to get her lunch. I don't need to be in here, but I knew she'd be taking her break now, so I'm fumbling with the coffeemaker.

Sophie looks up from her sandwich. "Do you need some assistance?" She has an expression that reads, *since when do you make coffee?*

Since she came to work here and I seem to feel the need to make time to see her, to figure her out … to be close to her.

Oh fuck, what's the definition of stalker?

"Got it covered, but thanks."

I can tell she doesn't believe me, but she gives me my way just the same.

She comes in here at the same times every day —always right before or right after everyone else. Sophie seems to like being alone.

She opens a personal-sized bag of baked chips, then checks her watch. She throws a chip in her mouth, picks up her cell from the table and makes a call.

This girl is so beautiful! She must have all kinds of guys falling all over themselves to impress her.

When she starts talking, she looks ... I'm not sure. Maybe concerned?

Shit! Now I have to hear what she's saying and figure out who the hell is getting her attention.

Is there a definition for an *infatuated stalker?* If there is, I'm sure it's not good. And yet, here I go, pretending I'm interested in what's in the vending machines directly behind her.

"Charlie, do you have your wristband on?" Sophie asks, then listens. "Very good. What's the rule? That's right—never, ever take it off."

Must be a nice wristband. I smooth out a dollar bill and run it through the slot.

"Remember, when you go to the playplace with Britt you stay close to her, do you understand me? If anyone tries to talk to you, you scream and run to Britt."

Very protective—she's such a mom. I'll admit,

I'm happy she's talking to Charlie and not some guy I'd want to destroy.

"I miss you, too. When I get home, we can play Ants in the Pants! I love you, too. See you when I'm all done with work," Sophie finishes.

I retrieve a blueberry yogurt from the machine and decide to take a chance. "I'm an adult, and my mom still worries," I say.

"Yeah, I think that's one of the two all-consuming motherly emotions—love and worry—I feel them both all the time," she explains.

"Mind if I join you?" I ask, indicating the empty chair at her table.

"Of course."

I sit and then shake my yogurt up as I consider her. She catches me watching. Her brow pinches, and she's so adorable.

"What?" she asks. "Do I have mustard on my face?" Quickly, she swipes a napkin over her mouth.

I laugh, "Not at all. I was just thinking about what it must be like for you …"

"For me—how?" Now she's watching me. *Curiously maybe?* Ha! *She probably thinks I'm an infatuated stalker!*

She's a good mom—always putting Charlie first—always taking time throughout the day to call and check up on her and remind her that she loves her.

"Must be tough being a single mother," I try.

"Sometimes it's tougher to be a married mother if the guy's a jerk." She drops her eyes and pushes a cherry tomato around her plate.

"I hear that. Too many assholes in the world," I agree, immediately wanting to know who the asshole is who hurt her so I can shred him.

"Exactly." She bites into the tomato hard, as if she's getting rid of some pent-up aggression, and it spurts seeds onto the table in front of me and into my yogurt. She just about chokes as she grabs a napkin to clean up the mess on the table.

I can't help but laugh, which sets her off laughing too.

"I'm so sorry!" she says, still laughing. "That'll teach you to sit next to me when I'm eating."

"Ah, so that's why you're always eating by yourself, huh? You don't want to endanger the rest of us?"

She smiles. "Something like that. Here," she says, starting to stand, "let me get you another yogurt."

"No way." I gesture for her to sit back down, and she does, hesitantly. "This one is perfect." I take a big bite and make sure to chew with dramatic flair. "Yum! Blueberry and tomato—my favorite! I'll have to make sure to sit here every day."

She busts up laughing again, and somehow,

she's even more beautiful—it's all I can do to stop myself from grabbing her and kissing her right there.

"Hey, do you have my personal cell number in your phone?" I ask, shaking the image from my mind.

"I have Silva's."

I'm so lame! "May I?" I ask for permission as I let my hand hover toward her phone.

"Sure."

I take her phone and plug in my number. "I'm going to program in my own ringtone."

"Okay …" she says with a questioning tone. "Does that mean I should be expecting a call?"

"Got to keep you on your toes." I finish and pass the phone back.

I hit send on my own, and hers begins ringing. "The Fighter" by Gym Class Heroes plays.

Sophie laughs. "Perfect ringtone for you."

I laugh with her, glad she likes it.

"You can call me anytime—if there's something you need …" *Or want.* "Don't hesitate."

"Thank you." She has such hypnotizing and thoughtful gray-blue-green eyes—they pull me in deep and hold me there. She doesn't wear much makeup—maybe a little mascara and lip gloss, that's it. She doesn't try hard to impress, yet she leaves a lasting impression on everyone she meets.

Stop staring, Josh!

"And remember, Charlie's more than welcome here," I remind her. When she first took the job, I set a space up in her office especially for Charlie, but she's hasn't brought her yet.

"Thank you," she answers simply.

Shit, she's finished her sandwich and starting to gather her stuff.

"Is it difficult to work with her around?" Can I keep her sitting here longer?

"Oh, no … Charlie's great." She apologetically shrugs one shoulder a little. "The atmosphere—fighters punching each other, spitting blood and knocking out teeth, the swearing—not really on the preschool curriculum."

Of course. Makes perfect sense. I nod. "Got it."

After she cleans up her space, Sophie stands up and walks around behind me. My entire body turns so that my eyes can follow her. She stops at the coffeepot. A second later, it begins to brew a fresh pot.

"There you go." She smiles. Almost … *flirtatiously?*

"Thanks." Is it wrong that I want to pick her up, wrap her long legs around my waist, and press her against the wall?

"See you soon." And she's out the door.

The doing-her-right-here-in-the-lunchroom thing probably isn't the best idea, considering people are coming in now. I smile into my yogurt cup as I scoop the rest of it out with my tongue. *I can think of other things I'd love to scoop out with my tongue.*

THE DAYS GO BY, AND THE WORD *INFATUATION* doesn't do justice or explain what I feel for Sophie because although it *is* intense, it's absolutely *not* short-lived. Nope, this doesn't feel like infatuation; it feels like hysteria, just like the title of that Def Leppard song.

What do I think about all day? Training and Dalloway? No—Sophie.

I've gone club-hopping with friends each weekend, and although I've met some fucking hot women, can I think of them or even flirt with them? No! I have no interest.

Sophie's busted my A-game and has taken up residency in my head. And that's a damn problem because every one of Sophie's massage sessions is becoming more and more sexually unbearable!

The one good idea I've had has been to continue invading her break time. Sophie never seems to mind. In fact, she actually seems to have started looking forward to me meeting up with her, mentioning nonchalantly after our morning session that she'll see me at lunch. One day, she even stunned me when she knocked on my office door and reminded me she was headed to lunch in case I wanted to join her. I was such a transparent idiot—I got up so fast, I smacked a stack of papers and my water bottle to the floor in one spastic move—as if she'd given me a two-second window to accept the offer. Fuck it, I made her laugh. And I love making her laugh. Sophie has an amazing fucking laugh.

We've talked a lot over the past couple of weeks—about philosophy, books, her schooling, Charlie, my job as a firefighter. But she never tells me anything about her past or anything personal.

I find myself wanting more. Wanting it all.

"EARTH TO JOSH. EARTH TO JOSH. COME IN, Josh," my younger sister Julia says as if she's Houston.

I tilt my head and look at her over the pot roast she made. It doesn't matter that she's all grown up; it doesn't even matter that she's married now. She still is and will always be my pain-in-the-ass kid sister.

"What are you thinking about?" she asks sweetly between bites of cooked carrots.

"Work," I reply. "And how's *your* work?"

At this, she smiles and perks up in her seat. I

can't help but grin a little. Jules is sweet and naive and one of the most caring people I know, next to our mom.

"Work is great! My latest novel made the New York Times list, and just in time for me to take some time off." She rubs her barely visible baby bump. Jules isn't even four months pregnant yet. She still has morning sickness, makes her husband Nate—our childhood friend—run to the store at all hours of the night for some really messed up cravings and has already started shopping and decorating for the baby.

Nate smiles at me and then at her. At least *he* noticed I shifted the conversation. She's so easily baited.

"Oh my God, what smells so good?" Livie asks ravenously from the kitchen.

I turn in my chair to see my brother Jake and his wife Livie—who happens to be Jules's best friend and Nate's younger sister—coming through the kitchen from the back door.

"I thought all I wanted was fried chicken and mashed potatoes until I smelled that!" she adds, beelining to the table.

Livie is about six months pregnant. She and Jules have been best friends since they were in kindergarten. They did everything together. Now, that's been extended to getting married in the same year and becoming pregnant only a few months apart. I feel my eyebrows come together. That's rather freaking scary if I dwell on the idea too long.

"Fried chicken and mashed potatoes sound good," Jules says.

"Really? Jake and I got take out. We can share!" Livie enthusiastically sets her bag on the dining room table and begins emptying it, revealing a huge bucket of fried chicken, a four pound vat of hot mashed potatoes, and corn on the cob.

"Hell, I won't argue. It's kind of nice with these two pregnant; we actually get some good food when Mom isn't around." I swipe a chicken leg from the container and quickly bite into it. I'm teasing. Our mom made sure all of her children could cook—especially the men. Most of us even enjoy it, especially when we're trying to impress a date.

"So what are you doing hanging out here, anyway, on a Friday night? Don't you have some smokin' hot woman waiting for you some-where?" Ah, Jules gets back on track, right back to where she was leading the conversation before.

"If I did, I wouldn't be here." I mean to say it sarcastically, but it doesn't really come out that way. It sounds more like …

"Ha! The Jackhammer couldn't get a Friday

night date? The world is ending! Tell me it isn't true." Jake is snarky and dramatic.

"Watch it, or you and I will have a Friday night fight card."

"That would be freaking fun!" Jake says excitedly. "We rented a couple of movies, but with you actually having a Friday night free, why don't we go hit the gym for a while and spar? Nate, you can take on the winner."

There'll be no telling him no now.

"Yeah, why don't you go?" Jules elbows Nate.

"Hell yeah!" He grins. "I'll grab a case of Molson for the event. It's been too long since I've seen a good fight." He pulls a chunk of roast from his fork with his teeth.

I roll my eyes. I practically live at the gym, so spending my free night there is ridiculous. *But I obviously have nothing else to do …*

"As long as Nate is buying the beer, I'm in," I say.

"Yeah!" Jake cheers and smacks Nate's shoulder. "Let's grab some stuff."

"I'm glad we started dinner before you all got here." He takes a drink of ice water, pulls away from the dining room table, and then kisses Jules on the crown of her head. "I'll run up to the house," he says, then adds to Jules, "Do you need anything?"

"I'm good, thanks," she says.

"I'll go with you." Jake jumps up from the table, full of restless energy.

After he kisses Livie on the lips, he snags a wing from his plate, and then he and Nate bolt out the door.

Nate and Jules have a newly built home a mile from the main house, which is still on the ranch property. It's perfect for them—Jules gets to stay close to Mom, and Nate is always on the ranch anyway. I know Mom would love it if all of us had homes somewhere on the family's property, which is vast and spans two U.S. states and three Canadian provinces.

Jake and Livie are staying in the guest house while they're here through the holidays. First week of the New Year, they'll be down in sunny Miami, where they have a condo. Jake, along with a friend of his from the Army, runs an extreme sports adventure business down there during the winter months. Jake has been conducting demographics and trial runs to see if the business could thrive here in the Williston area for the summer months. He and Livie don't want to live so far away from the family all year long, especially with the baby coming—they want the little one to be surrounded by family.

My oldest brother Caleb has been a missing entity lately. His girl Piper lives in Canada. So he conveniently works the ranches up in that area as much as possible. He usually stays at the family's log home in Alberta.

That gets me thinking—Caleb and Piper, Jake and Livie, Nate and Jules, and now even Sam (who would've seen that one coming?) and Kate. Just Will and I are left in the exclusive singles club.

I feel my sister's eyes burning into me.

"What *is* your problem?"

"Seriously?" Jules's brow knits together. "Usually, you grab food at your apartment, do take out from the gym, or get dinner at the firehouse most days of the week."

"I come home too," I protest.

"But I can't remember the last time we saw you on a Friday night," Livie now puts in her two sister cents. "Friday night's like the Holy Grail of date nights."

"Cut me some slack! Christ, you two are vultures." I roll my eyes, stand and pick up my plate to rinse it off.

"He's deflecting," Livie leans in to tell Jules.

"I haven't left the room."

"Oh, I know," Livie says to me, then turns to Jules and asks, "What do you think it means?"

"I think it means he's dating someone he doesn't want us to know about, and he might actually like her, so he's not fishing for another at the moment," Jules deduces.

"Did you both really just analyze my dating life?" I ask, incredulous.

"Of course." Jules's face is so serious as if she's getting down to business.

"My presence here tonight has nothing to do with women, dating, or not dating. I simply wanted to hang out with my family. And now I get the added benefit of beating the shit out of my brothers. Think you can handle that, little girls?"

They continue talking to each other as if I'm not even present. "He's full of bullshit," Livie says, and then Jules chimes, "Definitely."

"That's it! I'm out of here." I drop my plate back to the table and reach for my coat from the back of the chair.

"You know, we're planning a big Christmas party. You could invite her. It's not formal. It's easygoing." When Jules says this, she sings it.

I roll my eyes. "Tell the boys to meet me at the gym."

When I open the front door and step outside, icy cold wisps of air envelop me, reminding me that it's December in North Dakota. I shut myself inside my Gillet Vertigo, then tear out of the driveway, wondering how to hit on someone I said I wouldn't make the first move on.

SIX WEEKS UNTIL CHRISTMAS. I JAB RAY, MY sparring partner, in the eye. He staggers back a little before he shakes it off. *I wonder if I could get Sophie to come with me to the party?*

I send two fast fists into Ray's ribcage. *In two days, we'll all be flying to Denver for the rest of the week. I'll be meeting Charlie for the first time.* I block Ray's grasp as he comes in and tries to take me to the floor. I land a kick in his well-padded sternum.

I know Denver. Sophie says she's never been there before. I could set up an impromptu lunch or dinner with her and Charlie. That wouldn't look like I was hitting on her. Right? Maybe I can even get Sophie to be my—hell, I don't know what to call it. Wingman? Co-pilot? Any term but "date"—for one of the sponsor events. There will be two of them over the weekend.

Ray gets around me and attempts a choke-hold. I break free and throw him over my shoulder. His back slams against the mat. I hear the breath that's forced from his lungs.

The team always sets me up with one or two women for the photo shoots and promo galas, which usually consist of a benefit auction or fundraising dinner. Sophie might find it fun. *If we go as friends, she won't feel threatened, right? And she could learn more about the ins and outs of that side of the business. Oh, hell yeah! That sounds perfect!*

Just then Sophie walks by the ring. Her face is

freshly scrubbed and free of makeup. She possesses a natural beauty that's breathtaking. Deep brown chestnut waves of hair cascade over the shoulders of her crisp, white blouse. She glances at me from under her lashes. It's so subtle; if I wasn't looking at her precisely at this moment, I wouldn't have noticed.

But I do.

Her cheeks blush with a surge of pink when our eyes meet.

I feel Ray's legs wrap around mine as I hear his body slam to the mat and sense that he's taking me down with him. *Shit!* Immediately, my hip and shoulder connect with the tough canvas.

Sophie keeps walking by, pretending she didn't see anything, but I see the curve of her rose-petal lips as they form a smile.

CHAPTER SIX
SOPHIE

"Show me again." Charlie pushes her step stool to the wall in our bedroom, where the map hangs.

I giggle at her excitement. "Sweetheart, I've already shown you twelve times."

"But I can't remember *now*," she says.

"Okay, we have to follow the compass way, way up to the tip top of the U.S. map." As I say this, I have her point her chubby baby finger to the compass at the bottom of the map, and then slide it up to North Dakota. "You can't get much further north than we are here in North Dakota."

She repeats the words *North Dakota* and puts her fingertip over the yellow highlight I drew over the town of Williston. "That's where we live, right?"

"That's where we live." I can't help but study the map for a moment.

This two-bedroom apartment is Ayana's, and she's a great roommate, but making space in a single girl's life for a mom and a three-year-old tag-along isn't easy. Ayana likes to have her living room set up like most adults. I understand, but it doesn't make it easier. She has a fancy coffee table and art magazines, knickknacks and ornaments everywhere. Her walls are covered in beautiful paintings and photographs. It's a great place, but Charlie has had to learn to look and not touch.

I keep Charlie's toys here in the bedroom we share. In fact, I have the room set up as if it's her own personal school. On the walls are maps of the U.S., Canada and the world, an alphabet and numbers chart, a food pyramid, colors, and animals with their habitats. She has a learning laptop on a child-sized desk in the corner and a small table for puzzles and games.

In essence, it really is *her* room. I just happen to sleep in it with her. In the closet, I keep our clothes in a few plastic storage bins, neatly stacked. In another plastic storage bin, I keep my few treasures: a lock of hair from Charlie's first haircut, the pretty pink booties she wore home from the hospital, photographs of her growing and us together, a few pieces of jewelry and important documents—like her vaccination records, our I.D. cards and her "birth certificate" —I'm the only one who knows it's been altered.

That makes up the total sum of our personal possessions.

I remember the lesson we're in the middle of. "Tomorrow morning, when we wake up, we're going to ride in my boss's airplane," I say as she squeals and scurries across the bed with her arms stretched out as if she's the plane, "all the way to Denver, Colorado."

She bounces back to me, takes hold of my hand and traces my finger down till it lands on Denver.

"Are you going to put a yellow mark on it?" she asks innocently.

"Nope. It doesn't get a yellow mark." I leave the bed to finish our packing.

"We're not going to live there, though, right? We're going to come back home, right?" Her little voice stings my heart.

"We'll come back," I say without looking at her.

"I'm going to brush my teeth and get in my jammies!" Charlie screams way too loud, leaps off the bed and airplanes it to the bathroom.

Breathing deeply through my nose, I fill my lungs with air. I stop packing and regard the map. There is a lot of yellow on it. The yellow marker represents where Charlie and I have lived. It's complicated. For the first two years of her life, we moved to a new state every month. That required us to live in short-term lease apartments or hotels —and those usually weren't in the nicest sections of town. We stayed to ourselves, I used a new alias for every move, and I used an online program from a state university in Connecticut (where I had lived originally with my dad before he passed away so I could claim residency). After that, I found a mail service I could use as a personal address. It was legal—I still paid taxes to Connecticut—and they sent me my mail wherever I was. So, we survived on my school loans and grants. I studied and got good grades and even received some scholarships.

One thing I kept consistent—Charlotte. Depending on where we went, it was either Charlotte, Lettie or Harley, and then when she could say her own name, it became Charlie—a cute girl's name that could easily be a boy's. It was important for her anonymity.

Charlie crashes into my legs and wraps me in a hug.

"What's this hug for, ladybug?"

"Because I love you."

"I love you too." I hug her back. "Climb up and get under the covers."

She does. I close our suitcase and crawl in

next to her. She snuggles close, but my mind doesn't slow down.

I'd obtained enough credits for an associate's degree and really needed a fast-track career for the money for us to live. School loans did *not* give us enough. I heard of Williston, North Dakota, the booming, almost Wild West-like city that was offering workers in the area extravagant wages. I transferred my credits, put Charlie in daycare close to the college, and, in another six months, earned an Associate of Science degree with a certificate in massage therapy while I worked part-time at Walmart.

The job at the hospital was like a dream come true. Then, two months later, Josh North offered me the fantasy job of a lifetime! If it works out, I could even afford our own place where Charlie could have her own room.

My excitement and sense of security shift as the idea makes a metallic taste come up into my mouth. We've already been in Williston for almost a year. How much longer can I get away with *not* running?

I don't want to think of the answer.

When we have to leave here, it's going to be difficult for her. This is the place Charlie considers home.

ONCE WE GET THROUGH SECURITY, A MAN wearing a suit and standing in front of an airport buggy holds up a sign that reads, *Sophie and Charlie*.

"That's us," I say as I kneel down to retie Charlie's shoes. Charlie's new nanny, Brittani, stands back. She knows that when I'm present, I'm a hands-on mom.

I was seriously nervous about choosing a nanny, but Brittani came with excellent references —she just earned her degree in early childhood education and happens to be McGee's niece.

Suit man smiles. "I'm your ride out to the tarmac." He picks up our suitcases and sets them in the back of the buggy.

Charlie's so excited, and she pulls on my arm to hurry me up.

We're escorted to the other side of the airport before the driver continues through a gated area that leads us outside. December in North Dakota is not for the faint of heart. It's freezing, and a light snow is falling softly from the cloud-covered sky.

"Here we are," the man announces.

I let my gaze travel from the pristine private jet to Josh North, who stands at the bottom of the passenger staircase with the largest pink stuffed teddy bear I have ever seen.

A warmth spreads through me that I wasn't prepared for. Josh is 6'3" and 205 pounds of pure chiseled muscle; he's a powerful fighting machine, and here he is wearing a black North Face coat, distressed denim jeans and rugged work boots while holding this massive, fluffy, pink bear.

Our driver stops. Charlie is staring in wide-eyed awe at Josh and his offering. I pull myself from the buggy and lift Charlie to the ground. She stands close by my side, unsure of her next move.

Josh drops to one knee to get on her level. "You must be Charlie! I'm so happy to meet you. I'm Josh. I work with your mom."

Damn that boyish smile. It betrays a side of him that can be tender and gentle.

"I like your bear," Charlie says, peeking from behind my leg.

"Oh, this isn't my bear," Josh states. He turns the bear's face toward his own ear and acts as if he's listening intently to the secret the bear is shar-ing. "She says she's here to play with you on the plane ride."

"Really?" Charlie's smile grows instantly.

"Yep, and if you like her, you could even bring her home and keep her."

"Wow!" Charlie breaks free of me and runs,

throwing her arms around the teddy bear's neck and squeezing for all she's worth.

I smile as I walk closer. "It's going to need its own seat."

"You're probably right," Josh laughs and then says a friendly hello to Brittani.

As we ascend the stairs and board the plane, the captain and co-pilot greet us, along with one stewardess who leads us to our seats. The jet is luxurious, with subtle leather seats and couches and tables or trays next to them.

I'm surprised we're alone. "Where's the team?"

"McGee and Caruso have already been in Denver the past few days getting things prepared, and Silva's in a meeting with someone, some-where," he says. "Where would you like to sit?"

Charlie runs and flings herself and the bear onto the couch. She rolls while giggling and tangles her arms and legs around the new toy.

"Charlie looks happy," Josh says, obviously proud of himself.

"Yeah, she does."

Josh holds his hand out to a comfortable-looking armchair that faces another. I nod and unzip my coat.

"Please, let me." Josh quickly moves behind me and helps me slip the coat off before setting it aside.

I sit and watch, a little hypnotized, as he de-shoulders his own coat and then pulls his Broncos sweatshirt over his head. When he does, his t-shirt gets pulled up underneath it.

It doesn't matter how many times I see him half naked; I'm swept away each and every time. His eight-pack abs ripple and his chest flexes with his effort. As he stretches taller, the waist of his jeans dips low, revealing that sensual V-line—or Adonis Belt—like an arrow pointing downward to his …

I rip my eyes away just as his head resurfaces.

He tosses the clothes on the seat behind him and takes the seat opposite me. His black t-shirt clings to him.

I clear my throat. "How long is the flight?"

"Just a little over an hour. It'll give us some time to talk."

I see and talk to Josh every day, so why do I feel nervous?

We all buckle in for takeoff, and once we're in the air, Britt takes Charlie over to seats that face a table to put together some puzzles.

"I wanted to tell you about what the itinerary for this trip looks like." Josh takes some papers out of a briefcase beside his seat. "Today and tomorrow arc strictly training days   grueling and intensive. Time with you is going to be the best part of those days." He says this, and it fills my stomach with butterflies. What exactly does he mean?

He continues, "Friday and Saturday mornings and afternoons are packed with promos and photo shoots. They're boring, but you're welcome to come. Friday and Saturday nights, however, are significantly important. Friday night is Denver's Imagine There's No Hunger event at Hard Rock Café. It's casual attire, and a lot of Grammy award-winning performers will be there. Saturday evening, Nike is hosting a celebrity benefit auction featuring sports memorabilia at the Denver Performing Arts Complex. It's a formal black tie occasion." He pauses for a moment while he studies me cautiously. "I was wondering if you'd accompany me."

I can't find my voice.

"Don't say anything if you're thinking no." He lifts his hand. "Just let the idea set a bit. You'd have a blast; these events are really exciting," he cajoles then lays his hand over his heart. "I'd be the perfect gentleman," Josh swears, but a mischievous spark lights his eyes as he leans in closer to me. "And when's the last time you did something really fun?"

I haven't had fun for years, I think.

"I'm really camera shy," I lie. Well, not a lie exactly—I just don't mention the *reason* I'm camera shy.

"Then I'll protect you from the photographers." He smiles as if I said yes simply by contemplating it. "The only photographers will be at the red carpet entrance, but I know other ways into both buildings, and the photographers aren't permitted into the events. So you won't have to worry about that."

"Uh …" Am I going to make a bigger deal out of this than it is? He's not hitting on me; he's only asking me to some really fun-sounding parties. "I don't have anything to wear to either event," I respond finally. I'm stalling, and I know it.

"Hell, you have all kinds of shopping options in Denver. And to sweeten the deal, you can buy the clothes on the company's dime." He winks. He has it all figured out.

"Let me think about it."

"Alright, but don't wait too long—" He's about to say something else when his cell phone goes off. He snatches it from his pocket, looks at the screen, annoyed, then back to me apologetically. "I have to take it."

I nod.

Josh answers, "Hey, Silva." He stands and walks away down the aisle.

I lean back against the seat and peer out the window into the clear blue sky that surrounds me. I feel my eyes slowly close. The safety I feel up in the air and being here with Josh is unprecedented.

I WAKE AS THE PLANE LURCHES FORWARD. I FEEL the familiar sensation of landing and open my eyes.

Josh is looking at me with softness in his eyes. "Sorry. You looked so peaceful that I couldn't wake you."

I feel a little embarrassed and a little flattered, and I'm really hoping I haven't snored. I stretch and say, "Sorry, I think you had more you wanted to talk about."

"That's okay, we'll get another shot."

At that moment, Charlie runs over to us and, to my utter shock and surprise, leaps up into Josh's lap!

"Will you hold my hand off the plane, Joshy?"

"You bet!" *Joshy* answers and taps the tip of her nose with his fingertip.

Charlie giggles.

"How long was I asleep?"

"Long enough for Charlie and me to get to know each other better."

"Mommy, we played Go Fish, and I won!" Charlie crows. "We played dollies too. Joshy was Prince Charming."

Of course, he was. "I'm so happy you had fun." I reach out my arms, and she tumbles happily into them. I wrap her in an overprotective hug but keep my face light when I look over her shoulder to Josh, who looks like he just had the time of his life.

AFTER WE ALL CHECK INTO THE HOTEL—THE Four Seasons—McGee whisks Josh and me away to the training center. The place is huge, three times the size of the facility in Williston. It's packed with people, and Josh keeps me close at his side this time until formal announcements and introductions are made.

Josh speaks into my ear, "I have to go in the back and get suited up. Angie at the front desk is good-people. Get to know her; she'll give you the ins and outs and politics of the place.

I nod. "Got it."

It feels like a new sense of trust has developed between the two of us. I'd swear he can see when I'm uncomfortable, and he seems to know just what to do to help me feel more at ease.

Walking toward the front desk, the men and the women regard me with complete respect. I smile or nod politely back, realizing the depth of their devotion to Josh.

"Hey, girly! I'm Angie. Anything I can do for you, just let me know," the blonde-haired, blue-eyed woman who looks about the same age as me says and thrusts her hand out.

"Nice to meet you." I shake her hand.

She looks around us and sees there are no prying ears close by before she says in a hushed tone, "So, how long have you been working for Josh?"

"Less than a month."

She sizes me up a bit, then tells me, "You're the first woman masseuse he's ever had on his team. You must be good."

"Thanks."

"Here, come around the desk. I have an extra stool. You can keep me company."

"How long have you worked here?" I make conversation as I sit down.

"Going on four years. It's a great place to work, plus I get to be around my hubby more." She nods her head, indicating a muscled-up man who's working on a teardrop-shaped boxing bag. "Got to make sure the ladies are behaving themselves." She winks.

"The guy who looks like Charlie Hunnam?" My eyes do a double-take.

She laughs loudly. "That's my honey! He actually works as a stunt double for the real-life Charlie Hunnam."

"No way! You *know* him personally? *Sons of Anarchy* is one of my favorite shows."

"Yeah, he's a really cool guy." She smiles at her man. "But his stunt double—holy shit, he's hot!" She fans herself with her hand.

"Zero argument from me; the resemblance is wicked uncanny." And it is.

"Where did you meet Josh?"

"Williston. He busted himself up pretty good during a house fire and was in the hospital for a while."

"Sounds like Josh." She peers at me sideways. "You're not from Williston, though."

My heart pounds.

"My aunt is from Boston. You have a bit of that accent."

I smile with relief. "Yeah, I lived in Massachusetts for a time. Must have picked it up." So she won't ask any more about me, I say, "Are you from Denver?"

"Nope, met Cam in Hollywood. I was working as an extra on a movie he was stunting in. It was love at first sight," she answers. "Josh was called in for his fighting expertise and did some on-set training and choreography with Charlie and Cam for a while. Now Cam and I have a second home out here so he can train under the same gurus who work with Josh."

"That's exciting."

I'm immediately distracted from the conversation as I see Josh come out from the back wearing nothing but a pair of skin-hugging red shorts. His leg muscles are cut and corded in all the right places. He's barefoot. Josh has beautiful feet. His hands are wrapped with red tape. As he comes out of the hallway into the main area, I watch as he directs his gaze to the front desk. My heart skips when those rich, brown eyes meet mine. His expression, which holds what looks like concern, melts a bit into relief. He redirects his focus to the sparring opponent who waits in the ring to warm him up.

"Are you guys a couple?" Angie asks, startling me back to reality.

That was personal. "No." I shake my head. "Not a couple."

"Well, I think he would be if you wanted to," she says matter-of-factly.

My brows pinch down. "Why do you say that?"

"Um, because he watched to make sure you got over to me before he took off into the back, and now that he's back out, he's checking on you again." She tilts her head to look into my face and, in doing so, forces me to look at her. "I've never seen him so attentive."

That's easy to explain. "Some jerk in Williston tried putting his hands on me at the gym on my first day. Josh made sure no one would do it again." I can't help but smile at the memory of the guy going down to his knees. "That's all he's thinking about."

"Yeah, okay. If you say so," Angie quips curtly. "Want to grab lunch with me?"

"I would, but I should stay for now in case they need me."

"Do you like Chinese?"

"Love it."

"Good, I'll grab takeout. There isn't much estrogen in this place. It'll be nice to have a new friend," Angie says. "I'll be back in a bit."

"Sounds good."

Angie hops away from the desk, grabs her coat and purse from the back of her chair and rushes off.

Friends. I was definitely in short supply of those.

"Oh my God, Silva is trying to kill me," Josh whines as I press my fingers into his back, scrolling over his ribs.

"I think it's a conspiracy," I agree with a smile.

"Yeah, he wants to get rid of me so McGee can take my fights. They'll rename it the EUFC."

"What's that acronym mean?" I chuckle.

"Elderly Ultimate Fighting Championship." He laughs at his joke.

"Come on now, be nice. Dan Henderson is 44. That's not so old."

"You know that?" He sounds astounded.

"If I'm going to work for a UFC champion fighter, I think I should know a little bit about the sport." I smile, proud of myself. "McGee could be a contender."

"Don't tell me you're on their side?" he groans.

I laugh. "No way, I'm no traitor."

I warm Mandarin orange and other invigorating citrus essential oils mixed with organic coconut oil in between my palms before I spread it onto Josh's lower back. The scent is divine.

He groans, "God, you're good."

I wonder if I'm still *good* at other things.

"So, you and Angie hit it off?" he asks.

"Yeah, she's cool."

"I thought the two of you might get along. Her husband, Cam—"

"I know, she told me. How did you like working on set?"

"I should've known she'd tell you," he chuckles. "It was fun, but Hollywood is definitely not for me. Too much politics. I like being in charge of my own show."

"Control freak much?" I say lightly.

"Yeah, probably too much." Josh gets silent before his voice lowers. "Sophie?

"Yes?"

"Where is Charlie's father?"

I freeze. I haven't really gotten involved in others' lives for a long time—thus the no friends thing—but staying to myself keeps others to themselves, so I'm not startled and surprised by questions like this.

"Does he see her?" he tries.

"No." I grit my teeth.

"Child support?"

I wince as if I've been hit. He can't see me, and I'm glad of it. "No. He … isn't involved at all."

"Does he know about her?"

"Holy shit, Josh! Feel free to pry."

"Cool your engines, scrapper. I'm just trying to figure out the situation."

"It's not your situation to figure out." My tone is biting.

I think about how safe I felt on the plane, how he protected me from the asshole at Williston's gym, and then what Angie said about how he seems to be looking after me.

I also think about how people work and what makes them tick. What if I let Josh in? What if he turns into an asshole? In my personal experience, men always do.

"You're right. I apologize. That was terribly rude of me." His voice is soft.

I let that sink in, deep. "I've never heard a man say he was sorry before."

Josh is quiet, then says. "Well, you'll hear it from me often. I have a habit of saying stupid shit all the time. Not much of a filter, I'm afraid," he quips self-deprecatingly.

I work his muscles down to his feet. Usually, by about this time, my insides are clenching, and my panties are soaking wet from touching him like this, but not now. Now, all I think about are his questions and trust and fear and friendship, but mostly, I think about betrayal. Could confiding in Josh hurt Charlie or me?

Maybe it'd be a freaking relief to tell *someone*. I've been alone for so long, carrying this burden inside myself. By myself.

I want to know more about Josh, too. I want to dig deep inside and see what makes him so complicated. And, no doubt, I definitely want to sleep with him. Why couldn't we do that? So what if the friendship or the relationship or the job didn't last forever? Aren't people always saying you should live for the present?

Maybe I should try *that* and *not* spend my time trying to figure out the one hundred steps ahead of me.

He feels so perfect under my hands. Oh, how

his arms would feel around me … even for just one night.

But what if Josh didn't want me once he knew? What if he thought what I did was wrong?

Then I'd have to move on again. And Charlie? She would be heartbroken.

Fine. Let's say all of that happens. Whatever. It's not as if Josh knows him.

But would Josh turn me in?

The prospect of that is frightening, and I don't even know how I'd go about testing the waters.

Josh *is* a firefighter and they *do* work in conjunction with the police.

Better to keep my mouth shut.

CHAPTER SEVEN
JOSH

How in the *fuck* do I do the exact thing I tell myself I won't *fucking* do!? I pace across the carpet in my hotel room. My running shoes sink into the plush pile and leave tracks both ways.

"Answer your fucking phone, Caleb!" I bark into my unanswered cell. Back to voicemail. "Yeah, dickhead, this is only my twelfth message. ANSWER YOUR FUCKING PHONE!"

Okay, this isn't healthy. I set the phone on the table. Why am I so worked up over this woman? I just need Caleb to give me some words of wisdom or some shit—tell me how to make this fucked up situation better.

I *was* going to ask her to dinner. "Hey, Sophie, would you and Charlie like to have dinner with me tonight?" I mimic out loud. "I'm such an asshole!"

What made me think giving her the Spanish-fucking-Inquisition about Charlie's father was going to earn me a fucking gold star?

Honestly, I didn't think it was going to go in the direction that it did, either. I tried bringing the conversation somewhere else, but she was done. She actually told me it was better if we didn't talk so I could "relax more deeply." It was good bull-shit, though; I'd hand her that.

I sit on the edge of the bed in my room. Sophie's just a few rooms away. Def Leppard's "Hysteria" just came up on my iPod, and it's perfect. I'm in hysteria, and she's over there, hating my stupid ass.

A knock on the door brings me quickly to my feet and across the room. I pull it open, hopeful.

"Hello, Mr. North. Your in-house order is ready." The hotel's delivery guy is pushing a shiny silver cart.

I'm more than disappointed. "Yeah. Thanks." I remove a few bills from my pocket and set them in his hand. "I'll take it from here."

I pull the tray into my room and shut the door. Under the silver cover is beef stroganoff over fresh steamed green beans. It looks and smells incredible, and I am starving … but I'm not *hungry*, not really, not for food. I eat anyway, knowing my body needs it.

When I'm finished, I head into the bathroom.

Turning the faucet, I let the hot water run into the Jacuzzi tub. I pour a good couple cups of Epsom salt into it and wait till it fills. I'm just going to take a bath, watch a good skin flick and go to sleep early. I have to be at the gym at five in the morning anyway.

"I can fix this," I say determinedly. "I WILL fix this. Tomorrow is a new day."

JOSH
PAST

I'm sleeping when I hear the lock disengage and the door open.

"Time to get up, Josh," Cade says.

Fuck. "I like it in here." I roll over in the cot and face the wall. *Fuck getting up. Fuck him.*

"Come to breakfast. I know you're hungry."

Cade's footfalls go back the way they came down the hall. The aroma of pancakes and bacon wafts through the empty room. I sigh deeply, resignedly, and roll out of the bed. The fight happened last night before I had dinner—I'm famished. After I get washed up and dressed, I make my way downstairs and into the dining room.

Almost everyone is already at the table, but a few stragglers like me are still coming in. I make sure I sit away from Liam, who I'm not done hitting yet. The huge picnic-style table is about twenty-four feet long. This kid, Reese, is putting plates all around it. Seconds later, Darren comes stalking his way through the room and shoulders past Reese hard, knocking him against the table.

"What the fuck?" Reese is immediately up in Darren's face.

"Back off, Irish, or I'll fuck you up," Darren warns.

This is great entertainment, but unless someone swings soon, Cade will break it up before it starts.

"Are you assholes serious? Can't we just fucking eat without a fight?" Talon, a Native American kid with long black hair, rolls his eyes. He's maybe a couple of years younger than me and has been here a few months. "I'm getting so sick of this shit."

"Fuck you too," Darren shoots at Talon.

Now, Talon stands up and gets behind Reese.

Someone says something, and the first punch gets thrown. A few of the girls back up into the adjacent living room to get out of the way while a couple of others step back to watch the show. In a few seconds, everyone else is up fighting. There are about twenty of us, and it's a fucking ruckus!

Liam and I get to each other, and I fully intend on finishing what we started yesterday.

Liam swings. I duck and watch as his fist goes through the wall and gets caught in the plaster. I laugh until he kicks me into the table. The plastic cups rattle against the wood, and several fall to the floor. He gets his hand free, and we square off again.

A foghorn blares deafeningly through the room! Everyone stops and covers their ears.

Cade stands at the head of the table with the can and calmly announces, "Quinn has a special meal planned for us all. I expect us to act in a manner that shows we're grateful."

Quinn pushes through the swinging kitchen door with two monster platters stacked with pancakes. Behind her, Cade's wife, Debra, brings in a vat of maple syrup and a pan heaped with slices of bacon. It smells good. It smells like home.

"Look,"—Quinn drops the platters to the table, demanding our attention—"None of us wants to be here. We all come from shitty situations that we don't have the power to change. All we can do is change our own actions. We're lucky to be in a home like this one." She nods, and her soft blonde curls sway with the movement. "Cade and Debra are the best people I've ever known. Being here gives us a real chance to be okay!" Quinn's voice gets louder. "To make something of ourselves! To have a future away from our asshole parents, away from the gangs who don't care if we live or die, away from the streets! So get it through your heads, you idiots! Right now, we're all we have. So instead of all the fighting and cock measuring, we need to pull it together and have each other's backs. God knows nobody else does."

PRESENT

THE ALARM THAT WAKES ME REMINDS ME OF A boxing match.

Round Two, I think. I have to make things right with Sophie. Today's conversation is going to go very differently. I'll make sure of it.

At the gym, I'm going through the motions. Caruso shouts at me to put my heart into it. I try to make him think I am, but I'm really just watching the door. Sophie should be here by now.

Watching the clock is like a fucking torturous nightmare. Now, McGee is yelling at me, and his face is turning bright red.

Squatting, I wedge my fingers and hands underneath the massive tractor tire, then push it up and over.

"DO IT AGAIN!" McGee crows. People can probably hear him across the fucking street.

So I do it again, all the way across the floor and back again until McGee is satisfied.

Christ, where is she?

McGee tosses a rolled-up jump rope to me. "Work it out, loverboy."

I catch it and give him a death stare.

"Ha!' he laughs. "Put it into the workout."

I shake my head, and he walks off.

Lifting my sports bottle, I spray a stream of water into my mouth and then set my earbuds into place and hit play on my iPod. How many times can a human being listen to one song over and over again? Because honestly, Trapt's "Contagious" has been playing on repeat since last night, and all I can do is listen and chant it under my breath.

How the fuck has she done this to me? I haven't been able to stop thinking about her since I was discharged from the hospital. When she's near me, I feel relaxed and calm. When she's not, I'm agitated or nervous, wondering about what's going on in her personal life. When she goes home at night or has the day off, all I think about is what she's doing, if she's thinking about me, if she's safe, if she's seeing other guys, what she looks like naked …

When she finally walks through the door, I

almost lose it. I don't try to hide the fact that I'm looking at her. I don't try to hide the expression that betrays the feelings that are coursing through me—that I blew it and that she means something to me.

Sophie looks at me from under her lashes but then averts her gaze. She looks pained. I wonder if she's going to quit. Christ, I pray she doesn't quit! I hate that I pried and hurt her. I don't understand the buttons I pushed, but I'm sorry as hell that I pushed them.

She's so beautiful—so soft, so gentle. She's a loving, tender mother, and I can tell, because of the way she is with me, that she's a great friend. Sophie disappears down the hallway toward the offices.

Just like that, I want to take all her hurt away.

Now I perform like a fucking fighter. McGee, Caruso and Silva are watching me as if I have become someone else since the early morning workout.

"GET UP THE ROPE!" Caruso shouts.

I strain every muscle as I pull my body up the rope. At the top, I hit the buzzer, and everyone in the gym cheers. We all have a love/hate relationship with *the rope*.

Sophie is now sitting with Angie at the front desk. They talk and watch me intermittently, and I'd give my left testicle to know what they're saying!

Back on solid ground, Caruso hands me an electrolyte-replenishing drink, and I suck it down in seconds. "You want to run in or out today?" he asks.

"In." Watching her, I feel more settled than I have all morning. Knowing she's close. It really doesn't make sense, does it? Why can't I stop thinking about her?

Stop looking at her every millisecond. You look like a stalker! I shift my eyes and head to the treadmills.

I start flipping through artist playlists and stop on Van Halen. "Okay, Eddie, give me something."

"THAT ROPE KICKS MY ASS EVERY TIME," I GROAN.

Sophie's deft, hot hands are making my arm muscles melt like butter.

"I don't know," she says, "looks to me like you got the best of it."

She hasn't quit, and she *is* talking to me. At least a little.

My mind is going ballistic, trying to think of how to start a conversation without messing it up.

I remember how we found common ground over philosophy.

"Do you remember who said this one?" I ask. "Expose yourself to your deepest fear; after that, fear has no power … you are free."

"I should know," she admits. "Don't tell me." I hear a smile in her voice, and it's relieving.

"Okay, give me a hint."

She's playing. I can go with that. "'Break on Through.'"

"Not getting anything."

I sing, "Come on, baby, light my—"

"FIRE!" she comes in strongly. "Morrison." She sighs and adds, "He died too soon."

"Yeah, I agree, way before his time."

"Do you like The Doors' music?"

"Yeah, I like everything music, from classic and hard rock to grunge and metal to Yo-Yo Ma."

"That's a varied musical appetite," Sophie deduces.

I have an insatiable appetite.

"Okay, flip it over like a pancake," she says and then laughs. "Oh my God! I'm sorry!"

"Hey, I can flip it like a pancake." I roll over onto my back.

"I give Charlie massages almost every night before bed," she explains. "I use it with her so often … it just slipped out like it was normal."

I laugh with her. It's the perfect song.

"ABOUT TIME YOU RETURNED MY CALL, YOU miserable fuck!" I complain.

"Oh, relax, I haven't had time. What the hell is going on?" Caleb asks.

Why do I suddenly feel like an idiot? "I met someone."

Caleb laughs. "You're always meeting someone."

"This someone I want to invite home for Christmas."

Silence.

More silence.

Pissing-me-off silence.

"Say something!" I growl.

"I don't know what to say," Caleb exclaims. "You've never even brought a 'someone' home for dinner before, let alone a major family holiday. I think I need a drink for this conversation."

"Skip it. I don't think she'll come. I'm having a hard time getting her to come out with me at all," I admit.

"Have you grown a pair to ask her?"

"Fuck you. Yes. I invited her to both events this weekend."

"And she said no?" he reasons.

"She's said nothing."

"When's the last time you talked to her?"

"A couple hours ago." I'm alone in my hotel room—*not like me at all*—and what am I doing? Thinking about Sophie, of course.

"Alright, asshat, you either talk, or I'm hanging up," Caleb threatens.

"She works for me," I tell him. "The masseuse."

"Oh, yeah, I saw her at the hospital a few times. She's hot," he trumpets. "So you hired her … Ha! And now you want to date her. You're putting both of you into a precarious situation. No wonder she's not giving you an answer."

"What do you mean?" I demand.

"She's caught, man. She might want to say yes but doesn't dare risk her job. Really, you're not an idiot. Just think about it."

When I don't say anything, he continues, "Sleeping with the boss at night makes for an uncomfortable work experience during the day, don't you think?"

"Maybe I should fire her," I say.

"WHAT?"

I laugh gruffly. "I didn't think about the fact that I might have been sabotaging myself when I offered her the job, then pretty much dared her to take it by doubling the salary."

"You did what?" Caleb says, sounding mystified.

I explain it all to him, including the bet and what will happen if either of us makes the first move.

"Come on, Josh, what were you thinking?"

"I wasn't thinking, obviously."

"What is it about her you're so enamored with?"

"Oh, God, her hands alone—" I begin.

Caleb interrupts, "No! Don't need the imagery—SKIP!"

I sigh deeply. "Sophie is intelligent and philosophical. She's a deep thinker. She has a good sense of humor and is an amazing mom."

"An amazing *what?*" Caleb halts my train.

"She's a single mother to the cutest three-year-old little girl," I verify.

"Bro, you are so completely out of your league here. Back up and keep going. You do not want to mess with this."

He's suddenly pissing me off. "Why are you saying that?"

"Josh, that's not the kind of woman who *dates*. Single mothers want a mate. someone who is going to be a partner. Jesus, think wolves, Josh. Pack animals."

"Are you comparing Sophie to a wolf?"

"I'm taking an example from science."

"I'm taking a shot," I say and tilt my head back for some Jim Beam from the mini-bar.

"Female and male wolves form a partnership —they're both the alphas of the pack. They need each other for their own survival and the survival of the pups."

"Get to the point!" I snap.

"She has a pup, so she needs another alpha."

I let that settle in. "When the fuck did you turn into Oprah?"

"Shut up! I've been in a serious relationship for a while now, and Piper has a lot of friends. They talk."

Could I be that for her? Have I thought about the big picture beyond the chase? Beyond my dick?

"If she's been hurt, she's not likely to trust again easily," Oprah continues. "On top of that, you're her *pup's* bread and butter. Unless she feels confident enough in her career that she's sure she can get another job quick, she's not going to risk that security."

Sophie is … I don't know, Sophie—I want to be near her, spend time with her. I want to talk with her and listen to what she has to say. I want to be friends …

"She's got real baggage," Caleb notes.

That infuriates me! "Charlie is NOT baggage!"

"Oh shut up, hothead! I mean it as something you'd have to step in and help carry.

Responsibility, Josh. Are you really ready for that?"

I back down. I get it.

"You like one-night stands, no strings and no phone numbers." I wish he would just shut up. "You don't want to hurt her, right?"

"I hear you, Oprah," I bark.

How can I explain that those things—which I never cared about before—the responsibilities, the real relationship, the partnership … are things that Sophie makes me think about?

"I know, right? I'm always watching shit like Dr. Phil and Oprah, or I'm reading all the time—books, magazines, anything Piper needs." Caleb becomes solemn.

I close my eyes. I'm such a selfish prick that I forgot his pain. "How's she holding up, man?"

"Sick of being sick." Caleb sighs. "The doctor wants to admit her to perform some heavy tests. She won't do it until after the New Year."

"Isn't that dangerous?" I ask. "Some things should be dealt with quickly or …"

"Yeah, I know all of that. So does she. It's too close to Christmas, and she doesn't want horrible news so that everyone can then remember the holiday as the time when Piper was diagnosed with something …" He lets his voice trail off.

I want to say I'm sorry, but it's not enough. "She's in good hands with you, Caleb."

"Yeah, she is." I hear the pride and courage in his voice, and it makes me feel like breaking. "I love you, man," Caleb says. He's just like Dad.

"You too."

We hang up, and my mind is full of questions with no cut-and-dried answers. If I screw this up, the consequences could be severe.

I throw back another shot.

CHAPTER EIGHT

SOPHIE

Wednesday, on the plane, Josh asked me to the Friday and Saturday night events. Wednesday, on the job, he asked questions that made me batten down the hatches and run for the storm cellar. I did better on Thursday; at least I could talk to him again. Of course, it was a perfect conversation about philosophy and music … and who am I trying to kid? I want to know what got him into fighting, and why he doesn't have a girlfriend, and how he gets along with his family, but my questions aren't just innocent chit-chat. I want to know because … because I *care* about him.

Does he *care* about me? Is that why he asked those things? I rake my fingers through my hair. I have to stop.

"Mommy, are we going yet?" Charlie is having

fun jumping on the very springy hotel bed. "If we don't go, we could go swimming in the bathtub again."

"That was fun." Last night, I put one of my pink sports bras on her while I wore my white one. We pulled on shorts and slipped into the massive tub and played mermaids. We laughed so much and it was so much fun—her with her bubbly soda, and me with a couple glasses of Chardonnay. She made me take our photos with my phone.

I felt good and was proud that my very best friend was a three-year-old.

Today, Josh would be working with the press, doing interviews, and getting ready for the Hard Rock event.

I checked my phone earlier. He called a few times, and he left some texts. He also invited us to dinner last night, but I said I was too tired. I'm at a stalemate. I don't know what to do. It's complicated, and I can't seem to understand how to reach the surface for a breath. A crystal ball would be fucking nice. Not knowing what to do sometimes makes you do nothing. That's where I am.

His last text is from this morning, asking me if I'd thought about accompanying him to the Hard Rock and reminding me I'd have a great time. But I'm not scared of Josh. I'm scared to death of him! He makes butterflies rush through me at the mere mention of his name. When I see him, my blood pumps so fast, and my heart and pulse pound so hard, I'm sure I'm going to drop and have to be rushed to a hospital.

Josh is real. He's an honest, maybe even honorable, man. Yes, he has a reputation as a playboy—and I can bet it's well deserved—but if he ever settles down, he'll be more than an amazing lover. He'll give his whole heart away.

And maybe I'm an idiot romantic in a world full of liars and cheats and people whose hatred will wilt you. Projecting what I *want* onto what I *think* I know of Josh North is stupid and danger-ous. He's a fighter, for Christ's sake. He uses those hands for violence.

I remind myself that he also uses those same hands to save people.

And I'm back to being at a stalemate.

I take a deep breath. It's very unprofessional and rude to not give a gentleman an answer.

> I'm sorry. I won't be able to make it this evening to the event...

I type in the text box. I struggle with sending it. I struggle with not being able to give him a real reason why. I struggle with the simple fact that *I want to go!*

"Mommy, you're taking forever."

"Yes, I know." I hang my head and press send.

I GAVE BRITTANI THE DAY OFF, SO IT'S JUST ME and Charlie. I help her slip on her warm winter boots with the pink pom-poms, straighten her wristband, and zip her coat. She and Strawberry Shortcake smile up at me. I love being a mom. It's the most satisfying and important thing I've ever done. It's unconditional love.

She twines her little fingers between mine, and we're off. We take a ride in a yellow cab to the Denver Children's Museum.

Together, we paint masterpieces in the art studio, make amazing bubble creations that send Charlie into fits of laughter, dress up like back-yard animals and play in the tree fort. After an hour in the play market, we eat a delicious lunch in the museum's kid-friendly café and then bravely tackle the second half of the museum. After a while, Charlie's exhausted and needs a nap. I think I need one too.

We catch another cab back to the hotel. A couple blocks from it, though, a clothing store with displays I can't seem to resist catches my eye.

"Please stop here."

I pay the driver.

Charlie whines about leaving the warm cab. I

pull her through the boutique and find what I'm looking for.

She falls asleep on the dressing room floor while I try on black, faded skinny jeans, black platform heels, a white baggy shirt and a black faux leather jacket.

I study myself in the mirror. I haven't dressed up like this in a long time.

Smiling, I talk to the saleswoman about wanting to wear the clothes out.

"Do you have a big date tonight?" She's excited for me as she carefully clips the tags.

"You could probably say that." I'm trying to fight the rising effervescence within me.

A saleswoman stays by the dressing room with Charlie while I go up to the register to pay. Then I put my old clothes in the fashionable bag and sling it over my shoulder so I can carry my sleepy bundle outside to hail another cab.

"I HAVE A FEELING SHE MIGHT SLEEP FOR THE night," I tell Brittani. "Thanks for this."

"That's why I'm here," she says.

We have adjoining rooms, so there's more space for Charlie. She's crashed in the other room at the moment. Brittani's watching me fix my makeup while she reads from her Kindle.

"I like the smoky look. You look amazing!" she exclaims.

"Thanks." I pull a brush through my hair. "I think I'll leave it down. I almost never do that."

"It's sexy," she crows from behind her Kindle's soft glow.

"Maybe I should put it up?"

"Stop it! You, your hair and your makeup are perfect. Now go!"

I breathe through my nose. "Okay."

I can't believe I'm doing this!

"I'm nervous," I confess.

"Yeah, you are. It's Josh freaking North and a ton of music celebrities."

She has a point.

"And remember, if you see Adam Levine, I do expect you to commit a felony if you have to in order to bring him to me."

"Got it. Felony." I reach into the closet and grab out my big white scarf. "I don't want to get caught by photographers."

Britt indicates the scarf with a nod. "That'll work."

Standing on the edge of oblivion, I say, "Wish me luck."

"Good luck," she offers.

I smile and head out the door.

THE GIANT, GLEAMING, NEON GUITAR LIGHTS THE front of the modern building, sending the dark scattering. My adrenaline is flowing again as I step out of the cab. I'm a little late, which is probably a good thing since the photographers have run away to warmer places. I enter with ease, show my I.D. and the guest pass I got from McGee earlier—just in case—and weave myself through the crowd to find Josh.

I fluff the ends of my hair with my fingers and press my lips together one more time to keep the coat of pink lipstick even.

I've decided that tonight, there will be no heaviness. *Fun and light, Sophie.*

This is a neutral place where Josh and I can get to know each other on a different playing field.

The place is packed, but I catch a glimpse of Silva walking away from the bar. I follow him. My hands are trembling, and I rub them together to try to stop it.

Silva walks right up to him. Josh turns his head to the right. He's smiling, maybe laughing, and obviously having a good time. It makes me smile bigger. Josh takes the light beer bottle from Silva's hand and then turns his head to the left.

In that instant, in that moment in time, I feel

everything—everything I've ever felt, everything I've ever thought, everything I ever believed I knew—comes crashing down.

A pretty blonde on Josh's left enjoys having his bare, tattooed, muscled arm over her shoulders protectively, holding her right next to him.

She plants a lingering kiss on his cheek.

My blood feels cold. I try to urge myself forward. So what if he has another date?

Am I so easily replaced? Yes, I am.

Sophie, was it really even a date? Wasn't it simply a colleague thing? He asked me to *accompany* him.

I can't think clearly. *Damn it!* I can't focus at all.

The dim lights are disorienting, while the bright neon pierces into my mind.

The couple moves in sync toward a booth. I duck behind a decorative support beam and lean against it a little. He sits first, then pulls her in next to him so they're cozied up together. I can only imagine what their unseen hands will be doing!

I'm an idiot. I'm a fucking idiot! What was I thinking?

My stomach clenches, and my eyes begin to sting.

Shit! I need to get out of here before someone spots me. I turn and bolt out of the place, pressing through the crowds of people with my head tucked down

—just like the proverbial tail between my legs. *I should've known better!*

I CAN'T GET OUTSIDE FAST ENOUGH. I CAN'T GET into the cab and back to the hotel fast enough.

The elevator carries me to my floor. I'm nauseous as I unlock the door.

Oh, fuck. Britt is still awake, reading on her Kindle. She turns when she hears the door.

"What are you doing back already?" she demands. "Did you forget something?"

"I'm not talking about it!" I only pull off my shoes before Britt grabs me by the shoulders and guides me to sit on the sofa. "I said, I'm not talking about it. I'm tired, and I'm going to bed."

Softly, kindly, she says, "What happened, sweetie?"

I force it out. "He was with someone."

She waits before asking, "And?"

"And *what?*" I was stupid for going in the first place.

"I was under the impression that we *expected* him to be with someone else."

I wasn't *expecting* anything except for Josh *not* to have been wearing a blonde.

"Sophie, he's Josh 'The Jackhammer' North.

He couldn't very well attend the event without a date. He has a rep to uphold."

"Some reputation—being a man-whore." I feel like punching the wall.

"He is. It's true," Britt agrees. "But he's more than that. And besides, if he'd shown up alone, the press and his fans would've had a field day. They would've started pressing him to see if he'd gotten stiffed, and they would've printed all kinds of shit in the magazines. They've done it before."

Being McGee's niece, she would know. I hadn't thought of it that way.

She continues, "Josh is always in the news and the papers. He's always under heavy scrutiny—from local city news to national headlines. Wait a minute." Her expression changes, and her eyes grow wide. "You *like* him."

"I don't," I protest. I have to hide my face, so I open the blinds and turn a chair so I can sit and look out at the city's lights. They sparkle so beautifully they almost look like stars.

"It makes sense," Britt says from behind me. "You know, he just may like you too."

This discussion may now be the worst part of my night. At least before, I was humiliated all by myself.

"You should have gone all the way in like you were supposed to. You're his employee. It wasn't an official date."

"Thanks for the reminder, Britt." I'm miserable, and I'm wounded, and I'm stupid, and I can't figure out which feels worst.

"If you had gone into the party like a normal person—"

"Be careful. I can still fire you."

"You would have seen for sure what his reaction would've been," she surmises. "He could've dropped her like a sack of spiders. You don't know."

Or he could've kissed her and felt her up and taken her home right in front of me. I shake my head dejectedly. "I'm no good at poker, Britt."

She's quiet for a bit. Her arm reaches down from behind me, offering me a glass of juice. I can smell the alcohol she's mixed in with the O.J.

"Thanks." I take it and sip at it.

"I know we've only been working together for a short time, but I'd like to consider you a friend," she explains.

I close my eyes as the warmth of the alcohol pours into my system. I think about Ayana, whom I've known since I moved to Williston a year ago. I love her to bits, but I still keep her at arm's length—it's easier to leave and disappear that way.

"Thanks, Britt. I do appreciate your advice, even if it doesn't seem like it."

We sit in relative silence for a little while. I flip

the TV on, but neither Britt nor I are really watching. It's an infomercial for some cooking gadget that's supposed to make life *so* much easier. If only it could transform more than just my kitchen.

Britt keeps giving me these appraising looks as if she's trying to figure out how to convince me to head back to the party, but she doesn't push.

My phone bleeps with an incoming text.

"'Hey, scrapper, missed you at the party,'" Britt reads. "He calls you scrapper. That's so cute."

"Delightful. How about you don't read my text messages."

"I bet he's back in his room!" she says like she's struck oil. "Go talk to him."

"No way!"

She sighs in disgust.

"If he's not alone, I'm going to look stupid."

"If he's not alone and he bothered to take the time to text you, it means you're a hell of a lot more on his mind than she is."

She has a point. And the invite still stands for tomorrow night's party. I glance at my watch, and it is technically tomorrow.

Do the thing you fear the most.

I swallow everything in my glass, stand up decidedly and slip back on my shoes.

Britt watches me cautiously.

"I'll be right back," I announce and sweep out into the hallway before I lose my nerve.

If I overthink or stall, I won't do it. And even though I'm tempted to listen at his door, I don't. I just knock and brace myself for a giggling blonde in a towel to answer the door. When that happens, I'll be businesslike, ask to see him, and ...

"Hi." Josh stands in the doorway with a towel wrapped around his waist. Wisps of steam rise from his skin, where water droplets bead then break, and stream into the crevices of his muscles.

I tear my eyes from him to look past him. I don't see her. She's probably in the bathroom.

"Wow, you look incredible." He draws out the last word of his statement. By the time I get my gaze back to his, I see he's eating me up with his eyes from my head to my feet. "Never seen you dressed like that before. Looks good on you."

He goes from hungry to visibly upset before he can hide it. He closes his eyes for a moment as if a thought just hit him hard, then says, "Did you—?"

I cut him off. "Does the invitation to accompany you to the event tomorrow still stand?"

"Absolutely." He nods.

All I want to do is get out of here before she emerges and my courage dissolves.

"What time will you be picking me up then?" I sound like a freaking robot.

A smile hints at the corners of his mouth. "Six o'clock." Then he adds, "Would you like to come in for a drink?"

My breath hitches in my lungs and catches in my throat. "Um …"

"It's no fun being alone after a party." He opens the door all the way, turns and walks back into the room, leaving me at the threshold.

I take a cautious step forward.

"Close the door behind you," he says without looking back as he saunters to the bar.

I press my back against the door and lean on it as it latches closed.

Good God, I should leave, go right back to my room, because this … thing … right here and now … has nothing to do with business or casual … ness, or anything but pure want.

Josh walks back—still in the towel, mind you —and hands me a drink. "Don't look at me like that. You've seen me in less."

A small sound escapes my throat. Hoping he didn't notice, I quickly tip back my head and consume almost half the drink.

"What did you do tonight?" He sits and makes a triangle with his legs by resting one ankle against his knee. He sips at a glass of ice water.

He's baiting me! As soon as I realize it, my awkwardness evaporates. *Two can play at this game.*

I stride across the floor and perch on the edge

of his tightly made bed. "I got in a little sightseeing."

"Hmm." He nods. He seems to be momentarily flustered by the sight of me on his bed, but he regains composure fast. "What made you retire so early?"

"Just because I have Mary Poppins with me doesn't mean my job as a mom is trumped. I'm getting up early to spend the day with Charlie." I lean back a bit and cross my legs, swinging at the knee.

"How about a tag-along?" he asks.

"A what?" I'm confused.

"I'll finish up with promos around noon. Let me take you and Charlie to the aquarium," he suggests.

"Aquarium." I'm in a daze.

"It's one of the best in the country."

"Really?" Here I am, trying to play some sexy game of sharks and minnows and *trying* to be the shark when he up and asks me *and* Charlie to spend the day with him. "Why?" The thought in my mind just slips out of my mouth.

"Because it would be fun," he answers matter-of-factly.

"Fun." My leg stops swinging, and I sit up. Both feet are firmly on the floor. He's adding Charlie to the mix. I'm not sure how I feel about that.

"Charlie's an extension of you. She's what makes you who you are. Why wouldn't I want to hang out with the two of you?" And again, stone-cold fighter Josh North is tender.

I think of how he played with Charlie on the plane and how she wanted to hold his hand.

He can't possibly imagine what I'm going through right now. The overwhelming desire to jump, to say yes, to give it all to him and let the cards fall. But how can I subject Charlie to that kind of heartbreak? If … when he turns out to be an asshole, she'll be the one who hurts the most. Single mothers have hard choices.

I could lie to myself, trick myself into believing we'd just be going as colleagues and that Charlie could get just as emotionally injured by a nanny she grows attached to and has to leave as she could be by a man. I take a cleansing breath and stuff down the *potential dad*, screaming violently against my brain. It's not how I want to think.

Then, a realization spreads through me like sweet, warm caramel. He invited me in to show me he was alone in here.

I stand up and head to the door before I change my mind. "Tomorrow at noon, then," I say as I leave.

Before I close the door behind me, I watch the smile that comes over his handsome face. It's enough to bring me to my knees in surrender.

CHAPTER NINE

JOSH

This photo shoot is *not* ending fast enough.

"Come on, Josh. Where is that sinful, sexy grin every woman's panties drop for?" Darla, my photographer for the past decade, is trying to find me somewhere in the mess that I've become.

What the fuck? This should be fun. I have two models in little blue bikinis on the floor, each wrapped around one of my legs.

Oh shit! It hits me that I'm glad Sophie's not here to see this. Or Charlie!

"Oh God, I'm in trouble."

"What, Josh?" one of the models says, looking up at me with wanting eyes.

"What time is it, Darla?" I feel like I'm ready to jump out of my skin.

"10:30. Got a date?" she teases.

Yes, I do, as a matter of fact.

"Perfect!" she cries. I can hear the camera shutter take a thousand photographs. "That's the smile I needed."

I've worked with a lot of photographers, but Darla's the best. She does all of my exclusive shoots and usually works with the different magazines when they're looking for the best pictures of me. I've known her since I was a teenager, and she's easy to be around. It helps that she's family —Uncle Cade's wife's sister.

"That should be enough. Do you want to break?" she asks.

"Yeah, but I need to be out for the day."

"Great, I love a day off." She replaces her lens cap. "We're done, people! Have an awesome day."

When she announces it, the models whine in protest.

I beeline to the showers since my body is covered in a greasy oil that gives my skin a sheen for the photos. Scrubbing until my skin is clean, I quickly dry off and dress in the clothes I brought for my date with Sophie and Charlie—dark blue jeans and a nice, dark blue button-up with a white t-shirt underneath. As I walk back into the studio to get my coat and things, it's all cleared out except for Darla and a couple of people on her camera crew.

"So who is she?" She breezes past me and speaks it like a secret.

"How can you tell?" I pull my coat over my shoulders.

"Because I haven't seen you this happy since your brother came back from Afghanistan." She stoops to lower some equipment into a foam-lined case.

"That was … a long time ago," I quip. "Are you telling me I haven't looked happy for over a year?"

"Happiness is subjective," Darla explains. "You've appeared happy in that time, but there's an excitement in your eyes that hasn't been there before."

"Damn, woman! Don't you have a husband you should be giving shit to?" I crack a playful grin.

"Yup, he'll get an earful in a few hours. Guess you'll just have to be his replacement for the time being." She stands with her hands on her hips like she's scolding me. "Now, who the hell is she? I need to know in case she breaks your heart."

"My heart? Who says that's at risk?"

"No one has to, Josh. It's written all over your face."

THE LIMO FINALLY PULLS INTO THE FOUR Seasons. The moment the driver stops, I'm going through the lobby two strides at a time. My destination is the gift shop.

I have to play this smart. Too much, and I'll look like an ass; not the right gift and I'll still look like an ass.

Think.

It doesn't take too long to figure out that the gift store has a good marketing plan.

I scoop up the little gold bag and head to Sophie's room.

Deep breath, Josh. This is just a fun outing.

This is not just a fun outing. This is a deliberate, thought out, intentional scenario to see what *it's* like.

Being an older brother, I have some understanding of family dynamics, but I've never been fully responsible for a kid before.

Are you sure you're ready for that kind of responsibility? Caleb's words echo through my mind.

I don't know!

All this time I've been very content with my models in bikinis or taking out two women at a time and the fun and notoriety that came with that. None of it was real, meaning my emotions were never invested, I was just having a gluttonous, rowdy time. And upholding a bad-boy reputation worked well with the fans. Win-win all the way around.

When I first met Sophie, all I wanted to do was throw her down fast and hard and work out that insane craving she'd created.

I'd be a fucking liar if I said I still didn't want to eat her alive, but since we'd been working together so intimately—our talks, her open, kind and inquisitive personality … I want more. I've never wanted more.

I want to know more. I want to know everything about her. I want to experience everything with her. And I feel the strongest, most compelling urge to protect her, to possess her, and maybe even *love* her like nobody else.

At her door, I listen in for a second before I knock. I hear Sophie singing a song with Charlie about tying her shoes. It's so cute that I wait, and in a moment, the song changes to buttoning her coat. Being a loving mother is suddenly and automatically at the top of my list of desirable qualities in a woman.

I rap my knuckles twice against the door and call out, "Knock, knock."

"Who's there?" Charlie's happy, high-pitched voice rings out.

"Cows go," I answer and listen for her response.

"Cows go, who?"

"No, silly, cows go moo!"

I hear Charlie break into a fit of laughter, and Sophie opens the door, smiling.

"Clever," she tells me with a sweet expression.

She is naturally and amazingly beautiful. I think she might be wearing a little bit of mascara, but that's all. Her face is freshly scrubbed, and her complexion is porcelain and rose.

She turns and grabs a backpack then speaks out loud, "We have Goldfish and apple slices for snacking, a fresh set of clothes, a couple pull-ups, Kleenex and wipes. Oh, and three bottles of water."

She pulls the strap over her shoulder.

"I can take it," I offer.

She smiles. "I know. But I've got it."

She's wearing a pair of jeans with low-heeled black boots, a grey button-up coat, and a lilac scarf that wraps around her neck a couple of times while the ends hang haphazardly. Her hair is pinned up in a bun with a set of red, black and gold wooden chopsticks. Her deep brown hair has streaks of auburn that make it seem as if they don't want to stay in the bun. Her lips are a soft pink. I can tell she's wearing a colorless gloss or moisturizer. Oh, how I want to kiss her right here and now.

"Are there really sharks, Joshy?" Charlie takes my attention. I notice that she's wearing the same pink wristband pouch that she wore when I saw her on the plane, and I wonder what she's got inside. Probably some cute little treasures—it's the perfect bag for a three-year-old girl since she can't lose it.

"Just wait until you see everything. There are sharks and colorful fish, and I've heard that there are even—" I squat down to get on her level, and she comes closer, sensing special info, "mermaids," I whisper.

"MERMAIDS?!" she screams. "Really, Mommy, mermaids?"

"I guess we're just going to have to see." Sophie picks Charlie up and props her on her hip.

"You know, Sophie, I can take the bag. You don't have to carry it all," I say as we walk out into the hallway. As a single mom, I'm sure she's used to doing everything herself. I wonder if she'll let me in. It's a small gesture, really, just letting me carry a day bag, but I Googled the psychology of single moms—tough, independent, do it themselves and by their own rules—and I respect her strength.

She considers me for a moment.

"Mommy!" Charlie whines impatiently.

She fists the duffel's strap and hands it to me as if it's a test.

I think I'd better not lose it.

THE AQUARIUM IS HUGE, AND KEEPING PACE WITH Charlie is mind-blowing. We look in one tank for a moment, and if it doesn't completely enthrall her, we're racing to the next.

"This is a good workout." I laugh and glance at Sophie. "No wonder you're in such great shape."

"MOMMY, LOOK! IT'S NEMO!!"

We both laugh as Charlie yanks Sophie's arm to drag her to the *Finding Nemo* exhibit.

"That's Dory, and Gill, and Nemo's daddy …" Charlie points to each fish.

"Nemo is her favorite. This was a really great choice, Josh. Thanks." As Sophie says this, she doesn't actually look at me; she keeps her gaze on the tank.

I wonder what's going through her mind because she looks happy and deeply thoughtful at the same time.

We stroll through the underwater tunnel. Charlie sets her hand on the tank as if to touch the sea turtle that swims over to greet her.

"Do you have a favorite?" I ask Sophie.

"A favorite aquatic animal? Hmm … maybe the turtle."

"Why?"

She laughs lightly but nervously as she watches the huge turtle that is seemingly playing with Charlie. "When they're first born, they don't have much of a chance in life. Everything is set up against them, and it's do or die. They have no mother or father turtle to show them the way. They have to break out of a constricting shell, crawl up through the sand they've been buried beneath, and then run like hell to the sea before they're torn apart by some waiting predator."

"They really are underdogs," I agree.

"Joshy, what are these?"

While Sophie and I are talking, Charlie moves down the tube, so we catch up with her.

"Those are moray eels."

"They look scary," she says with a dramatic shiver.

In a second, they swim away, and Charlie screams! Both Sophie and I jump.

"SHARK!"

I try to calm my racing heart. "Does she always scream this way?"

"Always." Sophie giggles. "Wait till she catches sight of the mermaids."

Another half hour into our trip, I learned three-year-olds have two volumes, loud and louder.

At the touch pool, Charlie simultaneously screams and laughs while trying to get the courage to lay a hand on any of the creatures who circle by just under the surface.

"The triangle fish is going to bite me!" she says, sure of herself.

"That's a ray. They feel rubbery, a little like a Barbie doll's legs." I keep one from swimming further and stroke the rubbery flesh with my fingers before I bring it a little closer to her. "See, it's safe."

Her smile is so alive when she stretches her little hand over the ray's body. She laughs, "It does feel like Barbie legs."

Her giggle is contagious. Sophie and I catch it.

"Charlie, you're so brave!" Sophie praises her.

"Joshy keeps me safe," she decides, petting the creature I'm still holding.

How does such a simple, innocent statement from a child pierce through my heart and anchor itself there?

"LADIES AND GENTLEMEN AND CHILDREN OF ALL AGES, THE MERMAIDS HAVE ARRIVED!" an announcer booms through the overhead speakers.

Charlie squeals and pulls on Sophie's arm, then grabs my hand as well.

"We have to go this way." As I lead us down the corridor, I'm very much aware that Charlie's small, tender hand is in mine, holding it excitedly, trustingly. The comparison isn't lost on me; on the contrary, it's all I can think about. My hand is huge, monstrous and deadly, rippled with muscle and scars, while hers is soft and pure, tiny and loving.

I'm not the only one experiencing something deep and profound. Sophie is trying to secretly wipe her tears. The pain in her visage is so clear; I want to take her pain and eradicate it.

Another emotion I see in her eyes is hope as Charlie stands between us, holding each of our hands.

The three of us are linked.

CHAPTER TEN
SOPHIE

There is nothing sexier than a rough, dangerous man who can humble himself to play on a little child's level.

Charlie's absolute acceptance of Josh is unraveling me. Part of me screams, *get away from him!* Another part of me wants to reach out and take his hand with as much ease and trust as Charlie did this afternoon.

And what the hell is Josh thinking *anyway*?? I'm not a mind reader. Just because he's sweet on Charlie doesn't prove he has any substantial feelings for me.

How could I ever even *think* I could compete with the gorgeous and influential women he's always hooked up with, who can give him so much more than me? I'm not walking down any red carpets. They hang all over him like ornaments. They boost his playboy reputation. That's fine for them, but I am *not* an ornament.

I can't be.

I know I'm pretty and intelligent, but I don't have a celebrity's face or body. I keep healthy, but … I giggle out loud over the idea of Josh undressing me in a fit of passion and then getting spooked by the odd purple lines that run in rivulets down my abdomen.

Ah, stretch marks.

"Are you wearing stockings?" Britt calls from the other room, distracting me from my idiocy.

"Thigh highs," I answer.

As I roll them on, all I can think about is Josh rolling them off.

I can't help it! He's too gorgeous. I want his hands all over me. What woman wouldn't? What woman doesn't?

The event is supposed to be fun, and … Oh God, who am I kidding? There will be models and starlets, and if I could just get over the fact that *Josh* is accompanying me, maybe I could enjoy it.

I'd read the magazine articles and the internet news about how he often goes to a party with one woman and leaves with another or both.

That wouldn't happen to me. Right? Would he humiliate me that way? He'd humiliated other women.

Just focus on the party, Sophie, I reason, fighting down the feelings of hurt and embarrassment that are already rising in my throat at the thought of being abandoned. *It's going to be incredible, with or without Josh. If he takes off on you, he takes off. You can take care of yourself.*

Earlier that morning, I'd gone out to find a dress. It was easy. I chose a classic, sexy, almost vintage-style bronze gown that gathered about the waist and hips. It reminds me of something Grace Kelly, Jacqueline Kennedy or Marilyn Monroe might have worn.

I put on small drop pearl earrings and ask Britt to fasten the dainty strand of pearls that sits high on my throat.

"I love your hair down and long like this, in soft, wide curls. You're going to turn heads and break hearts." Britt nods, looking me over. "And your makeup is perfect."

"Mommy, let me buckle your shoes." Charlie works at the straps of the eggshell pumps. "You look like a princess." Her eyes are full of awe.

At that moment, Bruno Mars's song "Treasure" comes on the radio.

"Dance with me!" Charlie jumps up and grabs my hands.

"Come on, Britt, get in on this action," I say, extending my hand.

The three of us jam out together, singing that

we're each other's treasures. By the time the song ends, we're laughing and out of breath.

A second later, we hear a knock, then Josh's voice at the door. "Knock knock."

"Who's there, Joshy?" Charlie sing-songs, melting my heart.

"Iva."

"Iva, who?" She giggles.

"Iva sore hand from knocking so much!"

"Can I open it, Mommy?" Her excitement is revving up my own. I can barely nod yes.

I catch a breathless look at Britt, who smiles supportively.

Now, I keep my eyes focused on the door. Charlie opens it so wide she slams it against the opposite wall. My back tenses even more.

The moment seems utterly suspended in time, as if forever just occurred, and we are somehow standing in it together.

Josh wears a fitted tux—sleek, black, breathtaking. The fabric strains ever so slightly around the muscles of his arms and chest. His dark, perfectly cropped hair and white pressed shirt are begging me to destroy them. To rip each button and expose the gorgeous, cut chest that I know is underneath.

Damn, I'm in trouble. I'm quickly and undoubtedly losing all of my resolve.

"Sophie, you look like a goddess."

I hear his voice and register his words, but I can't move. I can't respond. The song that Taylor Swift sings with Ed Sheeran is now playing on the radio, and it sweeps me further into the present (possibly delusional) moment. But I can't deny that, for me, *everything has changed.*

Charlie races over and clings to Josh's perfectly pressed pant leg.

"Charlie!" I begin to scold.

"It's fine." Josh bends down and picks her up. "I have a present for you." He opens his hand over her face and lets a pretty pink, sparkly heart on a gold chain appear as if by magic.

She grabs it, screams, wiggles out of his arms and runs back to me, begging me to put it on her so she can look like me.

I still can't tear my eyes from him. "Have Britt help you like she helped me."

Taking the initiative, Josh sees my cloak in the closet by the door, carefully removes it from the hanger and walks around me. Every cell and nerve stand at attention as I feel his eyes examine my back before he drapes the fabric across my bare shoulders.

He comes back in front of me and holds out that strong hand that I'd contemplated so much earlier this afternoon.

Now, peeking out from under his cuff, a silver Rolex decorates his shapely, tattooed wrist.

I'm thinking I'm not going to make it to the event and that we could just simply walk out and straight into his room.

"You look like a prince and princess." Charlie giggles as if she's full of effervescent bubbles.

"The limo is waiting outside, my princess." Josh bows a bit, and I take his offered hand.

PEOPLE WATCH US AS WE WALK ARM IN ARM through the hotel lobby. I feel like Julia Roberts in *Pretty Woman*.

We step into the cold December night. A light snow is falling, and I wonder if I'm in a dream.

The driver comes around to open my door, but Josh stops him.

"Thanks, Pete. I've got this."

Pete moves aside, smiling. "Yes, sir."

Josh opens the door and takes my hand, helping to lower me into the vehicle before closing me safely in. In a moment he goes around to the other side and sits opposite of me.

His gaze is penetrating. His eyes are all over me. My breath quickens.

"You're the most beautiful woman I've ever seen," he says.

I would say thank you if I could. My mouth gapes open a little; I feel it. My eyes close. I can't handle the power of his scrutiny. My body and mind are rocked with primal need. If I don't get control of my thoughts, we won't make it to the event. Honestly, I don't even care anymore about anything. I want to feel him all over me. I want to feel the hardness of his frame hovering over my naked form and the sensation of him pressing onto me, inside of me, filling me, driving me, pumping with me.

It's over. I've lost the fight. I've lost the bet. I would do absolutely anything to have him inside of me now.

How did I do that? How did my emotions swing from feeling the very probable pain of Josh embarrassing and rejecting me at the party to an absolute surrendering to him?

Slowly, I allow my eyes to open. His black leather shoes shine, and I think about how long, wide and thick his feet are. Slowly, my gaze climbs, hypnotized by his very presence—the bend of his knees, the strength of his thighs. His hands sweep over the sides of his legs restlessly. My eyes glide to the muscled girth of his waist, then to that perfect stretch of fabric across his chest that again makes me want to rip his shirt like wrapping paper off a gift. His neck is gorgeous—thick with muscle and lines of veins. I want to bite and run my tongue across them.

I can't stop myself. I know he sees and feels

what I'm doing, but I'm too far past restraint. I drink in his sharp chin and the angles of his face. His strong, firm jaw clenches.

My eyes finally come to his and land there.

Josh is on fire. I can see it in him as much as I can feel my own burning.

Neither of us says a word.

My arousal forces me to press my legs together and reposition myself. Josh audibly but softly breathes at my movement.

I have to touch him. I'm desperate to quench this thirst.

I lean forward just the slightest bit before I feel the limo change course and stop.

We each watch the other, but before I have a chance or the nerve to say or do anything, Pete opens Josh's door.

Josh remembered what I said about the red carpet and photographers, and he ushers me in through an unoccupied side door where a host is waiting to greet us and lead us into the main event ballroom via the busy, crowded kitchen.

When we come out the other side, my mouth falls open in awe. I've never been to any formal event—no dances, no prom, no wedding—and have nothing experiential to compare this with.

The ballroom is stunningly elegant. Gleaming crystal chandeliers are suspended from a ceiling that is etched with beautiful, strikingly royal gold designs. Rich white drapes flow over each window. The floors are covered in a luxurious golden Persian style carpet, while a massive dance floor spans out in front of a stage, where an orchestra is playing, lending background mood. White-clothed tables are decorated with bouquets of white lilies and orchids, stately gold and white table settings and crystal long-stemmed glasses.

I feel Josh staring at me and feel rather green.

"This is beautiful," I say graciously. I don't want to appear like I've never been to a formal party. I remind myself to behave with poise and grace.

"Is that Peyton Manning?" I almost stutter.

Josh smiles. "Yes, it is. Let's say hello."

NoNoNoNoNo. Then something happens, and I feel Josh's hand on my back. He has *never* touched me before. It's *meant* to be casual. It's *meant* to lead me in the direction we're going.

It's innocent, but the sensation sends me reeling.

"Hey, Josh, good to see you, man!" Peyton and Josh shake hands.

I'm just shaking.

"This is Sophie Garner," Josh introduces me.

My mouth is suddenly dry. I clear my throat.

"Please, excuse me. I'm not used to meeting celebrities," I half lie. Josh's hand is *still* on my back.

"Is that what I am? Please, don't tell my mom. She thinks I'm just a football player," he says self-deprecatingly.

I laugh lightly at his attempt to put me at ease.

We talk for another moment before Josh sets up a lunch appointment with his sports colleague, and we move on.

He talks to several well-known celebrities: Johnny Depp, Serena Williams and Derek Jeter, among others. Josh introduces me to all of them, and they all seem very down-to-earth and magnanimous.

I'm trying to feel as if I belong here. I'm trying to stir up enough self-confidence to get through this unscathed.

Everyone is dressed to the nines—actors, actresses, athletes, models and significant others—they drip with jewels and wealth and status. I begin wondering why Josh didn't invite someone important.

A waiter comes by with flutes of champagne. Josh touches my arm to stop my motion, smiles at me and then takes two.

As he passes one of the elegant glasses to me, he says, "Believe me when I tell you, you're the most beautiful woman in the room, Sophie."

You'd think it'd be easy to receive the compliment. You'd think it would wash over me and excite me. He's being gracious and trying to get me to relax, but a part of me wants to believe it. A bigger part of me wants him to mean it.

We run into Silva, and I'm thankful for a familiar face. We begin talking when Josh abruptly says, "You're in good hands, excuse me for the moment."

Silva wears an apologetic expression, and there it is. Suddenly, I know what it feels like to come to a party with Josh. The reports of him screwing waitresses in the closet or leaving with a model on his arm who he didn't come with while his dates are left standing alone hit me full force. I feel the humiliation spreading through me and warming my face. Silva says something about how he's glad I could attend this evening and asks if I'm enjoying myself.

"This has been wonderful," I reply.

He continues asking about whom I've met and whether or not Charlie and I like Denver. I feel sort of bad for him; he's stuck here entertaining me. I find myself trying to appear casual as I answer and scan the room for Josh. I don't see him.

He could have gone to the bathroom, I think.

Taking a deep breath, I decide I'm not going

to let it show. This is not a personal betrayal. I'm hardly a date; I'm a business colleague.

I give Silva a soft, knowing look. "I'm sure you have friends and business associates to mingle with. I'll be fine here on my own," I say reassuringly.

Silva regards me with a look of concentration.

I lean in so my words aren't heard by anyone else. "You've been working with Josh a long time, and I'm not under any false pretenses." I lower my voice even more. "I've heard of his party exploits."

"Ah." He nods in understanding and then matches my hushed tone. "What you don't know, Sophie, is that Josh has been a whole different person since you came along."

I'm trying to process what he's said, along with the expression he's wearing, when I'm surprised by Josh's voice beside me and feel his hand on my arm. "Sorry, that took longer than I expected. Ran into Chris Weidman."

I respond, "That's fine."

Before I know it, I'm shaking hands with the middleweight champion.

Soon, we break away from them and move to another group and then another. To my astonishment, it seems that Josh is introducing me to everyone. My fear of him dumping me alleviates, and the notion doesn't cross my mind again.

What does stay on my mind are Silva's words, *"Josh has been a whole different person since you came along."*

Also, his touches are making my senses spiral. I can't read their level of … of *what? Intention?* That's a good word. Intention: *friendly* (his warm fingers press into my shoulder), *possessive* (his arm wraps around mine, connecting us at the elbow), *sensual* (the small of my back burns from the pressure of his full hand and how long it has lingered there).

Insane! I'm simply insane! I'm sure he means nothing by any of these gestures. It's just simple body language—politeness, gentlemanliness— certainly *not* meant to turn me on like a NASA rocket engine.

Still, I notice he treats me as if I'm the most important person at the party. He watches my comfort level and adjusts our situation accordingly. I must have a real tell as to when I'm uncomfortable around some people, because he reads it clearly and moves us on.

And, although I am obviously with him, many women simply ignore me and talk to him as if I'm not present, falling all over themselves to gain his attention. Politely but coldly, he acknowledges them briefly and then pulls me away.

Later in the evening, we dine. The food is sumptuous, but they don't hold my attention because I swear, even though there is plenty of space at our assigned table, Josh's leg presses against mine.

Deliberately?

Oh God, I hope so.

I like it.

AFTER THE MEAL, WHILE EVERYONE AT THE TABLE makes small talk, he takes my hand in his as if it belongs there. As if we're a comfortable couple.

"Are you enjoying yourself?" he asks me.

"Immensely. Thank you for inviting me."

"Then dance with me." It's not a question.

DANCING WITH JOSH IS GOING TO KILL ME.

He's not dancing with me, he's making love to me. It's not *Dirty Dancing* style; it's under the radar, full of finesse and thought out strategy. Each perfectly placed touch brings me closer, each detailed move heightens my growing passion and each sweep and press of his fingers leaves me more breathless.

It begins like any wholesome embrace—my right hand loosely cradled in his and his left hand placed saccharinely on my hip. He positions me a good six or seven inches away from him—I'm aware of the distance and the acuteness of his absence.

The song that plays tumbles note for note through my mind, but I can't recall the name of the popular song. Slowly, the fingertips of Josh's right hand trace the sensitive center of my palm and the length of my fingers, sending chills through my core and goosebumps over my skin.

He finds the inside of my wrist and stays there to follow the tracks of my veins and the lines of my tendons. The skin there is thin and absorbs the featherlight touches that warm my blood. Josh plays his fingertips slowly up my forearm and lingers at the inner bend of my elbow.

His attention to these near-erogenous zones forces my eyes to fall closed. Josh continues his ministrations up my bare arm until his right hand rests on my shoulder. I become acutely aware that his left hand has journeyed from my hip to the small of my back, where he's applied just enough pressure to bring our bodies close enough that I can sense his heat.

Josh's hand on my shoulder strokes up and under my hair. He uses its length as camouflage while he continues his assault on my senses. He massages my neck, varying the pressure from sweet tickles that titillate my entire body to needy, sensual kneading up into my hairline, which persuades my hips that they can no longer handle the distance between us.

I feel the tips of my breasts meet the contours of his chest while my belly and hips brush close enough to feel his own growing need. He twists his fingers into my hair, fisting the strands. The action nearly has me dropping my head back to moan. Instead, I reposition my face.

It's a bold parley. My soft cheek rubs against his chiseled jaw while my lips brush intimately against him, but only for a moment, as I whisper air over the curves of his ear.

At this, his right elbow bends as he uses his forearm to remove any space between us, and his body fully meets mine—hard and wanting.

A moan escapes my lips.

"Sophie." Raw and ragged, his voice strokes me as definitively as a caress.

I don't care about bets, or jobs, or appearances. "Bring me back to your room."

CHAPTER ELEVEN

JOSH

PAST

"I don't know what the fuck you expect of me. You want me to talk about my feelings? That's fucking stupid." I slump lower in my cold metal folding chair. Being forced to attend group therapy sessions sucks balls. Shrinks are freaking ridiculous! I don't talk when we're one-on-one. What the hell makes them think talking in a circle with others I hate almost as much as myself is going to make me "open up"?

Dr. Perfect is spewing some crap out of his mouth about how we're expected here at the house to act with respect toward each other. Dr. Perfect has never had a real problem in his life, I'm sure of it—he acts way too smart and positions himself like he has a fucking brick up his ass. Why does Uncle Cade hire assholes like this?

"Fine." I give up, annoyed. "I'll tell you how I *feeeeeeel*."

Dr. P rolls his eyes.

I sneer. "I hate this place, I hate my life, and I hate all of you."

Liam leans forward in his chair. "What the fuck is wrong with you, man? He's only trying to help!"

"Does he help you, Liam?" I'm sarcastically sweet. "Do you help him back late at night?"

"You're such a fucking asshole," Liam grates out.

"Truth hurts," I retort.

"You don't know the truth," my Uncle Cade's voice cuts through the room. He's just like my dad —his demeanor commands attention.

Instinctively, I want to apologize. I know how rude I was being. But there is no way I'm going to be fucking soft in front of these guys. The only truth is that I do hate my life … and most of all, I hate myself.

"Before going to med school, Dr. Hain was the leader of The Gods—a New York City gang," Cade informs me. "He was recruited when he was only thirteen years old by his older brother. As his initiation, he was expected to murder the principal of the local high school or be killed in front of the rest of the initiates as an example. He shot the principal, but it wasn't fatal, so he ran. The Gods murdered his sister in retaliation."

For a few moments, no one says a word or even makes a sound.

Quinn's soft voice breaks the silence. "I'm so sorry, Dr. Hain."

"So, how'd you get to be the leader?" Ryder, a thug covered in homemade tats and piercings, asks as if he doesn't believe the sob story.

"My brother and I exacted revenge for our sister," Dr. Hain says ominously. "We got a reputation for being brutal, and it equated to respect. Soon, we were kings of the gods."

Suddenly, the sweater vest and khaki pants he's wearing seem out of place.

"After I buried my sister, I didn't care about anything. I didn't care what I did or what happened to me or anybody else. I became known as The Interrogator, and I cut other kids up bad to prove myself ruthless. And for a while, I was."

Quinn shoots Ryder a scalding look.

"But the life caught up with me. I spent almost a decade in prison. It's no one's destiny to be in trouble, but when we get in it, it's our responsibility to get ourselves out of it, no matter what we have to do."

"How did you get caught?" Talon asks.

"I turned myself in," Dr. Hain admits. "Racketeering is business as usual for gangs, but when a girl the same age as my sister died from a bad cut in the drugs we were peddling … it opened my eyes."

"So you became a counselor to help kids like us," Quinn deduces.

There's a shift in the room. I don't know what it is, and I don't know about everyone else, but this does not make me want to share what lies deepest within me with the class. Instead, it makes me want to beat the shit out of someone. And get pounded in return.

"Fuck this shit." Ryder stands up and shakes his head. "I'm sorry about your sister and all, but this group session shit isn't for me. I'm going to my room." He stalks away even though he'll face consequences for leaving. Cade generously doles out the punishments that we earn, and group is mandatory. Ryder is an asshole, anyway.

I find myself staring at Dr. Hain.

He found redemption.

JOSH
PRESENT

I TAKE EXTRA CARE TO MAKE SURE THAT AT NO point from the dance floor to the hotel, do I lose physical contact with her. I have a feeling that if I do, I'll lose her.

Something else is happening, too. Fear. I'm an expert at hiding it, burying it and disguising it, but right now, I'm just holding it at bay.

I focus on the curve of her breasts, as the dress can barely contain them. They're so perfectly round, and I can't wait to get one in my mouth. In fact, I'm dying in the back of the limousine. I want to slide off her shoes and sensually massage each of her soft feet, but we're too close to the hotel. Instead, I let my fingertips play up her ankles to her knees as I wonder if the silk covering her legs is pantyhose I'll get to rip off or thigh highs I'll need to peel down. I'm at her knee as I consider going higher. I want her thighs spread apart, in my hands, around my face. And after she's soaked from my lips and tongue all over her sweetness, I want those thighs wrapped around my hips. The vision makes me forget myself, and before I know it, I realize my fingertips are now grazing against her soft skin.

Thigh highs. I'm in fucking heaven. If I slide my finger up another inch higher, I'll know what kind of panties she's wearing, if she's wearing any at all, and how wet she is.

I bring my other hand under her dress until

both are massaging her thighs, squeezing them and pressing them until they fall open. Her gorgeous eyes close as her head tilts back. My dick is throbbing.

The limo stops, and she lets out a sigh of disappointment.

I fix the fabric so it's back down over her knees, and we head out. Through the hotel lobby, I keep hold of her hand. The elevator can't go fast enough, and I keep wondering the entire time if she's going to come to her senses and leave me standing there, wanting her more than life itself.

That powerful, maybe careless, maybe very calculated thought—wanting her more than life itself—brings a primal force, an energy and action that I've only tasted before a serious fight, to the surface. But this, this is different. It squares me off against myself as Sophie's greatest defender and most violent threat.

Out of the elevator and into my room.

What the fuck am I doing??

When I close the door behind us, I'm in awe that she's made it this far without slapping my face. I take a step toward her, and Sophie's back is against the door while her eyes welcome me closer.

She knows me; she knows my reputation as a man-whore, and that's why she didn't want to get involved with me in the first place. But like the snake in the garden, I've seduced her. I've lured her here, and I'm a selfish bastard for it. I want her all to myself. I *need* the rush I get every time she gets close to me. I *have* to have her in my arms, in my mouth, underneath me. I *need* to have my lips and tongue over every inch of her. I *need* to bury myself so deep inside of her that I forget my own name. I'm jonesing like a druggy who got a little sample of the dealer's "best stuff" and desperately has to have a true fix.

And it means I'm a first rate prick, and I'm going to fuck everything up because Sophie won't be able to look at me the same when I'm finished. Things won't be able to go back to the way they were before. That means the consequence of me doing this to her tonight will be that I lose her.

"Josh …" Sophie's needful voice stops my mind and ignites my body.

I feel absolutely crazy—wanting to make love to her slowly, deliberately, savoring her, and at the same time wanting to rip this dress like a wrapper from her sweet candy body and fuck her raw.

What the hell is happening to me? My heartbeat is out of control.

I cup her beautiful face with both my hands— hands that can crush her. I can't deny that her very presence heals me, moves me. I can't say why or how. I have no words to define it, but touching

her face like this, and the fact that she lets me …
I'm mesmerized.

My fingers soak up her heat like every living
thing soaks up the sun for its very survival.

I gaze over her features in awe. I feel the
crack; a fault line begins to tear through the walls
I've built up around myself. "Do you know?" I
whisper. I want her to understand what I don't
understand myself. I want her to make sense of it.

Her eyes search mine for answers. I find in
them the reflection of everything I feel—want,
desire, fear, hope.

But in her eyes, I also see timidity, and it
makes me feel all the more predatory. I shake it
off and remember she wants this as much as I do.
She's the one who broke the rules to get it.

I work my fingers under her long brown hair
until I'm cradling the nape of her neck. "Sophie, I
have to know what you're thinking, what you're
feeling. You have to tell me. Are you happy? Are
you scared?"

Seriously, she answers, "Yes … and … hell
yes."

There are too many emotions coursing
through us both. I know she feels them.

Our deal was that if she made the first move,
she would stay with me for one night of unbridled
passion.

"What if I never want to let you go?" I ask.

"I'd say you better hold on tight."

Sophie's response brings a confident grin to my lips.

My hands leave her neck and trail across her bare shoulders, down her arms, and onto her legs. I kneel in front of her.

First, I pull off her shoes. Then my hands go on a journey up her sheer stocking-clad leg—ankle to calf, knee to inner thigh. Sophie sighs and leans her head against the door, surrendering to my touch. Slowly, one at a time, I peel the stockings down her leg and off her toes.

As I rise back to standing, I keep my hands on her perfect body. Enjoying the satin fabric of the dress against my palms and fingers, I only stop when I get to the top of the zipper at the back of her dress.

"You found that quick."

"I figured out where it was when we were on the dance floor," I say smoothly.

Sophie's unzipped gown falls haphazardly down her chest, around her hips and to the floor, where it gathers around her feet.

Oh, Christ! She's wearing a sheer nude corset and panties that become gasoline to my already active imagination, setting me ablaze. She's so much more exquisite than I ever imagined. The real-life Sophie is perfect and mesmerizing, soft and warm, and …

"Do you know what I've wanted to do since you came to my hotel room tonight to get me?" Her eyes betray her emotion—half shy and half animal.

"What?" *Jesus, I have to know!*

She unknots my tie, unbuttons my jacket, and then gathers my shirt in both of her hands and rips it down the seam of buttons.

"Oh fuck!" I breathe out.

She pushes the fabric of my jacket and shirt down over my shoulders by running her palms over the muscles of my arms, finally pulling the cuffs over each wrist until both the jacket and the shirt drop to the floor without care.

Sophie gazes up into my eyes. I hold that gaze and let the intense electricity crackle and charge between us.

She sets her hand over the center of my chest. I cover it with my own right hand. Together, our hands rest over the top of my heart—the heart she is claiming, the heart she's healing.

I realize we haven't kissed yet despite all of the touching. I'm dressed only in my pants and shoes, and damn, she's barely dressed at all. I smile and take a step closer, bringing my left hand under her jaw. I can't wait to taste her mouth—her sassy, bossy, gorgeous mouth.

Something makes me pause. She appears totally sexy, self-confident and ready to take me on, but at the same time, she trembles beneath me, her body betraying her nervousness. She's like a hologram—there's a flash of vulnerability, but then she tilts her head back demurely as her lips part to take mine, and I feel the heat of her thigh as she strokes it up my leg, coaxing me on.

I lean my forehead against hers while my fingertips play over the exposed skin of her chest and the plane of her collarbone. I watch and smile in satisfaction as her skin ripples with goosebumps at the sensation.

"I'm going to savor you," I tell her. "You know every ridge and contour of my body … it's my turn to learn yours. And as I do, Sophie, I'm going to claim you, every part of you, as mine."

"I'm yours … tonight." Her words breeze over my lips.

Tonight? She thinks I only want her for tonight. No wonder the vulnerability, no wonder the overconfidence. I hate myself for it; I hate that this is her opinion of me. I hate what I was before … before her.

Do I know what I want? I know I'd do anything and everything to change her opinion of me.

At this moment, all the fear I've been fighting, all of the old me I've been warring with, all the self-pity and loathing, is put down like a mad dog.

I know what I can be, and I know what I want.

"More than tonight, Sophie. More than tomorrow."

SOPHIE

Josh's words wash over me. It's okay that he doesn't mean it. It's okay that I don't have tomorrow to give him. I can pretend. Oh yeah, I can pretend tonight that he's mine. All mine.

Dear God, no one man should look as incredible as he does. It's just not fair.

I love his waist. Sounds silly, maybe, but it's thick and strong, and I love to sink my fingers into it and then count up his ribs.

"You look happy." He smiles down at me. He stands almost an entire foot taller than me.

"Yeah." I catch my bottom lip between my teeth.

"I want to know everything you're thinking." He searches my eyes. His deep brown irises are speckled with gold flecks. I've never looked into them this closely or for this long before. They're beautiful, like Tiger's Eye stones.

"I have to keep some of my secrets so I can

keep intriguing you with my mystery," I tease. I caress up his chest. Oh, I love the ripples of muscles and ink.

"Dear Christ! You shouldn't have this kind of power over me." He closes his eyes for a moment and sighs.

I like having this effect on him, but before I can really enjoy it, he catches himself. His eyes open, and there is a stern determination in them. I've seen this expression plenty of times now when he's sparring with an opponent and has had enough playing games.

"After the first round, you can call the nanny and let her know you won't be coming back for a while."

My eyes open wide.

"Sophie, I'm going to kiss you now, and you're going to feel it in your soul. And you'll know without a doubt that I'm yours and no one else's from now on." Josh's strong hands envelop my face; his thumbs brush over my cheeks. I marvel at how rough he is and looks and how gentle his hands can be. "I'm going to own your body, so you'll never have a need or desire for another man ever again. You'll feel it, and you'll know that you're mine too."

With that, his mouth covers mine. Finally, I taste him, and it seems like I've waited forever. He's heat and power, demanding and forceful. His tongue plunges into my mouth without ceremony, pushing in between my lips and wrapping around my tongue like it knows it belongs there.

And. Oh. My. God. *He knows how to move it.*

Josh swipes his tongue over the roof of my mouth, sending tingles shooting into my sex. As he does this, his steel body crashes into mine. He spreads my legs with his knee, positions himself between them and rubs his beautiful, hard cock full-on against me. It presses into my belly with the most delicious sensation.

Oh fuck! It's huge—thick and long.

His tongue tangles with mine before he pulls it from my mouth and catches my bottom lip between his teeth. He tugs on it, and I moan.

"All mine." He throws me over his shoulder and takes long strides across the room to the bed. "You're fucking perfect," he growls and sinks his teeth into the flesh of my ass.

"JOSH!"

"I love this thong you're wearing. I really love that I'm going to take it off you now." He peels it down with one hand.

I bend my knees, and he tosses it across the room. "Don't worry, baby. You won't need it again. I'm going to keep you naked all night and tomorrow, too."

One of his hands holds my ass while the other

investigates the corset. "Where are the eyelets?" he growls impatiently.

"On the other side," I tell him. "Looks like you'll have to put me down."

"And lose the advantage? Not a chance." Deftly, he swings me down and sets me so I'm straddling his knee, naked. "Oh, baby, your pussy is so hot."

"You made it that way," I pant.

His hands squeeze the sides of the corset together as he unhooks the eyelets several at a time until he's undone me completely. My breasts spill out from the confines. Josh drops the corset to the floor and drinks me in with his eyes.

"Beautiful tits." He wastes no time as he bends his head, lifts his knee and sucks the closest nipple into his mouth.

I get my footing on the bed and rub against his leg, welcoming the much-needed friction.

"No, no, no," he scolds. He gets his hands under my arms and lifts me away from his leg and up until my breasts are in front of his face, and I have no control. "That's better." He looks between them like they're an offering. "Mmm …" He uses his tongue to pull the second, neglected nipple between his lips.

I forget how strong he is. He's standing a few steps away from the foot of the bed. My feet are dangling far from the floor, but I figure out a way to get some leverage. I wrap my legs around him and lock my ankles.

"Oh, Sophie, don't you know what I do for a living?" Josh's words send a thrill through me. It's a warning and a promise. He's a sexy MMA fighter with a rock-hard body that he knows how to use. He could pin me to the bed or floor or couch or wall in more ways than I can imagine.

But I have my own weapons.

I untangle my legs and instead gently but firmly scratch my nails against his scalp just above the base of his neck. "Josh," I whisper.

His grip weakens. He lowers me enough so we're face to face again, our eyes searing. Slowly, deliberately, I nibble at his lips, the bottom one first, then the top. I dart my tongue over them, tasting, feeling, probing.

I need him inside me badly. I'm all for fore-play, but we've been engaging in foreplay since we met. I want this belt *off!* I want these pants *gone!* I reach down and tug at the leather of his belt.

He smiles under my tongue before he eats my mouth with his lips—kissing me with small, inten-tional movements that are driving me crazy.

"I'm not even close to letting these pants come off," he guarantees as he pulls down the bedspread and lays me over the satin sheets.

He climbs his gorgeous, still half-clothed body over the top of me and begins massaging me down my arms. So slowly, his fingers tickle my skin, press into the grooves of my muscles, and squeeze down until his fingers wrap around my wrists, holding them to the mattress.

"Now I know your arms." My heart pounds, realizing that he has me pinned. Not only my arms, but his body holds my legs immobile as well.

Josh stares down at my body, which is now obviously at his mercy. He bows his head and licks at the pink tips of my breasts, which harden beneath his gaze.

"I'm most defiantly a tit man—and yours have driven me crazy in everything from those boring, sheet-like scrubs you used to wear at the hospital to those pretty, baby-doll t-shirts you're always wearing at the gym. So round, so perfect—one for my hand and the other for my mouth." As he talks, he lets my wrists go and covers my left breast in his palm, squeezing while he licks and sucks at the right. "I've been dying every time you've leaned over me or when they've brushed up against me. Bet that wasn't on accident." He's playfully accusatory.

"Tell me you didn't like it," I counter.

"Oh, I loved it, but now you're going to get a little taste of what I've gone through." He moves to kneel between my feet and begins massaging up the front of my legs. "You know how hard you made me? Don't you? Of course, you do."

I hear the smile in his voice and see it through the sex-need haze in my eyes.

"Towels and compression shorts definitely couldn't hide or camouflage all this." He looks down and indicates the package between his legs.

I can't help but giggle.

"Yeah, you're laughing. You totally knew what you were doing," he insists, massaging the muscles in my legs as I'm watching him. "Kneading my muscles while I attempted to 'relax,' and it only made me harder. All the way up my thighs ..." At this, he comes up to the very highest point of my thigh. It takes every bit of willpower I possess not to jack my hips to make him touch the one place I need him to so desperately. "Just missing the sensitive area of my balls so that I had to hold my breath and stifle moans, begging you in my head to go just a little higher ... but no, you never did."

He strokes to the edges of my most heated place. "How's that self-control working for you now, scrapper?"

"You've proved your point," I whine.

"Not yet, I haven't. Not thoroughly. Flip, Ms. Garner, it's time to work your back.

I don't move fast enough, so Josh flips me impatiently over onto my belly. His hands begin up under my hair, coaxing tingles through my body by working my scalp with his fingertips. As he travels down my neck and shoulders, then down the planes of my back, I can feel from his strokes that he's growing impatient. I love how he's torturing himself as much as he is me. I thought of opening my mouth to call him on it, but realized that would be against my own best interests.

"This is the sweetest, curviest ass." Josh fills both his hands with my flesh.

"I can't take anymore!" I get to my knees and press that curvy ass against the steel rod in his trousers. We both moan in anticipation.

In a heartbeat, Josh strokes my vagina— spreading me apart to reveal the overflowing dam that has broken with all his attention. I'm breathless.

"I'm going to get you so high, baby." The pad of his thumb brushes over my clit.

I can't see him, can't touch him like this—he has all the advantage. Next, I feel Josh blowing warm air over my heat. His mouth is so close! The tip of his finger tempts my opening. He swirls the finger around almost absentmindedly until I scream.

"Please, do it!" I beg. "I need it. I need you."

"Yes, you do," Josh says as he licks and nibbles the skin of my thighs. At times he gently sucks my flesh into his lips.

I cry out and tuck my head over my shoulder to throw him a pleading look.

"Tell me." His voice is strong and sure. "Tell me what you want."

I'm quiet. I'm burning.

"It's just you and me. There are no rules. You're safe. You can let every inhibition go."

I'm shy. I hate it, but I am. I should have known a man like Josh would want animal lust. I want it too, but I'm scared to go there.

"Let me tell you what I'm going to do to you once you give me the word. I'm going to swipe my very hot, very hungry tongue over that gorgeous, wet and ready pussy of yours. I'm going to plunge my tongue as deep as I can get inside of you. I'm going to rub you with my nose, lips and chin until I'm full of you, full of your scent, full of your sweetness, full of your need. Because you can't reach me or touch me in this position, you're going to be clawing at the mattress and wringing the sheets in your fists as you climb higher and careen toward the most powerful fucking orgasm you've ever had—"

"Josh!" It's a plea.

"Sophie?!" He's not budging.

"Do it, please …" I say.

He doesn't move.

"Lick me."

"Lick you." His tongue plays up the side of my thigh.

"Lick my pussy, please lick my … pussy." I force it out. I feel empowered, sexy. Quickly, I lift myself on my elbows as Josh parts my legs and dives his hot, clean-shaven face between them, working his mouth over my vagina.

OH. MY. GOD.

Everything in my body shifts to focus on his ministrations. And he's right; it feels like deliverance, sustenance … salvation.

His hot tongue breaks me apart one swipe at a time. He's slow and purposeful, like he has all night. He stays, gently lapping at my clit until I feel the tremors shoot through my core.

"I love the feel of you swelling in my mouth," he says before dipping his tongue into my opening, making me whimper.

My forehead presses against the silken sheets as Josh's tongue delivers my pure wetness back over my engorged nerves.

I'm there; my hands fist the sheets, and I hear him growl and purr in gratification or satisfaction or both. I'm nearly screaming between pants for air and moans as the deepest pleasure I've ever felt begins to crash over me.

"JOSH!" My body comes so forcefully that the bed shakes as I tremble.

He throws me over so I'm on my back. I'm

fucking gone; I can't think past the desire, the heat and this man, ready to take me.

While I writhe on the bed with no self-control and probably no dignity, Josh is watching me, salivating as he undoes his pants, quickly stands up and pushes them off and away.

"You're taking too long," I whine and paw at my own breast and the broken delta between my legs.

Josh smiles at his handiwork and, in an instant, has rolled on a condom. "I'm going to bury myself so deep inside you.

"Yes," I beg and curve my hips up to greet the swollen monster between his legs. I hope this isn't our first and last time because I want to feel it in my hands and mouth and trace the thick veins with my fingers and tongue.

He fists his own cock and covers me with the full heat of his body. Oh, he smells so good, aftershave, musk and man. His muscles and skin radiate with heat, and I run my hands over his shoulders.

"I've craved you since I laid eyes on you," Josh says as his tip urges me open. I spread my legs further and squeeze his arms.

It's big and sears into my being as if I've never had sex before. He stretches me until I'm engorged with him. My teeth bite into his shoulder.

"Oh fuck! Sophie!" Now Josh is the one panting. "You feel so fucking good … I knew you would. Fuck, how I fantasized about this!" As he begins to pump in a slow, steady in-and-out rhythm, my body is consumed in a turbulent amalgam of deep, deep pleasure and white-hot pain from his size. "Oh Christ, you're tight! Come on, baby, relax your legs and let me have you."

I try. I'm excited and nervous. What the fuck?

"Look at me, Sophie. My eyes."

I do; they're soft and brown, filled with sexy wanting and power, but still comforting. Reassuring. He lifts my leg and settles it over his shoulder.

Oh my God, that's deeper! I'm about to protest, but his mouth closes over my breast, and he watches my face as he sucks and licks and waits until I melt into him.

The moment I do, I can feel it; the pain from my own tenseness fades. I accept him fully.

Josh stares intensely into my eyes. As I wonder what he's thinking, he smashes his mouth onto mine with a force that claims ownership.

His hips jack, his dick thrusts, and my greedy walls surround him and stroke him. I'm set aflame until there is nothing left of me except my oneness with Josh.

We release together with a violent force. Both of us have wanted each other all this time. Denied passion, when realized and reciprocated, is powerful.

Josh pulls me into his arms, my back curves, and I nuzzle into the front of his body. His hard chest is a protective shell around me, and his arms hold me strong.

And here I go again, pretending he's mine. Imagining that we could be a family. Pretending I could be loved like this. I soak up his warmth for just a few more minutes, relishing it, believing in it —sometimes fabricated faith is just as potent as the real stuff.

All too soon, I'm nudged into action. The tick of my watch, the change in his breath telling me he's falling asleep.

I wonder who he is in real life, in real-time. He's been on his best behavior; men always are when they're reeling you in.

My light and happy mood waxes ominous. What happens when a man as powerful as Josh becomes angry? I shudder.

Carefully, I slip myself from his grasp and light-foot it to the bathroom. Scenarios play out in my mind as I wash up. Angry because he steps on a toy in the middle of the night? Angry because he's sure you're sneaking around, fucking someone else? Angry because you burned dinner? Or didn't make his drink fast enough.

I breathe through the panic. *What am I doing*

here? Josh could break me in the blink of an eye. I remind myself how tender he is with Charlie. Unwelcome tears creep into my eyes. Falling for Josh North could be as easy as rain. Getting away from him when it turned sour …

I'm already as good as dead, I think.

I can't be here doing this! I should have kept the job at the hospital. I knew this would happen. And didn't a part of me want this to happen, beg for it to happen?

I won't regret it.

Josh North, don't make me regret it.

We're not a couple. One night doesn't create a couple. I'll be aloof in the morning and let things be as they always were. Honestly, that's probably how he wants it to be anyway.

"You're mine," Josh had said.

I could recall when those words would define a romantic possession, a feeling of belonging to one another and the adhesive of a loving couple. But that was before Jim said them, and they became a chilling threat and a deadly promise.

It's at least three a.m., and even though I know Charlie is right down the hall, safe and sound, my body shakes with trepidation. I have to get to her.

Quietly, I pull on my clothes. For a moment, I suspend all thought just to watch Josh sleep. My heart aches for him already. A tear runs down my face, and I brush it away impatiently. I can't let this happen. I won't let this happen.

Escaping the room—and my volatile imaginings—I get back into my own room. Charlie is asleep in my bed. I smile down at her soft, innocent form. She's never been hurt; she's never known fear at the hands of someone who is supposed to love her. And with all my strength, I'll make sure she never does.

As soon as the three months working for Josh are up, I'm out.

CHAPTER TWELVE

SOPHIE

"That was the worst wake-up I've ever experienced," Josh whispers under his breath while looking behind me, making sure Britt is really out of earshot.

"I doubt that," I say coldly and look out the window to our left.

"Ouch." He's upset, but I see more hurt in his eyes than anything else. I don't see the anger that I had expected.

Now he gets on a sexy little smirk. "Didn't I please you? Were you not satisfied?"

I sag like a rag doll in my chair, thinking about how much he pleased me. And damn it, I can't *not* smile!

"Yeah, that's what I thought, so why the Houdini?" He leans on his elbows over the table.

We're sitting at breakfast in the hotel dining

room. This morning, Josh knocked on my door so early that Charlie wasn't even awake yet. I pried myself away from her and saw through the peep-hole that it was him. I opened the door with the chain still engaged.

"Can't let you in, just got out of the shower," I lied, hiding behind the door.

"I'd like to talk to you."

I was sure he would.

"I'm hungry," Charlie called in a sleepy voice. The knock must have woken her, too.

"Perfect, I can take the two of you to break-fast," Josh said cheerfully.

I could tell from the look on his face when we met him in the dining room that he hadn't expected me to bring Britt along.

Now, she'd gotten up to use the bathroom, and I knew he saw this as his chance.

"Drink your milk, sweetheart." I push the cup into Charlie's hands to distract her and then lean in to meet Josh's face. "Don't get me wrong, I had a great night last night, but now it's time to get back to the real world. I know your M.O., I know your lifestyle, and you don't owe me a thing." I sit back up and take a bite of my eggs, trying like hell to appear nonchalant.

A wounded expression ghosts over him. "You don't understand."

Definition: I understand too well.

"I want to see you again," he tries.

"You see me every day."

"That's not how I mean."

"Can we see the mermaids again?" Charlie interrupts.

"Business." I poke my finger against the table. "We have a business contract, and I can't let myself cross the line … again." I'm dead serious.

"Who did initiate that first move, anyway?" Now his cocky grin comes out. Glad to see he's not daunted. "Come out on a real date with me."

"No." My eyes catch Charlie as her little head twists back and forth between Josh and me throughout our conversation.

"Dinner and a movie, nice and easy."

"No … thank you." I smile politely as a show for Charlie, who smiles back at me.

"Sophie, I want to spend time with you." He is almost pleading. "Look me in my eyes and tell me you don't want to spend time with me."

I can't. "Look, I'm not going to see you out of any business-related context, so if you want to spend time with me, you'll just have to … I don't know … teach me how to fight." I almost laugh. I had been about to say 'get hurt,' but I didn't want to jinx a superstitious fighter.

"Perfect!" He sits bolt-upright and looks like he won the jackpot at a poker table.

"What?" I hadn't meant it!

"What did I miss?" Britt asks as she slides into her seat.

"Sophie here is going to train with me and learn how to fight." Josh couldn't sound more proud.

"Really?" Britt looks at me, intrigued.

"Mommy's gonna punch!" Charlie throws a right hook.

"I can't believe you talked me into this," I bark.

"Hey, you asked me, scrapper." Josh grabs my waist in both his hands and just about lifts me off the floor. "You have to keep your stance strong and balanced. Get your right foot back behind you and lead with your hip because that's where your power is."

Josh literally forms his body to mine and moves me as if I were a puppet. "When you release your punch, your entire body needs to be behind it." My right knee is slowly pushed in by his right knee, and my right arm lays over top of his. As one body, we extend toward the canvas sparring bag.

"Is this how you train all your students?" I ask doubtfully.

"I've never trained a woman, but I'm definitely enjoying it."

I roll my eyes, but it's good-natured. I'm surprised he held me to this. I thought we'd only been joking that morning in the hotel, but here we are, after hours, in the Williston gym, just the two of us.

"What kind of workout routine do you normally do?" he asks.

"Dance aerobics and some yoga." I'm a little embarrassed. "Really, just to DVDs. I usually exercise when Charlie naps."

"It's been hard for you to get out and take time for yourself, hasn't it?"

"Yeah." *You have no idea.*

He gets serious. "Self-defense is an excellent discipline—mind, body, psyche."

Self-defense. What began as a joke is now making me wonder. Most controlling men do not want to empower women. "Why would you want to spend your time *off* teaching me fight moves?"

"Why is it so ridiculous for you to believe that I like you and want to get to know you more? And this is my world." Josh looks around the empty gym. "I'm comfortable here and never get bored with it. Besides, every woman should know how to defend herself. There are a lot of assholes out there."

FOR THE NEXT TWO WEEKS, BETWEEN HIS OWN training and working with the fire department (which he does part-time, and usually during the night shift), Josh spends all his free time with me. We begin running mid-morning at the local high school's indoor track. At night, when everyone else has gone home, Josh goes over punching, hits, kicks and full-body moves that will allow me to disable an attacker. He's very stern about proper "oxygen intake," or what I like to refer to as "breathing." He makes me drink a protein shake with him after every run, and he has me pounding the shit out of Buster, the sparring dummy. Just two weeks of dedicated practice has made a definite difference; I'm feeling stronger, more conditioned and more confident than I have in years.

"This isn't a fight for entertainment or to show how strong you are. Real fights are decided within the first moments. Punch the throat—it's an exposed, vulnerable place. Then go for the groin and get the hell out of there," he explains. "Now, do it."

"Do what?"

"I'm coming at you, and I want you to come at me for real."

I laugh nervously. "I can't do that. I can't hurt you on purpose."

"I guarantee you're not going to hurt me," he says. "I need to feel your strength."

I swallow the knot in my throat.

"You're scared," Josh states.

"Maybe—" I don't finish the word before he has me in a vice grip.

"Use the fear, let it fuel your adrenaline … channel it."

It works. My heart is pounding, my breath has quickened, and I need a place to put that energy. I jab an elbow into his ribs, and it loosens his hold enough for me to twist around to face him. He grabs my arms, but my instinct kicks in, and I remember the move to break loose. The instant my arms are free, my right fist slams against Josh's Adam's apple, and then the left heel of my hand connects with his nose. When he reaches up to protect his face and neck, I drive my knee into his groin. I feel the strong plastic cup cradling his jewels, but it doesn't distract from the lesson. I turn and run until I reach the far wall. When I do turn around, I see Josh smiling while blood from his nose runs over his teeth.

"Oh my God! Your nose!" I go running back to him. "I'm so sorry."

He's laughing. "Isn't my first bloody nose scrapper. I'm proud of you." Josh lifts me into the air and holds me against him. "Those were sharp, forceful jabs. You definitely would've gotten away."

I smile at his praises.

While hugging me, he walks over to the hook where his towel hangs, then grabs it and holds it over his nose.

"You gonna let me go?" I giggle in spite of myself.

Josh is quiet for a moment before he lets me down.

An awkward moment passes as we stand there and look at each other. I'm not sure what he's thinking, but I know what I'm thinking. I'm thinking I want to be in his arms again.

"I'm going to get you some ice," I deflect. "We don't want Silva mad at me."

JOSH KEEPS CONVERSATIONS BETWEEN US LIGHT and easy now, just like they were when we first started getting to know each other. We learn each other's favorite colors and foods, we discuss movies and books, sports, politics, the conditions of the world and, of course, philosophy.

A few days after we got back from Denver, Britt started to bring Charlie to the gym for lunch sometimes, and Charlie, Josh and I all eat together. At first, I wasn't sure I liked the idea, but Charlie begged and begged, saying she missed me and just wanted to let her giant pink bear say hi to Joshy again. In a moment of weakness, I said yes one time, and that set a precedent I hadn't meant to set. The guys in the gym are all so funny—as soon as Charlie steps through the door, they all stop fighting and act like perfect gentlemen until she's in the break room. It's really very sweet.

I thought lunches together would be awkward, but for the most part, they haven't been—just fun and light. It's obvious that Charlie adores Josh. I know I should put a stop to it, but there's a tiny part of me that doesn't want to. There's a tiny part of me that loves to see Charlie and Josh together, even when it tears me apart at the same time. One of the sweetest things I hadn't expected was the few times Charlie stayed past lunch, and Josh took the time to play with her in my office with the toys that he'd got for her—he just sat on the floor with the two of us sipping at make-believe tea and putting puzzles together—or whatever else Charlie wanted him to do.

Josh is disarming me in so many ways. He asks all about Charlie and learns that when he does, I can gush on forever. No one in my life has ever cared enough to ask before. He acts like he wants to know it all—her first steps, her first words, her favorite foods, her favorite games. I tell him about how she's already started reading and how much she loves to be read to. The next day at lunch, he comes in with a thick, heavy bag from Barnes and Noble stuffed with children's books and a cup of my favorite peppermint mocha. Charlie was thrilled!

He makes me feel like we matter.

That might make me more terrified than I've ever been because, although I know how to survive—close off my emotions, fight like hell and never surrender—except for Charlie, who gives and receives love so easily, so freely, I don't know how to matter to someone else. It should be easy, right? It should be natural. It probably is with normal people.

We matter.

IF I EVER HAD RESOLVE, IT'S CRUMBLING. THE tension between us is building and I don't know how to keep it from consuming me. There are so many reminders of our one night together—the brush of his muscles against me, the contour of his legs and the strength of his arms, working up a sweat as I throw punches into his waiting hands, or when he drives me to the floor in a hold I'm supposed to break. I know I don't want to break free anymore, and at the same time, I'm afraid I'm going to break because of him.

OUR NEXT SESSION STARTS OUT TOO QUIET. Gently, he wraps my hands in fighter's tape to protect them, but he doesn't look at me. There's none of our normal friendly banter or conversation. He doesn't say a word, but I can feel him smoldering, and I know that something volcanic lies underneath the surface. He's mad at me. I try to think why, but before I can come up with a sufficient answer, he grates, "Your training is almost over. I don't think I can divide my time like this anymore."

He stalks over to the mats and leaves me sitting there with my mouth gaping open.

Confused and reluctant, I join him. He says something, but I apparently don't move fast enough.

"When you do the roundhouse kick, you have to keep your hip positioned." He sounds frustrated as he grabs my waist impatiently. Manually, he shifts my hips to the correct position. "For Christ's sake, lean and balance," Josh snaps.

My brow furrows as his aggravation becomes contagious.

I push his hands off and away from me. "I can do it myself."

"Really? Prove it." He backs up and stands poised in front of me. "Come on and kick me."

I kick, but it barely connects.

"Is that all you've got?" he challenges, and it's not friendly. "Harder, scrapper, hurt me!"

"Fine!" I *want* to kick him. I *want* to hurt him!

Earlier today, when I was massaging him, it got rough. Lately, he's been Mr. Chaste during *every* massage treatment and *every* training session, never giving me any of his one-liners or sexual innuendos. Instead, he's stopped his rough-around-the-edges ways and dirty-talking mouth around me. And honestly, I'm *sick* of it. I know I said I wanted to go back to just a business rela-tionship with him, but now that I've gotten what I wanted, the lack of flirting is driving me insane. I can't keep myself from wondering why he's given up. It's not his style. I thought for sure I'd be fighting him off of me.

A thought hits me. *Maybe he's seeing someone else?*

Don't be absurd. He's had no time, I reason. *And what the hell? He's not even "seeing" me!* But it doesn't curb the jealousy the idea conjures.

Why hasn't he made another move? Did I suck so bad in bed? Disappointedly, I think, *It has been a while.*

I feel Josh's hand wrap tightly around my ankle. "You're not paying attention. Get your head in the game," he scolds as he lifts my leg and throws me off balance.

My hands meet the mat, and I bring up my left foot out of instinct, using his hold as leverage, and kick him hard, square in the chest.

He swears and tumbles backward before catching himself. I leap to my feet and get in a fighting stance. "Get your head in the game," I mock.

"So that's how you want to play?" He comes at me fast.

I deflect his first moves. He tries to grab me, but I don't let him.

I'm not disillusioned. I know he could get me down in a fraction of a second if he really wanted to, but since he isn't, I'm going to keep at it.

"How was the massage today?" I land two jabs into his forearms as he protects his face.

"It was awesome." He drips with indifference.

I kick him in the side hard and bounce back. "Fuck you!"

"Fuck me?" He's pissed off now. "What the hell did I do to you?"

"More like what you *haven't* done to me!" I shout and push my hands against his chest.

"What does that even mean?" he shouts back.

"Like you don't know." I take a couple of steps toward him.

"I'm done." He throws up his arms and turns to walk away.

"Why haven't you tried to have sex with me again?" Wow! Saying the words makes me more frustrated than ever. The jealousy just erupts out of nowhere and threatens to split my heart in half. How can I have such a whiplash of emotions? "Wasn't I as good as your other girls?"

"What?!" He's at me too quick and snags both of my wrists easily. "What did you say?" he demands.

"You heard me, *scrapper.*" I twist my arms and quickly lift them up while stomping on his instep. He falls hard; however, never letting go of my wrists, he takes me down with him.

He rolls onto his back, and I'm straddling him. "Let me go!" I'm pissed at myself. *How could I have said that out loud to him?*

"Not a chance!" He easily gets me on my back, pins me by my wrists, and moves his body over me just right so I can't kick or move my hips. I'm not getting out of this. "Tell me what you said."

I make a desperate, pleading face. "Don't ask me. Just let me go. Okay?"

"No. No, it is *not* okay." His eyes search me. "Not as good as my *other girls?*"

I struggle against him.

"Why haven't you tried to have sex with me again?" he throws the words back at me, incredulous.

"If you already heard me,"—I struggle against his grip to no avail—"why do you keep asking me to repeat myself?"

"Because I can't believe you said it!"

"Get *OFF* of me!" I scream in his face.

He lets go immediately and helps me to my feet. I feel the lump in my throat and the hot tears rising. I turn and start for the locker room.

"Do you want me, or don't you?" Josh shouts at my back.

I stop in my tracks.

I'm so confused. I grasp the sides of my head.

Do we really matter to you? How can I really know? When it's too late?

"I don't … know how …"—I pant in exasperation—"to do this!"

"Does anyone?"

I whirl around. "Yeah, Josh, some people have their shit together, they know exactly how to do *this*. I'm not one of those people!" I retort.

He takes a step forward, but I take a step back, and he halts, holding his hands up to steady me like I'm a frightened animal. "It's okay."

"It's never going to be okay," I whisper. I feel tears run down my face and look on, horrified, as Josh watches them.

"Have I made a mistake?" he asks.

"No."

"Have I hurt you at all?"

I shake my head slowly. "No."

"That's a good start, right?" he says.

"Why are you mad at me then?" I say through my teeth, trying to find firmer ground.

He shakes his head and rubs his temples with his fingers. "I'm not mad at *you*. I'm frustrated at myself because I want you! Because I don't deserve you, because I want the chance to prove myself to you. I care so much … so deeply … about you and Charlie."

I stare at him. He looks like he's on the verge of breaking. "I'm trying to be just your friend, Sophie, but it's not enough." He shakes his head. "It's not enough for me anymore."

"I'm scared, Josh," I admit.

"I know. I'm sorry." He takes a timid half-step toward me. "I'm never going to hurt you."

I swallow hard. Can I believe those words? Does he understand the context in which I put them?

"Maybe we should just square up now. I'll take the wages that I've earned and just slip out of your life, and things can go back to the way they were for both of us."

"No! No, don't do that." He looks like he's fighting ghosts. "Please don't do that. I don't want to go back to the way things were before you."

"Josh, you're not …"—my mind races for logic in the midst of the chaotic, emotional storm —"you're not the kind of guy to settle down, and that's okay. And even if you thought you were, I don't know what *I* am or what I can even be for *you*, but I know what I can't be. Our night together has left a tattoo on my heart that's never going to be erased. Your kindness to me and Charlie, I'm never going to forget that." That lump in my throat turns to a sob and escapes between my lips. "I'm not the type of girl who can handle a one-nighter. I thought maybe I could be, I really wanted to be, but now I want … more … and, Josh, I can't have more." I turn, ready to sprint down the hall, but Josh gets to me before I can.

He holds my arms in his hand and spins me to face him.

"Please let me go, Josh. It's better for both of us if you just let me go now. Forget everything I said."

I'm pulling away from him. He loosens his grip but doesn't let go. My back hits the wall in the hallway, and Josh's face is in my face, and there's no direction left to run.

"I want you, Sophie. I. Want. You." His eyes are red and wet. "Answer the question, do you want me?"

I nod.

He releases my arms and cups my face in his hands. "I want you, Sophie. I love you." His words penetrate me. "I love Charlie too."

"How do you know that?" I shake my head and feel his hands holding me, smell their masculine scent, feel their heat. I'm a broken mess. "What does it even mean? And what happens when you stop *loving* me, or her, or us? Do you even know what love is?"

"I've never been in love. But I know I've never felt what I feel with you with anyone else." Impossibly, he moves in closer until he's the only thing in my vision, in my senses, in my universe. "So we're going to have to figure it out as we go along. I can tell you, there isn't anyone else on this earth I'd rather figure it out with than with you. Sophie, you can want more because I want to give you more. You can have more … *we* can have more."

Can I believe it? Do I dare believe it? Can I not be afraid? Oh God, his hands are so strong and protective, like a shield I want to hide behind.

"I have secrets, Josh—big, ugly secrets."

"We all have big ugly secrets." He strokes my jaw with his thumbs. I melt when he does this. "I'll still love you, whatever those secrets are, and I hope you can still care for me when you see all my unsightly shit. We can do this. Let me prove it to you; let me prove myself. I'll fight for it—for you, for your love and for Charlie—harder than I've ever fought for anything before."

"Kiss me," I whisper through my tears, through his words, through the flurry of emotions.

He groans before he crashes his mouth to mine. I open my lips and allow him in. This moment won't end with a kiss.

One of his hands stays on my jaw, holding my face immobile, as his other hand slides down over my neck. He pulls me away from the wall enough so my head can tilt back. Josh gets full access to my mouth and deepens the kiss. Every emotion, every physical symptom—desire, fear, love, pain— all pool between my legs. The blood builds, and I ache for his hard, perfect body to take me again. I can't wait to caress his tattoos and muscles and bury my nails in the flesh of his back while he brings me up to heaven.

CHAPTER THIRTEEN

JOSH

PAST

I let Ryder's fist slam against my jaw. Since when did I become a pain junkie? Does it matter? For the moment, it takes away the crushing sensation in my chest that I can't deal with and the memories I can't forget. Every night, I close my eyes, and every morning when I open them, Taylor is there, dead. Time and distance won't change it. I'm not going to wake up one day and find him alive again. This is it. The hurt will be endless, and the only way I can get relief is through the physical pain.

I clip Ryder's nose and hear it break. It makes me laugh when he cusses and spits a mouthful of blood onto the floor.

He's on top of me in a minute, hammering

my face. Left, right, left, right—until I taste my own salty blood and feel my jaw knock out of place. I decide I'm not going to fight back today. I'll let him knock me to hell and back. I deserve it after everything I've done.

Right—that's for my mom and dad, who had to send me here because I was too far gone to be forgiven.

Left—that's for my brothers and my sister, who have to pretend I went off to camp, never admitting that I actually let them down, along with my parents.

Right—that one's for Taylor, who was my best friend and will never see another day …

Left—who will never play paintball with us again or draw another picture …

Right—who I couldn't save.

Left—for the kid whose life I destroyed because of it.

"CADE!" a girl's voice drifts in through the haze. "LIAM!" she screams. "Stop it, Ryder, you're killing him!"

"Jesus Christ!"

I watch through swelling eyes as Liam pulls Ryder off of me.

Just let him get it over with, I think, but I can't move my jaw.

"Look at me, Josh! Can you hear me?" Quinn is in my face now.

She's the prettiest girl I've ever seen. Too bad she's Liam's. She's faithful, too. I know it for a fact because last week, I grabbed her ass, and she sprained her wrist when she hit me so hard. She lied and told everybody she tripped on the porch steps. I felt fucking awful—I must have apologized a hundred times. I hadn't meant to hurt her.

Quinn is always saving puppies and shit.

I don't want saving anymore.

JOSH
PRESENT

WHEN I KISS HER, I FEEL THE FRACTURE IN THE walls she's put up around herself. She can hardly stand; her body becomes slack and weak as if she's finally letting go of the heavy load she's carried on her own for much too long. I pick her up, and she wraps her legs around my waist and her arms around my neck, and I hold her there. We're both breathing hard and heavy from the eruption of emotions.

I'VE BEEN AT MY WIT'S END FOR THE PAST TWO weeks, ever since Denver. All I've wanted was round two, and she's been refusing to give it to me. Damn, the woman has iron fucking willpower! Silva warned me not to frighten her off. He likes her, he said, and he likes me better when she's around. Prick. But even then, I knew he was right; she has an effect on me, one that I've been becoming quickly addicted to.

Teaching her to fight has been a sweet sort of torture. She's been killing me (and my dick), wearing those little workout clothes—sports bras and tight black shorts that hug the curves of her pretty ass like a second skin.

Beyond all of that, though, is Sophie—the way she's been working out and training over the past two weeks has told me more about her than I could have possibly imagined. She hasn't been training to spend time with me like I thought. It's no ruse. It's obvious that Sophie's fighting a demon, a ghost, an unseen force, with deep-seated fear and trepidation. In my line of work, I've trained plenty of boys and men for both the octagon and the firehouse, and I know when they're fighting a hell of a lot more than a sparring bag, more than the flames.

Watching her has made me wonder, *What's Sophie fighting?*

I mentioned it to Uncle Cade one day on the phone, and he said, "You're going to have to hold her loosely. Let her know that you're there for her but don't smother her. She'll run faster from that shit than anything else. And most importantly, stop all your infuriating playboy moves."

That advice was nearly impossible to follow. Not flirting with Sophie was like not breathing, especially when she was so damn close I could taste her.

But Cade had apparently been right. She'd been working shit out, and my not being up in her face, but being a safe place for her to land, brought her closer to me.

And now, here she is, back in my arms, and it's fucking amazing!

She begins clawing at my shirt. "I want your hands all over my body, Josh. I need to feel you inside of me again."

Nothing exists at this moment except me and Sophie. I lean her against the wall so I can use my hands. I tilt her head and start kissing and sucking on her neck while my thumbs graze over her already-hard nipples. I yank the sports bra over her head and toss it to the floor. Once I get my hands firmly on her back, I push her sweet tits out to me and suck each one deliciously. She moans, and her hot pussy covers my very hard, very throbbing cock. I stop sucking to move up to her mouth and lick her lips, then grip her tongue between my teeth as I sink my hand down the front of her shorts, under her panties and right to her heat.

"Oh fuck, Sophie, you're so wet," I groan into her lips and tickle one finger through her folds before teasing her clit. "You're so swollen." I sink one finger inside of her.

Her head drops, and she pants with uncontrolled breaths. "More."

I take my finger out and bring my hand to my mouth. I suck on two fingers, tasting her and watching her while I do.

"Mmm ..." I purr. "So fucking delicious."

Her eyes become hooded, and her nipples get rock-hard against me. I take her mouth as I push two fingers into her. She moans around my plunging tongue, and I love it. I swallow each sweet noise as it shoots vibrations of electricity into my stomach and through my needy dick and balls.

Touching her feels so good; I'm ready to come with zero friction.

She cries out as the sensations continue to build within her. I stoop my head to grab her nipple between my lips, where I roll it, then flick my tongue over it.

"The massage table, it's still up," she manages.

She doesn't havc to suggest it twice. I take my fingers from her—which makes me immediately feel the loss of her heat— support her ass and back and keep kissing her as I maneuver us down the hall toward her office, where the massage table still stands.

I can't stop kissing her; two weeks has just been too long.

"Hold onto me," I mumble against her lips and feel her smile. That makes me grin.

When her arms are secured around my neck, and her strong thighs clench me between them, I stretch my arms to feel for the walls and doorway. I find the threshold and carefully walk us through it. Sophie's now giggling, and it's beautiful. I love that I'm part of her "working it out" process and, even more, that I'm making her happy.

"I want to be on top," she says between kisses.

"I'd love that," I tell her and work my boxer briefs down around my thighs while I get into my desk for my wallet. I fish out a condom and let the briefs slip to my ankles, where I kick them off.

I sit, leaning my ass against the massage table, and she straddles me, kneeling. We both pull her shorts and panties off—we obviously can't get to each other fast enough.

"Let me touch you," she purrs, and I swear I almost come. I feel it pooling, ready to explode. My dick becomes painfully hard as her sweet, soft hands grip the shaft and massage it up to the neck, where she pulls at it, lengthening it. "I've wanted to touch you for so long now."

I think back and remember how she never had a chance to feel me with her hands our first time.

She tickles around the tip, dipping her finger in the overflowing salty liquid and sucking it off her finger.

"You're going to make me lose it, baby," I warn.

She smiles at the power she realizes she has over me. Her fingertips continue down my length to my balls, where she cups and massages them. My head lolls back, and a growl rises up through my chest. She's going to kill me, and I think there is no better way to die.

"I can't believe how big you are, how perfect. And I love your tats, all of them—they speak so much about who you are." She grazes her other hand over the lowest part of my abdomen, over the black script there that reads, *Remembrance. Redemption*, along with the date *10/17*.

The motion thrills my skin.

"Let me roll it on." She takes the foil package from my fingers and rips it open. As she scrolls the latex over my rod, she says, "If this becomes a regular thing, I may need to invest in some form of birth control." She meets my eyes. "I'd really love the experience and feel of your flesh inside me."

"I've been tested. Your call, scrapper." Her fingers are driving me insane.

"Scrapper, huh? I'm the scrapper." She smiles, and I know she means we both are.

I can't take it anymore, so I lift her by the rib cage and position her over my dick. "Slide me around your sweetness."

Sophie reaches her hand down and swirls my head through her soft folds. I can imagine the feel of her with no barrier, and since she said it, I'm not going to stop thinking about it until it's a reality.

I feel my tip enter her and watch as she slowly lowers herself onto my dick, which is burning with need for her. Burying myself inside her is the greatest fucking feeling in the world. Her muscles clench me, squeeze me, milk me.

"Fuck me hard, Josh," she whines.

I move my hands to her hips, lifting her up and down over my cock as my own hips piston faster. We move in time together. I fill her up entirely. I can feel the soft bump of her cervix at the end of my cock, and every nerve that fires inside her walls makes rippling sensations move over my dick. The pleasure is too much. I'm squeezing her hips hard enough to leave a bruise. I start to let up a little.

"Don't stop. I want the roughness; it's a good kind of hurt," she whimpers.

I can feel myself grow harder and more rigid at the sound of her voice. I pound up and into her with long, deliberate strokes until she throws her head back and screams. I love it—no hotel room walls.

"I'm going to lose it, Josh!" Sophie cries, her gorgeous tits bouncing in my face.

Laying a hand over her shoulder, I pull her hard down on me, and she clamps tighter. "Lose it, baby," I tell her and pull her breast into my wet, wanting mouth.

The spasms inside her walls go off like fireworks, bringing me with her. I shout out her name as the surging magma in my belly and balls erupt.

When we're both spent, I collapse back against the table, and she lies on top of me, resting her head on my chest. The feel of her there comforts me beyond reason. I never realized a woman could make me feel this way. I hold her tightly against me. I'm not going to let go, not for anything.

She's fidgeting with the neatly tied bow on the present while she chews the inside of her cheek.

"Don't be nervous," I reassure her. "They're going to love you."

"Some people don't like—" She swallows, and it's audible, "prepackaged families."

"They're not like that, Sophie. We're not like that."

"CHRISTMAS LIGHTS!" Charlie yells and points out the SUV window. I had to rent it; my Gillette Vertigo is only built for two. I'm seriously thinking I'm going to have to shop for one.

Sophie lets out a deeply held sigh.

The lights Charlie sees are on my family's ranch. When my dad heard a child would be spending Christmas Eve and morning with us, he spared no expense. It looks like Disney World.

"Trust me, all this—" I wave my hand to indicate the fanfare, "is for her."

Charlie laughs excitedly.

"If it gets awkward, you'll bring me home, right?" she whispers.

"Of course." I squeeze her knee. "I think you're going to enjoy yourself, though."

A few days ago, I'd finally gotten up the courage to ask her if she was visiting family for Christmas. She wouldn't elaborate, but simply told me that she'd just planned a quiet holiday with Charlie. Even though we'd only been officially dating for a little less than three weeks at that point, I took a chance and invited her to meet my family.

By the time I park the SUV, she's wringing her

hands. I put a gentle hand on her cheek and turn her to look at me.

"You're perfect," I say, and she lets out a staccato breath. Leaning into her, I kiss her lightly glossed lips and taste her warmth mixed with coconut and strawberries. I look into her eyes and smile. "It's going to all be okay."

"Joshy kisses Mommy." Giggles float to our ears. We both smile. Charlie has a sweet way of relieving tension.

She nods, and we step out into the North Dakota cold.

Charlie has no fear; she goes running through the larger-than-life blowup Winnie the Pooh menagerie of characters that my dad set up.

"Did I hear car doors?" My mom comes stepping out through the front door. She's petite with light brown hair and looks just like my sister. She's bathed in porch light, wearing a pair of black skinny jeans and a white silk blouse with a green and red holiday sweater over her shoulders.

"We're home!" Charlie announces.

"So you are!" my mom answers with just as much enthusiasm. She goes down to one knee. "You must be Charlie! I'm so excited to meet you. I'm Suzanne. You can call me Suzy."

"Suzy." Charlie points at my mom while looking for permission from Sophie.

"Say, 'It's nice to meet you,'" Sophie coaxes with a smile.

"Nice to meet you." Charlie jumps into my mom's arms, and Sophie smiles apologetically.

A moment later, Charlie sees the tree behind my mom's back. "Christmas tree!" she says and runs into the house.

Sophie takes a step toward my mom and extends her hand. "Hello, Suzanne, I'm Sophie."

My mom ignores her hand, and scoops her into a hug. Sophie is so taken aback by the gesture, it takes her a second to recover and hug my mom in return.

"Josh has never brought a girl home, so you must be very special."

"MOM!"

"Get over it," she throws at me. Then, giving Sophie a kind expression, my mom says, "We're going to be great friends." She keeps an arm around Sophie's shoulders and herds her into the house.

"Not even a hug from my own mom," I mumble, laughing, and walk up the step into the house.

"Holy shit! You really do exist!"

"SAMUEL NORTH! Watch your mouth!"

"Sorry, Mom."

It's complete and utter chaos. Everyone is mobbing Sophie and Charlie as if they're celebrities, doting on them with hugs, handshakes and kisses. I stand back and watch the rushing onslaught—my mom and dad, my sister Jules and her husband Nate, and my brothers Sam and his girlfriend Kate, Jake and his wife Livie, Caleb and his girl Piper, and then Will. I'm overcome with love for my family. They accept Sophie and Charlie without question or hesitation. I'm proud to be a part of this family.

I think of the year I lost *him*. I always do when something stirs my soul too deeply. When he was ripped from me, I completely lost myself and hurt a lot of others in the process, but my family never gave up on me. The callous apathy I let grow around my heart that year kept me separated from the family I loved and who loved me. I've learned that sometimes, we go through things in our lives that can alter us forever. But now, watching Sophie and Charlie, it feels like a piece of me is being made whole. I'm filled with the prospect of Sophie and Charlie becoming my family. My own family. That could become a reality. I want it with her.

Will she want it with me after she learns what happened?

CHAPTER FOURTEEN
SOPHIE

J osh's family is wealthy, so wealthy, in fact, I've never even *been* in a home as beautiful as theirs, and I feel instantly out of place. Not good enough would also hit the nail on the head.

It's gorgeous, lavish and professionally decorated. Interestingly enough, it's not museum-like, even though it could cross that line—it's more homey and comfortable. Both Josh's mom and sister are in name brand, designer clothes and shoes.

Josh takes my coat. I'm dressed nicely in a silky silver dress from Target and tall, black leather boots. I smooth my dress down over my legs.

The other women, Piper, Kate and Livie, are all dressed very casually. That's good, makes me feel less like I'm sticking out.

Everyone's being so down-to-earth, genuine and friendly, it soon evokes natural openness from me. In fact, no one's the least bit stuffy or putting on airs.

Josh talks incessantly about his family; it's obvious they're very close. They're all so at ease with each other. I find myself observing them and the way they interact. They laugh easily together. All the brothers seem like rowdy hooligans. I can't help but laugh a little and wonder what it must have been like for their mom to raise all four of these hellions.

They each possess a restless energy that seems to require constant motion. And they also bounce that energy between them, because when one sits and gets comfortable for a moment, another takes his place, pacing, talking, entertaining someone else, eating or teasing. The teasing seems to range from good-natured bantering to good-natured competition—bets made, demands to prove oneself, wrestling matches on the floor, chasing around the house. It's hysterical, and even Charlie is enthralled and entertained by them.

Caleb is the oldest and holds himself with an extra dose of decorum. He and his father, along with Nate, seem to fall easily into business discussions of ranches and oil fields. All three of the men wear nice but casual button-up cotton shirts, jeans and work boots or cowboy boots. They're not fancy.

Now, seeing Caleb and Josh, the second oldest, I wonder how much influence Josh has had on his younger brothers. It seems like a lot, between the athletics and tattoos—but they're also each very much their own individual personalities.

Something else—I don't know if it's because of Josh's line of work or sports or what, but he holds himself a little differently than the rest of the North boys. There's a roughness he has that the other boys don't seem to have about them, a hardness in the eyes. Except now that I look closer, I see some of it in Jake and Josh's brother-in-law Nate. They're both a little guarded, like they've been through something, and they're not sure if they're going to let you in. I know I'm right because it takes one to know one.

All of them are rugged, gorgeous and powerful men, there's no doubt, and something that moves me deeply is the way they treat their women. Each of them is caring, considerate, devoted. They serve them, touch them tenderly, talk about them as if they're the greatest women in the world and put them on pedestals. Except for in novels and movies, I've never known any men who treated their girlfriends and wives with such deep respect and honor.

It all seems too good to be true. I feel like

Alice after she fell through the rabbit hole—disoriented and in a whole new world.

Josh takes a seat next to me and hands me a local Montana-brewed beer. "I see those wheels spinning, scrapper," he whispers. "You gonna run?"

"I'm still deciding," I reply.

"If you do, take me with you." He pushes his leg against mine.

"Enough boring talk about work, sports and fantasy teams," Julia says, standing up. "I think it's time for something much more family-oriented before dinner."

Her brothers look at her like they're debating whether or not to throw her outside in a snowdrift.

She bounces to a large wall lined with bookshelves.

"No!" groans Caleb. "Come on, Jules! There are a hundred other ways you could torture us."

"Yes, true." Her voice twinkles sweetly, like a Disney character. "But none quite so rewarding and sinister."

Caleb rolls his eyes.

"Oh, Jules, it's a great idea," her mom, Suzanne, chimes in. "And we have several new initiates to the North family. They need to see what they're getting into."

Livie is laughing like she's totally in on the

whole thing. Piper and Kate look at me like maybe I know something. I shrug my shoulders apologetically.

"We should start with these." Jules, as everyone calls her, turns and is weighed down by six of the thickest photo albums I've ever seen. They have to be five inches wide each!

"Hey! What are you doing?" Nate jumps up from the couch and, in one long stride, is taking the heavy books. "That's totally too much weight for you to be carrying," he scolds lovingly. "That's my job."

"Of course, you're going to aid and abet her," Sam quips.

"Why shouldn't I?" Nate retorts. "None of my embarrassing naked baby photos are in them."

He sets them down on the rich, cherry wood coffee table in front of the oversized couches.

"I'm not shy." Jake leans comfortably back into his seat with his hands behind his head—the epitome of relaxation. "Livie's seen it all."

"Really?!" Will fires. "I don't need that image in my mind."

"I didn't mean it like that!" Jake laughs. "Idiot. I mean that she's already *seen* all of my baby pictures. What the hell is wrong with you?"

"Alright, alright, enough," Suzanne says, taking it all in stride. "Piper, Kate and Sophie, you ladies will definitely want to get in close. Won't want to miss this."

"Her first time here, and you're going to do this?" Josh feigns embarrassment.

"Yes," says his mother. "Now move out of the way so Sophie can sit next to me."

"Fine, I'll be exiled with the rest of the guys, but I'm not going far. I have a feeling I'm going to have to defend myself." Josh joins the guys, who are now setting themselves on the furniture on the other side of the coffee table.

Kate squeezes next to me with Piper on her other side. Suzanne sits beside me, too, with Jules and Livie next to each other. I can tell those two are close.

Josh positions himself directly across from me. He's smiling as if he approves of this activity. Sam, Will and Caleb, however, look somewhat mortified. Makes me wonder exactly what's in these photos.

"Does anyone need a drink before we get to storytelling?" Colt, Josh's dad, asks. A couple of people ask for refreshers. I'm amazed at these men.

He disappears into the dining room. Everyone waits for him.

Meanwhile, Sam and Will are conspiring together to snatch and grab the book they're featured in.

"I'm sure you were the most beautiful baby there ever was," Piper says to Caleb adoringly.

"Naw," Jake laughs. "He had cauliflower ears as big as his face."

Everybody laughs, and I'm grateful for the tension release. Caleb stalks over to the couch to punch Jake in the shoulder, but Jake deflects it, and the two begin trying to monkey-bump each other.

I can feel Josh's eyes on me, so I lift my gaze up, and sure enough, I am right. My heart flutters at the attention.

"And here we go." Colt passes around drinks and then takes a seat across from Suzanne.

Suzanne opens the first book and reveals a gorgeous photograph of her and Colt from their wedding.

Colt peers at it for a moment with the expression of a sweet memory on his face, then smiles at his wife. "Best day of my life."

"How long have you been together?" Piper asks. Piper's naturally beautiful. She has long, flowing, auburn hair, wears almost no makeup and is dressed in jeans, pink cowboy boots and a pink checkered western style blouse.

"Twenty-eight years," Colt answers. "We've been inseparable since high school."

We all smile.

"There I am, pregnant with Caleb. I carried

him really low. My mom said she was sure it was going to be a boy," Suzanne tells us.

"Right, and your dad was convinced—" Colt begins.

"It was a girl," they finish together and laugh at the remembrance.

"And there he is. Eight pounds, nine ounces," Suzanne gushes. "He was perfect."

"Still am," Caleb calls over his shoulder; he and Jake are still at it.

"This is my mom and dad." Suzanne points to the photo of a couple that's holding baby Caleb. "They both passed away several years ago."

"I'm sorry," Kate says.

"Thank you." Suzanne smiles at the photo. "He passed first, and then she followed him a year later. They couldn't stand to be apart."

I'm caught up. I gaze at the picture until Suzanne turns the page. I've never seen love like that. I look around the room and have a feeling most of them will have that same kind of love— timeless.

I don't dare bring my eyes to Josh. I feel like my thoughts are exposed. Do some people deserve love more than others? Did they live their lives in a certain way? Or were they especially good in a past life, maybe? Why do some people have near-instant success, and others work their fingers to the bone for a meager and hungry existence? I fall short of answers. But I can't argue that true love doesn't exist now because these people are testaments that not only does it exist, but it thrives. I wonder what it must have been like being raised by two people who loved each other—and you.

"And here I am in the hospital, about to give birth to Josh," Suzanne exclaims. In the photograph, she's lying on a hospital bed while Colt stands right next to her, holding her hand.

Now, I let my eyes fall on Josh. He smiles and shrugs.

I shouldn't make this about me. It isn't about me at all. But their great wealth of love and joy reminds me all too acutely of my great poverty and pain.

At the mention of Josh's name, Charlie leaves her crayons and comes crawling up onto my lap. I hug her thankfully. She is all my love and joy.

"Picture of Joshy?" she asks.

At the same time, all of them coo, "Aww," at the radiant cuteness of her saying Josh's name.

Josh ruffles her long, curly, unruly hair, which is the color of autumn wheat. "You want to see a picture of me when I was a baby?"

She nods with glee.

He turns the page to the sweetest photo of Colt holding Suzanne in his arms while she holds baby Josh. They're looking at each other with such awe and amazement.

I want the photo, to put it in my pocket and remember, when the world is at its worst, that somewhere there is something very good.

They belong to each other in a way I've only ever imagined.

This entire family *belongs* together.

"I love Joshy," Charlie declares. Then she bends and leans forward in my arms and kisses Josh's picture.

Everyone thinks she's adorable, but my own fear creeps in, and I wonder what the hell I'm doing and what I've gotten us into.

CHRISTMAS EVE DINNER IS SPECTACULAR. THERE is pineapple ham, roasted turkey, and every side dish and dessert imaginable. I know I'm going to gain ten pounds.

"Give me your hand," Livie, who sat next to me, says and puts my hand on her tummy.

A moment later, I feel the little kick. We both grin ear to ear.

"I *loved* that feeling, maybe more than any other in the world," I confess.

"Oh! Jules and I are going to have to grill you about labor and childbirth!" Livie exclaims enthusiastically as if I'm an expert or something.

"I'm not a guru," I say, disqualifying myself.

"Are you kidding? You have experience!" she insists.

My experience won't be anything like hers. "Sure."

Jules is all over it. "Ha! Great. Let's help clean up, then we'll take her away for a little girl time."

"Mommy, I'm sleepy." Charlie swipes mashed potato-crusted fingers across her eyes.

"No, no, don't."

My warning is too late. She begins crying as the salt in the potatoes starts to sting. And, of course, she presses more potatoes into her eyes, trying to rid herself of the first offense.

"I'm sorry. It's getting late for her." I stand and pick her up against me, dabbing at her eyes with a moistened napkin.

"I'll show you to our room." Josh jumps up and helps get my chair out of the way.

Our room? "Thank you." Poker face.

As I take the lead from the dining room, I grip the handle of Charlie's day bag to bring with me.

"I can get that," Josh offers.

"Thanks, I've got it."

He draws his eyebrows together, but he doesn't argue. He shows me up the stairs.

More than ever, I feel guarded. Charlie kissing his photo and announcing that she loves him scares me to the core. He's just another person to hurt her, to leave us. Josh says he loves me, loves us. He might not when he learns where I come from. What I've done.

"This is the room my mom prepped for us." He opens a door and turns on the light.

It's exquisite. A large, four-poster canopy bed is set near a set of glass French doors that overlook a prairie that sprawls for miles in every direction. A small, pink princess bed sits close to the adult bed.

"Mommy!" Charlie forgets about the potato problem and wriggles out from my arms to throw herself on the little, just-her-size bed.

"My mom likes making homey, feel-good touches like this. Hope that's okay," Josh tells me.

He's sensing the change in my countenance. "It's beautiful."

"She really can't wait to be a grandmother," he explains, shifting from one foot to the other.

"She'll make a wonderful grandmother," I agree.

"What's a granmudder?" Charlie rolls on the bed.

A strange expression crosses Josh's face, and I rush to deflect the conversation. "Charlie, we have to get you out of those dirty clothes before you can get into the nice, clean bed. You know that."

But Josh is still studying me carefully. Perfect, more unanswered questions to avoid.

I see the bathroom off to the side of the room.

"I'm just going to clean her up," I say. "Please don't let me keep you from your family. I'll catch up with you once I get her to sleep."

"Let me help you." Josh opens the bag and begins to lay out her pajamas, her diaper and the books I packed for her—*Mouse Paint* and *Goodnight Moon,* her favorites.

"Josh, I have this." My tone snaps more than I mean it to.

"Alright." He nods, then kneels, and Charlie leaps into his open arms.

"Night night, Joshy." She hugs him tight, and my heart constricts in my chest.

"Night night, sweetheart." Josh hugs her back and closes his eyes.

I cover my mouth with my hand. I'm overcome, and I don't want him to see it.

"Go wash your hands," he tells her, and she runs to the bathroom sink.

He swoops me into his arms. "What's wrong?"

"Nothing." How did he stage this coup?

"You have no poker face, scrapper."

"Come on, Josh." I push him away. "I've had enough tonight." Moving to my overnight bag, which Josh must have carried up here earlier, I toss it onto the bed so hard it bounces. I rip the zipper open, grab fistfuls of my stuff and throw them on the bed, too.

"I know that look in your eyes," he says softly.

"You don't know anything," I snap back.

"Yes, I do. It's fear. And that's all it is—a word, an emotion that will ruin everything good in your life." Josh yanks his shirt off. "Fear quotes —you've read them all. I have these permanently inked into my skin for a reason, Sophie. I know fear intimately in all its forms—pain, rage, jealousy, despair. It comes and stays, burrows and roots into your heart, and darkens your soul with shadows you think will never go away. You can't let it. You have to fight it and believe in the sun, even when it's night and the fear has made you a coward; you have to reach in and dig deeper than you ever have and pull out the fortitude you don't even think is there."

He takes my face in his hands. "You're a fighter—I know it, I see it—just like me. I see you fight for her every moment you breathe." He looks to Charlie, who is standing quietly, watching us.

"Don't give up." He looks at me for a second more before he walks out of the room, leaving me standing there with his words running through my veins like insulin giving life to a diabetic.

"Is Joshy mad?"

"No, baby, Joshy isn't mad. Let's get in your jammies." I take off her pretty, ruffled holiday dress, now stained with cranberry sauce and blueberry pie, wash her up with a warm, soapy cloth and pull on her soft, flannel nightgown with the reindeer and snowmen on it.

I tuck her into the pink princess bed. "You know I love you more than anything in the world." I press my lips to her forehead, breathing in her beauty and love.

"I love you, Mommy." Her little hands are wrapped around my neck, and I could cry from the sheer power of her unconditional love.

Right then, Josh comes into the room and closes the door behind him. "I have a goodnight song to play for you."

Charlie smiles and snuggles deeper into her pillow.

Josh taps the screen of his phone and sets it on the chest of drawers. The music begins to play, and I immediately recognize the iconic song "Fools Rush In."

He holds out his hand to me.

I close my eyes, overcome with emotion.

He pulls me into his chest and buries his fingers into my hair, singing the words to me while Charlie giggles from her bed.

"I can't help falling in love with you."

Wearily, I drop my head and take in his strength. I let him lead as he sways me gently, here in the guest room of his parents' home on Christmas Eve, with Charlie watching us, full of innocent joy.

"Love can get through anything. It finds a way." Tenderly, he brushes my cheek. "I know you're bruised, Sophie. I see the broken. Let me fix it."

Before I know it, the song repeats, and we dance through it again.

I won't be the one to let go.

"MOMMY! MOMMY, WAKE UP!"

"Charlie, stop jumping on the bed," I groan sleepily.

"SANTA CAME!" She's shaking me with all the power of a gale-force wind.

"He did!?" Josh crows next to me as if he's already drunk a pot of coffee. "Let's go see what he brought!"

He bounces out of the bed like Tigger from Winnie the Pooh and pulls on a t-shirt. He's wearing green plaid flannel pajama bottoms.

I sigh. *Plaid never looked so good.*

He grabs my robe and holds it open for me. "Get it on, beautiful."

"Ha! I'm not going down there in my robe and pajamas. You're lucky you get to see me like this. I have to brush my teeth, comb my hair, fix my makeup …"

As I'm talking, he rips the blankets off of me

—luckily, I'm wearing a pretty yet modest pajama set—and throws me over his shoulder!

"What are you doing?!" I demand.

"I know you're not doing all that! We've got presents to open," he says as he tries to get out the door.

I get my hands up just in time and grip the doorway, my fingers like a vice. "You will let me at least brush my hair and fix my face," I warn.

"Hey, Sammy, could you give me a hand here," Josh says like they're going to move a table or something.

"Of course," Sam chirps back.

Freaking morning people!

Next thing I know, I feel Sam's fingers assault my ribcage, the most ticklish place on my body.

"NOOOO!" I howl.

"We all have to go down just as we woke up, a mess. It's tradition. Get used to it," Sam lectures through his attack.

I scream in a fit of laughter and have no choice but to release my grip.

Josh pulls hard and fast, so I can't regain any leverage. "Stick close in case she gets any more ideas."

"No problem. Jake and I just had to go through it with Kate, too. I don't think she's too happy with me, though. Unlike you, I forgot her robe." Sam holds up a light blue bathrobe while wearing a Cheshire cat grin. "Hell, I think she looks better without it. But she wasn't too thrilled about greeting everyone in her Victoria's Secret camisole and short set."

He and Josh laugh, while Charlie tries to go down the steps as quickly and as carefully as possible.

Josh lowers me onto the couch and covers me ceremoniously with the robe, lifting it high and letting it drop over me as if it were a blanket. Even over my head.

"Thanks," I mumble from beneath the cloth.

Piper and Caleb wish us a Merry Christmas. They're curled up together on the loveseat across from us.

"Merry Christmas," I say, realizing I'm pretty happy.

"Merry Christmas!" Jules and Livie come out of the kitchen carrying trays of delicious-looking, flaky turnovers and glasses of eggnog and begin passing them out to everyone.

Nate turns on the stereo system, and Harry Connick Jr.'s "Have Yourself a Merry Little Christmas" is playing.

"Nate!" the guys all protest.

"Get off my case! Christ, it's the radio. What else do you think they're going to play on Christmas?"

"Don't touch the dial; it's my favorite,"

Suzanne's disembodied voice cautions from the kitchen.

"Is this one *mine?*" Charlie is nearly screaming as she points to some seriously large gifts—several are bigger than she is. "IS THIS ONE MINE TOO?!"

"We have to wait just another few minutes, sweetheart."

The only Christmases she's ever known have been celebrated with just me. I would wrap two things I already owned just so she could hand me something. I always tried hard to buy her at least three new things—usually a new set of clothes and two new toys. Last year, I was able to sign her up for Toys for Tots. This year, with her turning three years old, my new job, and coming here for Christmas, I got her a couple of extra presents. But five presents under a tree that looked like Paul Bunyan chopped it down and dragged it into the North's house along with what could have easily been a couple hundred packages … Well, I get the feeling she's going to have some serious present envy.

Everyone is filtering into the room, brightly saying good morning, hugging and kissing. Josh puts a cup of coffee into my hands, and I've never been so thankful.

I look up from under my lashes at him with grateful eyes. "I forgive you."

"Thank you," he says and sits in a butterfly yoga pose on the floor in front of me.

Kate walks over to the couch with coffee in hand and sits close to me, folding her legs underneath her. "I didn't know about the tradition. Sam didn't even let me wash my face," she complains. She's stunningly beautiful, with thick, long, blonde hair the color of spun gold from a fairytale and ocean-blue eyes.

"Me neither," I commiserate. "At least they gave us coffee."

"Yeah, I guess they're redeemable," she grumbles playfully.

"So, this is your first Christmas here, too, then?" I try.

She nods. "Yes."

"How long have you been seeing Sam?"

"I've been *seeing* Sam since September. I've been *dating* him since October."

It sounds like a private joke. I go a different route. "What do you do?"

"Oh! Josh didn't tell you. You wouldn't have understood what I meant about September." She shakes her head. "I was Sam's university professor."

"*You?* Really? I'm sorry, you don't look old enough to be a professor." I'm very surprised.

"I was a very young professor. I earned my degrees in accelerated courses. Sam and I met on the first day of school. He hit on me." She smiles. "Anyway, it took a month of him asking me to coffee and a few other incidents for me to agree to go out with him."

"Nice." I think for a second. "You said '*was* his professor'?"

"Yeah, now I'm a co-writer for his band."

"That's incredible."

"And she's training for an upcoming surfing competition in southern Cali," Sam adds.

Kate smiles up at him, and he bends down to kiss her.

"I'm sorry we took so long!" Suzanne says as she and Colt come in from the kitchen.

"We were taking care of a few last-minute touches," Colt puts in.

Once everyone has said Merry Christmas to Josh's parents and we all have a drink in our hands, Colt raises his glass and says, "A toast. To our ever-growing family. May your lives be filled with many years of beautiful holidays."

"Cheers," we all say in unison.

"MOMMMMMMMMYYYYYYY!" Charlie is going to self-combust.

"Sorry, daffodil! Let's find a present marked for Charlie." I get up from the couch and join her under the tree. Josh joins me.

"Oooh, this is going to be so much fun!"

Suzanne says animatedly. "Those closest to the tree, start handing out the presents."

Charlie screams, picks up a gift that reads *Will* on the tag and gives it to Josh. "That's for you, Joshy. Merry Christmas!"

"Thanks, Charlie, it's great!" Josh tries to hug her, but she's not having it; she's rushing to the nearest, biggest, wrapped box.

Oh, jeez, why didn't I think about this happening? This could seriously ruin everyone's morning, especially if she starts crying. I start to dig in to find one of her presents.

"Charlie, looks like this one is for you," Josh says and pushes the hugest present of the lot toward her.

There must be some mistake.

I begin to protest. That is definitely not from me. But I'm close enough to read the big tag that has Charlie's name written neatly on it. Her eyes become as big as saucers, and her smile lights up the room more than any Christmas lights ever could.

I look at Josh. He's smiling at Charlie and watching her, along with everyone else. She's so excited that she's shaking as her fingers work themselves under the folds of Christmas wrapping, and she tears it off as fast as she can.

She screams for joy!

Standing as tall as her is a gorgeous, pink

wooden dollhouse with elegant, white Victorian trimming. She throws herself at Josh.

"Thank you, Joshy!" Her delighted squeal makes everyone laugh.

"You're welcome, Charlie. I'm happy you like it!" Josh spins the dollhouse around to show her the rooms full of furniture, dolls, pets and other accessories.

They begin playing with it together, and I'm seriously holding back tears. Josh is hard, and strong, and tough, and tattooed, and here he is playing pink dollhouse with a little girl, a little girl who is falling in love with him as much as her mommy is.

Gifts are passed around and exchanged, and everyone hugs everyone else. Jules cries when she opens a bracelet with a diamond charm that Nate gives to her. He blames the tears on pregnancy hormones, and she slaps him and then kisses him. Piper throws her arms around Caleb's neck when she sees that he bought them tickets for a winter Australian getaway. Kate gives Sam a silver Omega Seamaster watch, and he freaks. Then she opens his gift—a bottle of Clive Christian No. 1 in a crystal and diamond bottle. It's one of the most expensive perfumes made in the world.

All of a sudden, I'm pretty sure my gifts to Josh and his parents are *not* going to measure up!

"Oh, Colt! This is perfect." Suzanne beams,

holding up a piece of gold paper. "Cruise tickets to Belize."

"It leaves before the New Year." Colt kisses her. "I thought we'd enjoy that."

"Sophie," Josh says, pulling me from my thoughts, "you still need to open yours." He passes me a gold envelope decorated with a green ribbon.

"Thank you," I say in nervous anticipation as I open the envelope. "A weekend of pampering at Arrowwood Resort Spa." The smile spreads over my face. I think of facials, manicures and massages, which I would never get for myself. "Josh, this is so thoughtful." I hug him and plant a chaste but excited kiss on his lips. "I've never heard of this spa, where is it?" I look over the certificate.

"Minnesota." Josh smiles. "We're there for training in a week."

"That's a perfect surprise. Thank you so much." Now, tears well in my eyes. "It's the sweetest gift anyone's ever given me."

"I'm sure you've had better," Josh says disparagingly.

"Nope. Never have." I feel the tears and pinch the bridge of my nose to stop the rush of emotion. "That was a lot to spend on me, Josh." It had to have been a few hundred dollars anyway. Same with Charlie's dollhouse.

"No, it wasn't," he says, brushing an errant tear and leaning in to whisper, "I would've done more. I just didn't want to frighten you off with something elaborate like vacation tickets or diamonds."

I laugh as he puts me at ease. I recover and say, "It must be your turn."

I pass him a thick box wrapped in white freezer paper that Charlie smeared her handprints and fingerprints on in green and red paint.

She comes over and matches her hand to one of the prints. "That's me, Joshy!"

"It is you!" he says, acting surprised. "Will you help me open it carefully so I can keep it?"

"Yes." She nods her head determinedly, and the two are cautious to open it along the tape line, so as not to rip the paper.

Josh rolls the paper carefully, secures it with a little piece of tape, and sets it next to him. "Just see what I do with *that* present." He touches his finger to the tip of her nose, and she giggles, her laughter musical.

He looks toward me with contented eyes and opens the box. His brow knits as he pulls out the menagerie of sleek black photo frames of different sizes.

"Sophie!"

"Do you like it?"

He shakes his head, and my heart freezes.

Josh spreads the five frames on the floor in front of us. "I love it." He grabs me by the back of my neck and places a totally *not chaste* kiss on my lips in front of everyone.

Each photo frame contains something different about Josh—two display the fear quotes he has tattooed on his skin from Emerson and Twain in calligraphy script. Another is a photograph of him when he won his first title fight. He looks so amazingly proud in the picture, lifting the golden trophy belt over his head for the world to see. The fourth is when he received a Firefighter of the Year Award from the governor of North Dakota for heroic acts of bravery and valor.

Finally, the fifth is an empty frame. I tilt my head to the side and graze my fingers over the glass. Josh probably doesn't get how much of an inspiration he is to me and, I'm sure, others. I'm taken back to last night's conversation and the irony of my gift to him. I explain, "This one is for a photo of the next accomplishment you achieve, despite the fear you may have to fight to attain it."

Josh stares at me, speechless.

Another moment passes, and I think maybe I messed up. I'm about to apologize when Suzanne comes in closer to get a better look.

"Sophie, that's beautiful."

Everyone makes a comment, but Josh is biting the inside of his lip.

Shit! He's not smiling. At all.

He doesn't look up from the frame as he says softly, "I love you more today than I did yesterday, and that was enough to choke the life out of me. And I loved you more yesterday than I did when I first told you I loved you."

"Boy,"—his dad sighs and lays his hand on his shoulder—"that's the way the real stuff works."

Josh smiles and takes my hand in his, lacing our fingers together slowly.

Soon, more presents are opened. Everyone got a gift for Charlie, who is making out like a bandit. But a half hour later, there are still hundreds of gifts left under the tree. I realized a little while ago that most have no names, but different colored stickers.

Colt announces, "Looks like it's time to get dressed and make the Christmas run. Charlie, how would you like to help Santa?"

Next thing I know, we're packing all the rest of the presents into the back of Colt's, Caleb's and Nate's pickup trucks and Josh's rented SUV.

"We're a Christmas train!" Charlie dubs it from her car seat.

"What is it that we're doing?" I ask Josh.

"It's another tradition."

For the next three hours we distribute the gifts throughout the community—to homeless shelters, children's homes, senior homes, the Boys and

Girls Clubs, a battered women's shelter, local foster homes and hospitals.

"Your family does this every year?" I say through fresh tears at the smiles we've created.

"It was a way my mom and dad came up with years ago to show how grateful we are for the financial blessings and good health we have." He laughs at the memory. "When they started it, Sam, Will and Jules were still really young. They had some serious issues with giving out what they thought should have been theirs. Oh God, they used to cry until Dad thought up that *'helping Santa'* line. It worked."

"It's incredible." I can't think of words to describe how I feel about giving like that or how I feel toward Josh and his family.

It makes me fantasize about being part of them.

It makes me pretend Josh is Charlie's daddy and we're a family.

Finally happy, finally safe.

That's dangerous.

CHAPTER FIFTEEN
JOSH

"That was one hell of a Christmas," Dad says and brings the beer to his mouth.

We're sitting on the inner door porch my mom had built a few years back. The wood stove in the corner adds heat and a warm glow, while the glass walls and ceiling offer an incredible view of the night skies. It gives the illusion of being outside. My dad and I are having a moment alone out here, and alone time in a family as large as mine can be rare.

"Sophie putting the little one to bed?" he asks.

"Yeah." I watch a shooting star streak across the darkness. It's brilliant.

"I'm assuming you're going to introduce her to your Uncle Cade?"

"Definitely." I smile.

"Have you told her yet?"

The smile dissolves quickly. I take a deep breath. "No, sir. Not yet."

"Didn't mean to deflate you, son. I just wondered since you're going to Minnesota."

"I've started to tell her a few times now. I just … I don't know how she's going to react. I just found her, Dad. I don't want to lose her."

"It's been nearly a decade, Josh. Why would you be afraid of losing her?"

"I don't know. Some women would shy away from a man with that kind of violence and darkness in his past."

"Not if that man became a man like you, and not if she's a good woman. The right woman will love you more for what you had to overcome."

"I always thought that when I got involved with a girl, I'd go slowly, you know? Open myself up a little at a time," I muse. "But it's not like that with Sophie. I don't want to go slow; I want to love her *now*. I can't fight the intensity that she creates in me. I don't want to, either. And I don't want to hold anything back. I want to tell her everything."

"I know exactly how you feel. I felt that way with your mother." He takes a drink and says, "You should jump."

"Really?" I'm almost surprised at his advice.

"You've always been a deep thinker. You count and examine every step in front of you before you take it. She's the first woman you've brought home to meet your mother and me. She's special, and you know it." He examines the situation. "It's also obvious that you're ready to take on the role of step-father."

I take another deep breath. "She's been hurt, Dad, and she has secrets that I can't press her to share. Anytime I try, I have to stop because she becomes this skittish creature, ready to run. I don't know who Charlie's dad is, or where, or what kind of relationship Charlie has with him. It looks to me like he's not in her life at all," I explain. "And call me crazy, but it's like Sophie's always cautious—checking her surroundings and looking over her shoulder—it's very seldom I catch her completely relaxed."

We sit quietly together and empty our beers. Dad pulls two more from a small cooler next to his chair and twists them open. I take the second cold glass bottle gladly. This isn't an easy conversation.

"You know, Josh, by telling her what happened to you and confiding in her that way, you're going to build trust. You sharing the deepest parts of you first may just be what she needs to feel secure in opening up to you."

That makes sense.

"Now, something else to think about—you're concerned she's going to hear your past and take off. Well, if she does, then you know it wasn't meant to be. The woman made for you is going to accept you for you, just like your mom did me," he says. "But she could be thinking the same thing —what if she opens her heart to you, and you don't like what you see? What are you going to do then, Josh?"

"There couldn't be anything in her past that would make me stop loving her," I say, shaking my head.

"Seems to me, maybe she feels the same way … yet you're both hiding," he says slowly. "Maybe you should man up and come out first."

I nod. "I get it, Dad."

"OKAY, SO MINNEAPOLIS IS WHERE YOUR MASTER for Jeet Kune Do, the martial art created by Bruce Lee, is." Sophie seems to be making sure she gets what I'm telling her.

"Yes."

"Your master also just happens to be your uncle, who got you into mixed martial arts in the first place," she relays. "I think that's great. I can't wait to meet him."

Its two days after Christmas and we're on our way to the twin cities. The flight is only a little over an hour. We're playing Candyland with

Charlie, who won't move from the Princess Lollipop space.

Christmas was a real game changer for our relationship; I can feel it and see it all over Sophie's countenance. She liked my family and they liked her. And that night we talked about fear, it felt like we went over a hurdle, or maybe dodged a bullet.

I realize that our next week here in Minneapolis, what I'm going to show her and tell her, and how she reacts, is going to either fortify us or obliterate us, just like my dad said. I think his advice is sound.

My gaze wanders to my laptop case. I brought a memory book that's filled with photographs, newspaper articles, letters and journal entries that explain more about my life and choices than anyone knows besides my parents and my uncle … and maybe Caleb. He knows more than the others. None of us brings it up. Who would want to? Talking about it is like a visit to hell.

Sharing my life story with Sophie is going to be like cutting my fucking guts out with a butter knife.

When I think about it too deeply, my knees start going to goddamn Jell-O, and my hands shake. I keep reminding myself of the pretty speech I gave her in the guest room at my parents' house about fear.

Yeah, eat those words, asshat!

"MAKE THE CALL, SCRAPPER." I'M SMILING AT Sophie and her dilemma.

Britt's trying to stay out of it as she walks away to stare absentmindedly at a painting in the Hyatt Hotel lobby. Charlie is a little mini-scrapper, just like her mom, who's standing defiantly with her arms folded over her chest.

"I want to sleep with Joshy," Charlie demands.

"I know, Charlie. You told me," Sophie says with what seems to be perpetual patience.

Since Sophie made the concession of allowing us to sleep together at my parents' home, now that we're traveling for business, she's faced with deciding if she and Charlie will get their own room again *or* if they will share a room with me.

She's frigging hysterical. She wants to say yes, but because of her rep and the way it'll look to Britt and the team … I figure I'm up against one hell of a fight.

Charlie stomps her foot. Her very angry face is so cute I have to turn away so she won't see me laughing.

"This isn't going to be an issue," Sophie decides stubbornly. "Josh, I would appreciate it if you would honor our original agreement in this business atmosphere. I get my own room with Charlie adjacent to Britt."

Charlie's chubby bottom lip juts out in the cutest pout I've ever seen.

"Please don't look at me that way," Sophie says. She looks around her and at me, flashing a little smirk. She bends down to her knee to talk to Charlie more intimately. "We can still go and sleep in Josh's room sometimes if you want."

Charlie jumps up and down, clapping her hands. "YAY!!!"

"I liked that," I tell Sophie.

"I'm sure you did."

WE GET OUR STUFF IN THE ROOMS, AND AFTER Charlie's settled with Britt, Sophie and I take off. The taxi stops on the gritty south side of the city, in front of The Core, the training center that I co-own with my Uncle Cade. I hold the door open for Sophie, and we walk inside.

It's interesting, the places in our lives that become home and the stories behind those places. I smile automatically. I love this place; it means so much to me.

The Core consists of three levels, a level for each type of training gear—the mats, the weights and the bags. We enter on the ground floor, which has the mats. An instructor is training a class of young children. They watch in the wall of mirrors as they punch and kick.

I lead Sophie around to the back, where the offices are. I turn my head and smile at her, so excited she's here with me.

I knock on the door.

"Better be important," a gruff, deep voice calls out.

"Oh, I guarantee it is," I call back.

"Get your ass in here!"

I shove open the door, and my uncle is already coming around the desk. I reach out to him as he immediately spreads his arms wide, passes me and pulls Sophie into a big bear hug.

"Oh!" She is startled and looks at me to see if this is all okay.

He pulls her feet off the floor. "I knew you'd be beautiful," he gushes.

"You know, if you'd hugged me first, she'd know who you are by now," I quip.

"I've been hugging you long enough. She's prettier."

I roll my eyes.

"Josh has never brought a woman to meet me, ever."

"I guess you and the folks back in Williston have that in common." Sophie smiles. "I'm honored to hold the title."

"I'm Josh's Uncle Cade, Colt's brother," he informs her.

He still hasn't put her down.

"I'm Sophie—"

"Garner," he finishes for her. "I've heard all about you. Did you bring Charlie with you?"

"She's back at the hotel."

They're having the entire conversation with her still in the air.

"Aw, too bad. You'll have to bring her with you tomorrow. We'll get her punching the bags in no time."

Finally! He puts her feet back on the floor, holds her in front of him and examines her. "She does look like a scrapper," he says to me without taking his eyes off her. "He's teaching you self-defense moves, right?"

"Yes, he is," Sophie says, blushing.

"Good. Everyone should be equipped." He stares at her for another moment, then states, "She really is very beautiful. You've done well, Josh. Don't muck it up."

"Cade."

He points at me. "Every man should be warned." He looks back at her. "How's he doing? I know he's handsome, but sometimes all that punching takes a toll on the brain, and testosterone does that anyway, so fighters are doubly screwed."

She laughs. "He's wonderful."

"Aww, she likes you. She's cutting you slack."

He grabs my hand and pulls me into a back-slapping hug. "The kids are going to be so excited to see you."

"How are they doing?" I ask.

"This new batch is doing great; they're getting stronger and starting to believe in themselves. We do have a new boy. He's fourteen, just came in last week, and is having a damn hard time. Mom's a junkie. He doesn't know who his dad is, and he's watched a parade of assholes slap his mom around. I think he's been sexually assaulted, too, but he won't talk about it."

Fuck. I hate hearing how people treat each other so badly. "Has he been staying out of trouble since he's been with you?"

"A couple fights with a few of the other kids. He's just mad and hurting. He'd love to meet you, though—Jackhammer."

"Absolutely." I see Sophie trying to put together what we're discussing. "My Uncle Cade runs a long-term residential home and halfway house for teens."

"That's beautiful," Sophie says, visibly moved.

"When they come to us, it's from all kinds of situations and backgrounds," Cade tells her. "What we do is get them in here, to The Core, and then we teach them how to harness the power of their emotions for good and healing, for their own inner and outer strength. They start lifting weights and learning how to kick, and soon, they feel strong, like they have some control over their out-of-control lives. Their self-esteem grows, and they become secure with who they are in a way they may have never experienced before."

"I'm in awe." Sophie nods. "That's incredible work."

"Yeah, I love them," my uncle says. "And this big gorilla here comes out once a month or so to train not only himself but the kids, too."

"You do this?" She turns to face me.

"Yeah, I've been involved since I was fifteen," I tell her, feeling like a dick for not having told her *any* of it in fear of having to tell her *all* of it.

"Why didn't you tell me?" Her brow knits in curiosity.

"It's a long story. I promise I'll make the time to tell you."

"Good." She smiles again. "What a fabulous cause. I'm really impressed."

"This place will be really hopping this week, what with six classes a day, weight training and the divisional finals coming up. We have kids and adults of all ages who train here," Cade explains.

"I'm excited to be a part of it, even if it's just observing."

"Oh, are you kidding?" Cade begins. "I can't

wait to see how Josh's doing getting his girlfriend in fighting shape."

Sophie laughs. "He's really only just begun."

"Good, then you can kick his ass for me on the mats." Cade winks.

"Oh, Christ." I'm laughing.

Cade checks his watch. "The kids are hitting the bags about now."

"Let's go."

After I put our stuff in my office, we lock it up and head upstairs to the bags. We walk through the door, and about fifty kids shout my name and moniker and come up to shake my hand or bump fists. Most of them, I know, but a few are new. A lot of times even when the kids are placed in foster care, they still come here to continue their training goals for free. Kids in foster care pay nothing.

"Can we get your autograph?" The request is shot out once, and it has a ripple effect. I take a couple of Sharpies out of my back pocket—red and black— and start signing gloves, t-shirts, sneakers, water bottles … whatever they want me to.

We stay about an hour, talking with them, showing them some training tips and techniques, and I remind thcm that I'm going to be there through the week and we're going to learn a lot and have a really good time.

Cade excuses us. "So, take a minute to grab some protein, change and meet me on the private mats in about ten," he says as we go down the stairs to the offices. "Get ready, Sophie. You'll definitely have your work cut out for you this afternoon after I'm done kicking his ass."

"Yeah, yeah, old man," I scoff. "I'll meet you in ten."

"Come on, Sophie," I plead. "Now I'm in pain in more ways than one."

"I said *Noooo!*" she teases. "You'll be okay until tonight, lover boy."

"I have evidence to the contrary." I grab her hand and put it over my ever-hardening dick.

"I cannot risk Cade coming through that door," she reasons and then snatches her hand back and begins to laugh.

"Yeah, you know you caused it." I reach out and snag the hem of her t-shirt. "You can't expect to rub me everywhere all seductively, press your gorgeous full tits against me and blame it on *reaching*—" I make one-handed air quotes, "then tell me you're not going to finish what you started."

"I never said I wouldn't finish it. I have every intention of *finishing* it when we get back to the hotel." She's giggling and attempting to pry my fingers from her shirt.

"Lock the door, woman."

"Cade's smart, Josh. He'll know exactly what's going on."

"And he'd understand!"

Cade walks in at that moment without knocking. "I heard my name. What would I understand?"

Sophie blushes and shoots me a death stare.

"That Sophie wants to stop by the hotel to change and get freshened up before we meet at home for dinner with the kids," I say, covering the situation. She *will* owe me.

"Of course, that's not a problem," Cade tells her.

"Oh, good. Thanks," she says while packing up her gear and avoiding his eyes.

I *will* get her at the hotel.

"We'll be there on time," I assure Cade.

AFTER WE GET BACK TO THE HOTEL, SOPHIE immediately takes me to *my* room, where we have one fucking hell of a quickie.

Christ, that woman is hot!

I'm grateful for the diversion because I know that, in just a little while, I'm going to be reliving the pain and the hurt I've spent a lifetime fighting.

"How do I look?" Sophie's dressed casual classy, wearing blue denim skinny jeans that I'd love to peel off of her, a white blouse, a waist-length cream colored jacket with gold buttons and long gold earrings.

"Yeah, why don't we call and cancel? Tell him something came up?"

"I guess that means I look nice?"

"More like decadent and good enough to eat. Literally."

"AROUND THE TABLE, WE HAVE DILLON, ASHER, Jenna, Michaela, Robby, Sander, Landon and our fraternal twins, Chantal and Terriese." Cade goes around and sets a hand on each of the teenager's heads as he says their names.

Several of these kids weren't at The Core this morning. A few say hi, others nod their heads, while some roll their eyes. I don't blame them. I'm just another adult, and they figure I will come and go.

Cade's wife, Debra, comes out of the kitchen carrying a tray of lasagna, with two more kids behind her, carrying more trays of lasagna and salad.

"And—" Cade adds the last introductions, "this is Dwane and Michelle."

They smile and say hi.

"The lasagna smells great!" I say, inhaling the aroma.

"Homemade by the kids," Debra states proudly. "I can't wait to taste it."

"Everybody needs to remember," Michelle begins, "this one—" she points to lasagna number one, "is full-on Italian style, with ground beef, sausage and four cheeses. And this one—" she points to lasagna number two—"is vegan, made with Tofurky sausage and soy cheese. And the final one is gluten-free; it's made with rice noodles."

"Let's give thanks," Cade says. We look at our plates or at each other. I watch Sophie out of the corner of my eye. "We want to express grateful-ness for our lives, for each other and for our futures. Thank you that we're together and can learn more from each other and become stronger than we can on our own. That we can be and do anything we set our minds to, no matter the obsta-cles in our way. Amen."

There is a chorus of *amens* around the table, and the digging-in begins. Debra leads a discus-sion with the kids about their day, but all I can think about is that I must be out of my freaking mind.

What was I thinking by bringing Sophie here? I could have kept my life with her compartmentalized. She didn't need to know. Now she's sitting here at this ancient table I've sat to eat at too many times to count. Why did I do this? My head is spinning.

I consciously clear my mind and work immediately to fill it with positive thoughts.

I'm thankful Sophie and I are together because she makes me feel like a better person. She makes me feel like I can do anything, and she makes me happy.

Happiness and joy are concepts I've long since put away. I have a vibrant career, a wonderful family who loves and supports me, satisfying volunteer work working with Cade and the kids, and I have great friends who know me and understand me. But a feeling of elation—the power of pure, real happiness—I haven't experienced that for years, or at least I hadn't until Sophie came into my life.

She's an addicting substance that, once you have it, you know you can never live without it again. Sophie is my happy.

So *why* on fucking earth would I want to tell her about a past I can't go back and fix or make right?

"Aren't you hungry?" Sophie asks me in a quiet voice.

I've hardly touched my food. "Yeah, I'm starving," I say more boisterously than I need to. I shovel several forkfuls of the lasagna into my mouth. "Wow! This is great!" I exclaim through the mouthful of food. "You guys did a good job."

I can tell the kids who made it by the smiles on their faces.

Could telling her bring me further, deeper redemption?

Or deeper condemnation?

I swallow half-chewed food as the answer surfaces at the forefront of my mind.

I can't fucking get rid of my past. It's a part of me that makes me who I am, and it was a life experience that's come to define me.

If I want to share myself with her, I have to share *all* of myself, especially this.

The idea of actually going through with it terrifies me. I reach under the table for her hand. I need to feel her strength. She smiles and laces her fingers between mine while keeping up with the pleasant conversation I've been ignoring.

I make a conscious effort to tune in for the remainder of the meal.

After dinner, everyone participates in cleaning up until the kitchen and dining room are spotless, then we meet in the "family room." This is the way things are run here at the home. Next, we'll watch a movie or Cade or Debra will read aloud to the kids from a popular book.

And I think I might actually explode if I have to go in that room and sit like I'm fucking fourteen again. I can't handle it, not with Sophie here, not holding this secret like a deadly poison that I'm afraid will ruin my life *again*. The poison that landed me here in this home in the first place.

Everyone is filing into the family room and choosing their spots. I can tell who the new kids are because they sit off by themselves. They don't trust anyone here yet. They're also so used to rejection that they close themselves off so they might not suffer again. Of course, they're suffering in it anyway, and it breaks my fucking heart. Then there are the callous ones who put on a tough façade to convince everyone that they don't need anyone or this fucking place. And, of course, the couples—it happens a lot in coed group homes—a boy and a girl fall for each other so fast it'll make your head spin. They gravitate toward each other like an asteroid to the moon's surface. They don't care that they'll crash and burn. They're just trying to create a makeshift family and have someone who loves them.

They're all here. It's the same thing month after month, year after year, and only the names and faces change.

Why does the world have to be so goddamn, fucking cruel?

I hear Debra start talking from the family room and realize I'm standing outside of it.

Trying to appear nonchalant, I lean against the wall.

I'm not going in there.

"I know we're in the middle of reading *Lord of the Rings*, but Cade wants to do something a little different tonight," she says. Several of the kids moan in protest, but others don't give a shit.

"Relax," Cade says as he walks in. "It won't take forever, and when I'm done, you guys can play Xbox."

An ecstatic cheer goes up from the kids. I can't help but laugh.

Cade grabs a kitchen chair, sets it in the middle of the room, turns it backward and straddles it.

"I'm going to take you back in time, back when The Beatles' 'Let it Be' was the number one song on the radio and the Chevy Corvette Stingray was the sexiest car on the road. I was thirteen years old."

"That must have been the days of the dinosaurs," one of the kids quips, and Debra taps his shoulder.

Cade continues, "My family lived on a farm here in Minnesota, in Elk River. The summer heat had become so oppressive, my older brother Colt and I spent most of our time in the pond— when we could get away from our mom and dad, that is. They always seemed to have an endless list of chores."

The kids laugh at that. It's always good to hear about when adults were kids doing kid things. But I know this story. It's a killer, and I wonder why he's telling it tonight. It's not one he brings up often. It's usually when he's trying to work on a kid's heart, to let them know that he's been there, that life sucks balls, but if you keep fighting, you can have a happy ending.

I notice I'm still standing in the doorway. Sophie's sitting next to Debra on the loveseat. All of the kids are chilled out on the floor or on one of the two sofas in the room. Uncle Cade has everyone's undivided attention.

"A storm rolled over us, violent, turbulent. It happened so fast we didn't even see it coming. We came up out of the water and were standing on the bank, putting back on our shoes, when we saw a streak of lightning that blinded us both and, almost immediately, heard the roll of thunder over our heads, followed by the most sickening crash. A second later, we saw angry black smoke billowing up into the sky—ugliest thing I've ever seen." Cade stares at the far wall. His eyes are wide as if he can see it happening all over again.

"Colt and I ran like hell toward the house and into a nightmare. That lightning had struck the barn, and it was a fiery hell on earth. Then, everything happened so fast. Our dad was standing outside the barn door, screaming for our mom. She and the horses were trapped inside— you could hear them screaming, too. The combination of my mom's cries and the horses' panicked screams will never leave my memory, not ever, no matter how old I am. A summer breeze can still hit me just the right way, and I'm thirteen years old again, standing there watching everything in my life being ripped away from me. There will never be enough years to remove it."

He grows quiet for a moment. Debra gets up from her perch on the loveseat and goes straight to the kitchen. She brings Cade a glass of water. He takes it from her hand while looking up to her with grateful, emotion-filled eyes. She sits on the floor beside his chair, reminding him she's there.

Everyone's silent. No one moves.

"And then, before we can reach the hilltop, Dad runs in after her—into the fire, into the flame, into the smoke. Colt and I … we're almost there. I can feel the heat, hear the crackling wood … but we're still too far. We weren't fast enough. The roof of the barn collapsed. Neither of our parents came out alive."

He drinks some of the water. He lets the tears roll down his cheeks without bothering to hide them. My uncle and my dad are the two toughest men I know, and they're not afraid to expose themselves. It makes them fearless. It makes me idolize them.

"Before we barely had a chance to process what had happened, the bank sold off our land, our home and all our belongings until there was nothing left. Then, they sent Cade and me to two separate foster homes. After that, everything became a fight—fighting for survival, fighting other kids, fighting adults and the system they forced us into. First few months, we spent a lot of time in detention for constantly running away, trying to find each other. But see, Colt was almost eighteen when our parents died, and they threatened him with adult charges—like kidnapping. When he came of age, he tried to get custody of me, but because we'd been labeled delinquents, the courts didn't think he'd be fit as a guardian. So they kept moving me from boys' homes to detention to in-home foster care and back through the circuit again. My brother tried to keep in contact by calling and writing letters, but with them always moving me and records not being public information, we lost each other completely."

Debra reaches up and holds his hand. The gesture pulls me away from the fear that has kept me in the doorway. All I want now is to be close to Sophie, to feel her strength and her love. I sit next to her on the loveseat. She wipes her eyes, and we hold each other's hands. Her realness brings me peace.

"It would be five long years before we'd be reunited."

Most of the kids make an audible expression of disgust or surprise or both.

"He'd found work in North Dakota as a ranch hand training horses and was already building his own herd. He'd gotten married to his high school sweetheart, who had stuck through it all with him, even when things got more than messy. He was building a life for himself." Cade shook his head.

He continued, "I hated horses—never wanted to see another one as long as I lived. But over the years, I'd watched every Bruce Lee movie ever made—probably a million times over. They were the only thing that gave me some sanity, some control. I began copying what I saw and learning his moves on my own.

"When I turned eighteen, I walked out of that fucked up system and began seriously training in every discipline of the martial arts I could. I also became a firefighter. I hadn't been able to save my parents, but I could sure as hell save others. I spent years replaying that day in my mind, wondering what would have happened if Colt and I hadn't gone swimming, if we hadn't been messing around. Would things have turned out differently? Would we have been able to save our parents? I blamed myself for a long time.

"You're probably wondering why I'm telling you all of this. I'm telling you because every so often, a group of kids comes through that needs to know that what happens isn't always your fault. Even when it is, or you make the wrong choices based on what's happening in your world, it does not define who you are or what you can become. There is redemption for all of us, but you have to dig deep for the courage and move on from where you are."

Uncle Cade stood up. "I expect to see all of you up bright and early to work at Core. My nephew, the light heavyweight UFC champion, will be there to work with each of you." Our bloodshot eyes meet as he looks directly at me and holds my gaze. "I'm proud of you."

At that moment, I know. The story, his words, it had all been for me.

CHAPTER SIXTEEN

JOSH

"Cade's story is so powerful." Sophie stares out into the night at the lights of the twin cities. We've just made love, and she's wrapped in a thick blanket with her hands around a steaming cup of tea.

The clock reads 10:23. I watch her, knowing what has to happen, but I steal myself mentally away for just one more moment—one more moment where I'm not tainted in her eyes.

"It's obvious the two of you are very close and that he's had an incredible impact on your life. The similarities … you must have idolized him as a kid. What an amazing hero to look up to—daring firefighter, MMA trainer. You even look like him, you know. And when did he and his wife decide to start up the group home?"

"Slow down there, scrapper. That's an interrogation." I pinch the bridge of my nose and run my hand down my face. "Aren't you tired of stories for one night?"

She turns toward me, all seriousness. "Why would I tire of hearing about your life or what's made you who you are?" She comes and sits on the bed next to me.

"Truth is …" I take a deep breath and leap, "You may not like me much after you hear my story. It's not a pretty tale."

She studies my face and then says, "Try me."

"The press doesn't know. The records were sealed because I was a juvenile, and my family never talks about it."

"Josh, I'm sorry." Her eyes are full of concern.

"It's awful to remember, but there isn't a day that goes by that I don't. And I've never told another soul, and I'm scared as fuck to tell you."

She nods in understanding. "You have my heart, Josh."

"Yeah, well, you may just want to take it back after you hear what I have to say."

"Trust me." Her soft hand strokes my face.

I pull back from her touch and sit up, facing away from her. I can't watch the expressions on her face.

"I'm sorry." She sounds hurt, like I've struck her.

"You have nothing to be sorry for," I assure

her. "I'm sorry I didn't tell you sooner, like when I knew I was falling in love with you. It would've been honorable to let you know and give you a choice before you fell in love with me, but I was selfish. I didn't want to let you go."

"Josh, you're torturing yourself. I wouldn't change the relationship we've had for anything."

I only hope that's true. And that hope is sketchy at best.

I get up and go over to the desk where my laptop case is. With trembling hands, I take out the scrapbook I brought to share with Sophie and hand it to her.

"My best friend was a boy named Taylor. We became friends in eighth grade after he and his mom moved to Williston from Minot. We bonded over Batman comics. He was a talented artist; his dream was to work at DC or Marvel. That first photo is of me and him at a Comic-Con." I peer across her lap at the picture. "He was funny and full of life—he never hurt anyone." I flip the page, and my eyes follow the lines of our homemade comic strips. "We created comic books together. I'd make up the stories, and he'd draw the pictures. I kept them all."

I watch as her fingers turn the pages I haven't looked at in years. As she turns them, I see the potential that will never be realized. I mourn it as

I breathe in, and with my exhale, I release it into the universe.

"The kids in school picked on him about shit like his ears and his face, telling him he was so ugly no one would ever love him, and that's why his dad left him. Sometimes, the words turned into fists. When my brother Jake and I were around, no one dared—and the two of us got into more than a few fights, shutting some of those assholes up and reminding them not to touch him.

"For a while, it worked, especially when my high school-aged brothers intervened. But by the time Taylor and I reached our sophomore year, the bullies had changed their tactics. They'd whisper to him in the hallways. In the classrooms, when he walked by them, they'd scrawl taunts on paper and stuff it through the grates of his locker—*queer, gay, faggot, you shouldn't even be allowed to live.* How does anyone say that to somebody else?"

I feel it again, the helpless rage. "He tried talking me into ignoring his bullies; he told me that's what he did." I reach out and touch his photo. "But they didn't stop, and without me intervening, it got worse.

"Fucking kid was just trying to figure his shit out. His mom drank too much, his dad abandoned them, he didn't get good grades, and he didn't get girls … he didn't try either. He was unsure of his sexual orientation. So fucking what?

Who the fuck cares? He didn't fucking bother anybody!"

I can't look at the next page, but I turn it for Sophie. It's his suicide note. I know it by heart. It's scarred into me.

"The bullies caught up with him on a Wednesday after school when I had football practice. They beat the hell out of him. When he made it home, he put a bullet through his head with his mom's shotgun. October 17th." I'm whispering, forcing the words out. "I'm the one who found him."

"Oh, Josh." I hear Sophie, but her voice sounds so far away.

"The blood was … everywhere … all over his bed, his wall, the floor." I try to center my breathing to get through this, but the hurt is pressing the air from my lungs. "The note was on his desk."

It simply reads, *"I can't take it anymore. I'm sorry, Mom. I'm sorry, Josh."*

"At that moment, I turned into someone else. *Something else.* The first person I went after was the leader of the group of bullies, Eric. He was tough and fought back, but I beat him badly. I knew when I'd broken his nose—I enjoyed seeing his blood running down his face and into his mouth. He deserved every hit I delivered … every hit except for the last one."

JOSH
PAST

I'M COVERED IN TAYLOR'S BLOOD. IT'S ON MY arms, my face, my clothes … my hands. If only I'd kept up my vigilance against his haters, this wouldn't have happened. The note on his desk flashes through my mind as I pull his body up off the floor and out of the pool of blood he's soaked in to look at him. But it's grisly—his head is destroyed. Only tattered portions remain intact. The rest of it is in pieces on the floor and wall behind him. I scream his name, but he has no ears that can hear me and no face to look into.

But because of his shirt I know it's Tay— Spiderman fighting Doc Ock. He'd drawn the picture himself, and his mom had it made into a shirt. One of a kind.

I did this. I didn't take care of him. I hadn't protected him like I should have.

I want to shout and wake him up. I want to go back and rewind everything just a few hours. That's all I need to fix this. A few fucking hours!

Eric.

It doesn't feel real as I stumble out the door and run, full-out, the three blocks to Eric's house.

His mom and dad will still be at work. I want to hurt him.

I'm going to fucking hurt him … bad.

He and three of his asshole friends are smoking cigarettes on his front porch when I tear up the lawn. I don't say a word. I grab him by his shirt and throw him to the ground.

"What the fuck, North?" Eric growls. "If you came for a fight …" He stands back up and puts up his fists, ready, then takes a good look at me. "What the hell is all over you?"

"What did you do to him!?" I shout.

"Aww, Taylor?" He looks behind him at his friends, who are laughing. "Queer-boy needed to be taught that you don't fuck around with other people's shit."

"What are you talking about?"

"He tripped over a jack in auto shop and thought it'd be a good idea to reach out and touch my car so he didn't fall." Eric laughs. "He should have let himself fall."

They're all laughing. Tay's dead. I'm covered in his blood.

"I don't know why you hang out with that ugly fucking faggot anyway." He reaches into his jeans pocket and pulls out a small white stone. He holds it out for me to see.

It isn't a stone.

"Here. This is Taylor's tooth. I knocked it out

of his face this afternoon. Want to give it back to him for me?" he laughs.

I hit him hard. I watch the tooth fall to the grass and stare at it. I know I have to remember to pick it up after.

When he hits me back, it's like I wake up. I start pounding the shit out of him. He moves, and I follow relentlessly. Eric's friends come off the porch for a better look. They yell shit to taunt and threaten me while they're cheering him on, especially when he gets a couple of punches into my ribs. I think about how they must have cheered him on when he was beating Taylor, how they would've ganged up and all got their hits in.

Eric steps off the curb and into the street when I land an angry fist on his chin. His feet come out from under him, and he falls backward, his head slamming hard against the heavy iron bars of the storm grate. His eyes roll back, and he goes utterly still before his body starts to shake and jerk around, his head slamming repeatedly against the iron.

I just stand there and watch him. I've seen this on a TV show—he's having a seizure. I hadn't known the drain was there, but I don't care. If he dies from it, I don't care. He deserves it for what he did to Taylor.

"Holy fuck!" one of his friends shouts as he fumbles for his phone.

The other guy grabs Eric by the shirt and lugs him up onto the grass. He yells that he doesn't know what to do and then starts shouting for help.

I have no sympathy, no remorse. I feel nothing but a hollow, empty sort of rage. I walk over to the grass and find the tooth.

"I'm coming back for each of you for what you did to Taylor," I warn and walk away.

JOSH
PRESENT

"No one could talk to me after that." I walk to the window. "I pounded the shit out of each of those boys. And I didn't stop there. I kept fighting. My parents grounded me and made me see a psychologist, but my rage burned so hot I couldn't stop it. Even when my parents told me Eric had been diagnosed with epilepsy because of the injury to his head and had to go on seizure medications, it didn't stop me. In fact, I got worse. I got expelled and began hanging out with a rough crowd who'd go around starting fights with kids from other schools, at parties, anywhere. That led me into get into trouble with the law.

"My dad sat me down and told me all the shit

I was doing wasn't going to bring Taylor back and that it was time for me to get away for a while because by staying there, where it had all happened … I wasn't going to get better. That's when my Uncle Cade came and got me."

Sophie is crying softly. She lifts her hand to stop me from continuing as she makes her way to the bathroom. I hear her blow her nose and run the water. When she comes back out, she's patting her face with the towel. She goes to the mini fridge, opens a bottle of water and hands it to me.

She doesn't say anything, and I don't want her to. I don't want her judgment or her pity. Now that I'm in it, I just need to finish it.

"I lived at the group home with my uncle for almost two years. I made a lot more mistakes, got into more fights, had some arrests—but no matter what I did or how far I went, I couldn't drown out Tay's voice, or his face, or his drawings, or what his horrific death looked like, or the despair he must have felt that made him pull that trigger."

I'm crying now. *Fuck!*

"I feel responsible for his death, Sophie. And on top of it, I hurt Eric so bad he'll have epilepsy for the rest of his life. *I did that.*" I poke my finger into my chest. "And even though I didn't physically pull the trigger on Tay and I didn't purposely bash Eric's head into a storm grate, my actions and inaction created a horrible mess.

"My Uncle Cade taught me to control myself, focus the pain and fear and use it to strengthen myself. He taught me how to release the rage and to give it up, accept my part in what I'd done and let go of what wasn't in my control or power to change. He did this through what worked for him —martial arts."

Exhausted, I fall onto the sofa. "I haven't fought off the mats since." Then I add, "After I had my shit together, Uncle Cade showed me the ropes of firefighting and how I could pour that raw energy into saving people's lives."

I can't look at her. I don't want to see what she's thinking—can't stand the thought that she might look at me differently now, without the love in her eyes. Instead, I simply say, "There, that's my story, Sophie. It's the ugly truth, and you're going to do what you want with it. If you walk out of here and out of my life, I'd understand that."

"Remember. Redemption. 10/17," she says. "The tats on your lower abdomen. *Remember* for Taylor and *Redemption* for you."

My nose and eyes sting, and I can't say a word, not a fucking word.

Sophie comes and sits beside me, and her fingers lace with mine. I still can't bring myself to meet her eyes.

"I'm sorry." It comes out like a whimper.

"Josh, you have nothing to be sorry for."

277

"I have a very unstable peace agreement with forgiveness, and it's even harder to believe anyone else would forgive me."

"You don't need to be forgiven anymore, Josh —not by me, not by them, not anyone. You're the best man I've ever known, and you've reached redemption many times over because of the way you live your life." She's still beside me and that unstable peace feels more secure, more solid. "I know now why Cade told his own story and, more importantly, why he told you he was proud of you. I know I am. In fact, somehow, I love you more."

I finally look up into her eyes and see the sincerity there. Those eyes tell me everything I need to know.

I cry, no holds barred. It's been a long time since I opened the dam, and the rush of emotions doesn't stop for a while. She holds me, and I let her.

I feel like it's a great moment of weakness.

She tells me she's never seen me stronger.

CHAPTER SEVENTEEN

SOPHIE

M y plight weighs heavily on my mind. I'm holding a bad hand of cards in a game where the stakes are way too high.

I think of scenarios that have no point or value since they aren't even based in reality. What if I'd never met Jim? What if, instead, I'd ended up in Williston earlier in my life? Josh and I could have fallen in love, and then *he* would have been Charlie's father. It's stupid, I know, but I can't help it. The reality crashes in soon enough—Charlie wouldn't be Charlie without Jim. Because of that, I'm grateful. He hadn't meant to give me a gift, but nonetheless, she is the single greatest gift of my existence. I wouldn't change a thing.

What I *really* wish is that, when I first found out I was pregnant, I could have seen Jim for what he was. I wish I wouldn't have been self-destructive and that I wouldn't have told anyone about the pregnancy and had instead run far, far away. Maybe he wouldn't have chased me then. Maybe he would have messed with some other woman— the wrong woman—and some hulking dad or brother would have killed him.

That's not what happened, though. So, then I start making up other death scenarios—like wishing he'd wrapped that new, twenty thousand dollar sports car he was showing off in town around a tree. The one he bought after telling me he wouldn't pay child support, and if the welfare department didn't believe me, he'd give me the bruises to prove it.

These scenarios that play out in my head are a real waste of time and thought. They pose no solutions.

I think maybe they're just a distraction, so I don't think about my true needs. My desires. To think about those things hurts the most. That pain cuts to the quick of my soul. But my soul is masochistic; it obviously wants the agony because as Josh sleeps next to me in the new morning light, I dream that he's really mine.

I can easily picture a log home on the North Dakota prairie. We'd have a few shade trees, flowering fruit trees, maybe a winding stream and a few horses. We'd have a swing set for Charlie in the backyard, a sandbox and a treehouse. She could go to school, meet other kids and have friends. Josh and I would be married, and Charlie would call him Daddy—*oh, how she'd love that.* She would have grandparents, aunts, uncles and cousins who loved her, something I could never give her.

But that's not the reality, is it?

"My reality sucks." I barely breathe, and I think about the fear tattoos on Josh's ribs.

Being with Josh would pull Charlie and me out of anonymity. I've already taken a risk by working for a public figure and am thankful he doesn't have a flurry of paparazzi always hunting him.

I conjure a weak smile. *They're probably afraid of being on the receiving end of Josh's MMA career.*

What I can do now, because I only have today, is prove to Josh that my love is real, that my acceptance of him in the light of his painful confession is one hundred percent and nothing less.

So that's what I live for—today.

"THAT'S THE NEW KID I WAS TELLING YOU ABOUT. He's been here an hour and won't leave the heavy bag except to get water," Cade explains as we watch the young, angry boy pound his fists like hammers against the bag, his face set with fury. His pain is palpable, and it makes me want to go to him, put my arms around him and take away his hurt.

"Maybe he just needs a friend who doesn't pry into his shit for a while." Josh looks frustrated. He strides off toward the boy and begins jabbing at the bag next to him. It doesn't take long for the kid to recognize Josh, and the two strike up a conversation.

He's the greatest guy I've ever met. I'm better for knowing him.

"That boy's got it bad, Sophie," Cade says to me, his eyes never leaving the scene before us. "I've known him his whole life, so I can tell."

Why does this make me blush?

"Well, good. I see you have it just as bad," Cade observes, then turns and walks away. "Feel free to work out if you want."

I START IN THE WEIGHT ROOM. PICKING UP A FIVE-pound dumbbell, I begin some reps. It's beautiful here, not the aesthetics of the place, but what's happening within it. There are at least twenty kids in here, ranging in age from thirteen to eighteen. They're set up in small groups, with four extremely athletic, muscle-bound men working with them, teaching them how to lift, motivating them to move past their limitations, and praising them for a job well done and good effort. The kids smile; you can see the new pride radiating from them, and I wonder how often they've experienced that in their lives.

One of the men notices I'm watching. He catches my eyes and throws me a flirtatious smile. He's strikingly handsome with light color eyes and dark hair in a short crop. His arms and legs are covered in colorful tattoos. I'm not ungrateful for his attention, so I smile back in a way that says *just friendly* as I go back to my workout.

Once I'm finished with a circuit, I go upstairs to the bags. This time, I remember my iPod. I blast "Bring It" by Trapt through my earbuds and work on the hits, punches and kicks Josh has taught me. It's very empowering to work out with a UFC title holder.

After a good hour, I shower and head to the private mat room to watch Josh train. I always give him a complete rub down, but when I know which muscles he's put the most stress on, I can give them some extra attention.

When I get there, he's already sparring seriously with a partner who isn't Cade. I get closer and see it's the same man I saw in the weight room. These two aren't playing around; they're going at it as if a belt were at stake. I'm definitely taken aback. Usually, Josh's partners are there to challenge and strengthen him, and these two look like they're fighting for real. Concerned, I look to Cade, who's standing off to the side, watching them with a huge smile on his face.

At that moment, Josh pops the guy in the eye, breaking the skin that had become swollen there. Blood trickles down his face. The guy smiles at him, then notices me watching and gets in a hard strike to Josh's nose.

Josh dances back and checks his nose. "You're fucking lucky it's not a bleeder."

"Aw, you mean like my eye, douchebag? I might have a hot date tonight." At that, he turns and winks at me.

When Josh follows his gaze to me, he turns back to him and smiles. "Not with her, you don't, Romeo." Josh gets his arm around the guy's neck and takes him down to the mat in a flash.

"Too bad, bro. I saw her first." The guy slips out of Josh's hold and gets the advantage.

You'd think I'd be ruffled over the fact that they're "claiming" me like I'm the title prize. But they're much too funny to make me feel threatened. Actually, it reminds me of the way Josh plays with his brothers.

"Boy—*and I do mean boy*—there is nothing you could do to interest a class-act woman like that," Josh harangues.

"You mean like how I'm about to beat your ass right in front of her?" the guy declares.

"You're pretty good for a *featherweight,* but I don't think you should get your hopes up too high," Josh quips back.

"Dude, you're such a prick," he laughs. They both roll away from each other, laughing. I notice Cade is laughing, too.

"Liam," Josh begins, holding a hand toward me, "meet my girlfriend, Sophie Garner. Sophie, this is Liam Knight."

"Man, you really did see her first! Asshole." Liam reaches over and shoves Josh playfully before looking over at me. "Oh, please excuse my language, Sophie … and my flirting earlier."

"You flirted with her? You have a death wish!" Josh pushes him back, but it's not quite as playful.

Liam laughs, and they both walk over to me.

He reaches out his hand to shake mine. "It's very nice to meet you, Sophie." He doesn't let go of my hand. "How did you meet this loser?"

"I'm part of his team. I'm Josh's massage therapist."

A triumphant grin spreads over Josh's face.

Liam brings my hand to his mouth and kisses it before letting it go almost reluctantly. Then, he turns to Josh. "You rcally are an asshole."

"I WAS WONDERING WHAT THE DEAL WAS WHEN I walked in and saw the two of you seriously going at it," I tell Josh later.

He laughs. "You should have seen when we were kids and *really* going at it."

I'm excited to meet the others Josh lived with in the home. These guys are close enough to call themselves brothers.

"This is it," Josh announces as we pull up in front of the red brick warehouse.

"The House of Ink and Steel," I read the red neon letters written in graffiti-like tattoo script. "Tattoo and Piercing Shop."

"This is Liam's dream realized. He owns it," Josh tells me. "But we've all worked here at one time or another—some of us still work here. Liam is an incredible artist. The best I've ever seen. Talon is amazing with design work. And Ryder does pretty decent script. The rest of us learned how to pierce or run the books. It's the best shop in the twin cities, even voted best by *Ink Magazine* four years running."

"Very cool," I say, looking at the impressive artwork painted onto the inside windows of the shop. Huge, long, colorful dragons flank the doorway.

Josh opens the door. "Come meet the guys."

We step through the foyer. The front room is painted sleek black; comfortable leather sofas are situated into a semi-circle for easy conversation; a red and black Persian-style carpet warms the black and red checkered linoleum floor between them. The walls leading through to the shop are deep red, while the trim is the same sleek black as the front room; artwork adorns the walls in black frames; a long glass case forms an L shape in front of one wall, displaying an array of body jewelry, gauges, enhancements and modifications.

There's a beautiful woman working behind the counter. Delicate tattoos trail down her arms, and she has several facial piercings and wears a yellow, vintage dress that compliments her jet black hair.

She smiles, and her silver chin post sparkles. "Josh!" She comes around the front and hugs him.

The heat of jealousy begins in my gut, and I try to keep it away from my face. I smile, too, but it's definitely forced. Plus, I'm not tattooed—at all —and for some reason, I feel naked or incomplete without them now that I'm standing in front of her.

"Adrienne, this is my girlfriend, Sophie," Josh says. "Sophie, this is Adrienne. She's been working at Ink and Steel since it opened."

"I basically live here," she confides in Sophie.

"Adrienne and her girlfriend Gwen live in the apartment above the shop," Josh informs me.

Girlfriend, Gwen. *Perfect.*

"It's so awesome to meet you, and I love your body art," I compliment her.

"Aww, thanks." She hugs me and whispers in my ear. "Girl, it must be love because he has *never* called a woman his girlfriend. *Ever.*"

When she straightens back up, she masks her expression as if she'd said nothing at all.

"Are the guys in the back?" Josh asks, thumbing in the direction of the tattoo alcoves.

"Yessa. Game's already started. Oh, and Sophie, if you play, know that Reese and Ryder cheat." She winks and starts back behind the counter. "Good seeing you, Josh. Hope to see more of you, Sophie," she sing-songs.

"I don't know who I need to worry about more around you: Adrienne or the guys." Josh takes my hand, and we walk through the long hallway toward the back of the shop.

There are eight tattoo and piercing alcoves—four on each side of the hallway. The black and red design changes back here, and each alcove is a different color, or several colors, or purely art composed on the walls. An artist is in each station, working with a client, and the hum of the needles' motors is unnerving.

"I've always hated needles." I shudder.

"Thus the virgin skin," Josh growls like he wants to eat me.

"Would you like me and my skin better with a tattoo?" I inquire.

"I will love your skin any way you want it."

We come to the end of the hallway, and Josh knocks three times on the dark, ornate, wooden door.

"Are you going to have to tell a knock-knock joke?" I ask playfully.

He laughs. "That's only when the mob boss is named Charlie."

A peephole slides open and closes again just as fast. "It's Josh," a voice calls out.

There's a bunch of rowdy laughter as the door opens, and five impressively gorgeous men sitting at a table turn to see who came in.

"About fucking time, North," says one of the men. His blond hair falls to the top of his shoulders. A tattoo of a beautiful woman in a flowing gown takes up his left arm. He's wearing a white tank top, and I can see a bit of script across his collarbone.

"And you brought Sophie." Liam is the one who has opened the door and smiles at me charmingly as he leads us over to the card table. "So watch your mouths, asshats," he says and then adds, "And now all you losers can lay a twenty in my palm for doubting me about her existence. And, Sophie, welcome to the House."

"So, you are for real." One of the guys stands up, shoves a twenty in Liam's hand and walks over to greet us—I mean *me*. He's imposing and remarkable. "I'm Ryder." Both his hands close around mine. "Ryder Axton."

Ryder is tall, long and lean; every muscle I can see is cut and defined. His dark brown hair is cut short, and his green eyes are set like sparkling emeralds. He's wearing a pair of black leather biker pants and boots along with a plain black tank and leather vest. He has two small black gauges in each earlobe, and his arms are covered in lots of black tats—a Celtic armband around his forearm, a set of wings holding a heart in the middle of his chest, and I catch a black scorpion on his bicep.

"You're going to frighten her off, Axman," the blond says, leaning back in his chair. "Sophie, I'm Reese—"

"Witherspoon," one of the guys quips.

"As in *Reese's*—the peanut butter cup candy." The stunning and flirty blond finishes with a wink. Reese has a silver barbell through his eyebrow. His blue eyes are intense. "Josh was supposed to be my card partner tonight, but I can see he's been engaged much better elsewhere."

"Oh, for Christ's sake." Josh pushes Ryder's hands away from mine.

Ryder laughs and points his index finger in Josh's face. "That's right, brother, you definitely better watch out." He bows his head toward me "It's *very* nice to meet you, Sophie." As he turns back toward the table I see the words *Iron Order MC* on the back of his vest, and the skull in the middle looks up at me with evil mischief in its eyes.

Josh leans into me. "Told you I had to watch out for them."

I instantly remember what he said when I met Adrienne.

"I'm Talon." The finely sculpted man stands up and leans in to shake my hand. He has strong, prominent facial features and stands a little taller than me. His pitch-black hair is cut into a striking, wide Mohawk, gelled up about three inches high and colored red at the tips. The sides of his head are buzzed short—but not shaved—with two half-inch red stripes on each side. His ears are pierced with two black plugs, a silver cuff on the high curve of his right ear and a silver barbell through his left. He wears a black Nine Inch Nails t-shirt. But what I find really intriguing are the tattoos on his arms—several intricate, black-inked mandalas, among other spiritual symbols.

"I'm an artist here at the House, and I'm also

a personal trainer at The Core," Talon continues charmingly. "And don't worry about us at all. You're family now; any one of us would give our lives for you." He nods, and I'm taken with his heartfelt and serious declaration.

"He's right about that," says the next guy moving into my proximity. "My name is Chase— Chase Diaz Wolf." I put my hand in his steady, strong grip. His skin is richly tanned; he has long, dark hair to the middle of his back, and dark, almost black eyes. Chase is tall, thick and broad-shouldered; his muscles bulge beneath his black thermal shirt.

"Spanish *and* Native American?" I ask with a smile.

"Spanish on my mother's side and Ojibwe on my father's." He nods and gives me a friendly smile in return.

"My mother was Spanish, Diego." The moment I say it, I feel the familiar pit in my stomach. It's too bad that even trying to be proud of my heritage brings up her memory and makes me feel sick.

"Your father was English then? Garner?" Josh adds.

"Yes." I press forward to cover my expression. "And you are?" I ask the guy waiting on our left.

I pin him at five foot ten. He's lanky and has deep, red-brown hair, shorn short in the back and unruly on the top; his bangs fall over his forehead. He has stormy gray-green eyes and pale skin with a few errant freckles; a small silver loop is set through his right eyebrow, and his right ear has a silver gauge and a silver barbell down through the middle. He has a light beard scruff and a mustache. He wears a white shirt with a black leather jacket.

He offers his hand, and I see tattooing all the way up onto his fingers.

"Connor Callahan," he tells me. "Brains of the operation. Great to meet you, Sophie. We don't usually get beautiful women in the back of the House."

My eyebrows lift in question.

"Meaning this is where we come together to unwind and just be ourselves," Josh explains. "So we don't bring dates back here."

It is completely a man cave—card table, pool table, dartboard, flat screen, stereo and a stocked bar.

"That makes you tremendously special," Connor states.

"Yeah, you get to see us with our pants down," laughs Reese. "Proverbially speaking, of course."

Connor rolls his eyes and heads toward the door. "Let me get the two of you a beer."

Josh smiles down at me. "Well, Sophie, you've

just met my *second* family, the brothers of Ink and Steel."

"Do you give a t-shirt to the survivors?" I ask in a quiet voice.

All of them laugh.

WE PLAY BULLSHIT.

I'm losing at the card game.

But I'm the best when it comes to *bullshitting* Josh about my reality.

I feel it here. There's no escape from it.

I hate myself.

I hate Jim for having turned me into this.

The ugly truth is that he still owns me.

I didn't think about it before. Life has been such a challenge just to survive, to keep me and Charlie safe. Now with Josh in my life, I realize with a painful force that I am *not* free.

And keeping it a secret from Josh is eating me up.

Josh has been one hundred percent open with me through our entire relationship. He's gorgeous, honorable, honest and kind. He works with high-risk kids in need; he loves his family and is a loyal and faithful friend.

And I know without a doubt that he loves Charlie and me.

And what's more, I know that he's *good* for us.

"The judge isn't going to be able to tell who the criminal is, Connor, you or the defendant," Reese wisecracks.

Josh tells me, "Connor studied law at the University of Minnesota. He works for a fancy firm now."

"Yeah, my whole plan is coming together; I really love fucking with their minds after having such a successful career as a juvenile delinquent." Connor smiles. "Oh, pardon me, Sophie."

"You're fine, really," I assure him. "Reese? What's your line of work?"

"Work, ha!" Liam laughs. "He got a fancy scholarship to U of M for football."

"I do love to play on and off the field." Reese is funny and charismatic, and I can't help but smile at his antics. "I'm pretty good at ball and keep the university's stats high, so they keep me around."

"Rider is a bounty hunter and runs with the Iron Order Motorcycle Club, so God only knows what other businesses he's into," Josh says, helping me get to know each of them more. "Chase is still undecided and divides his time between working here and on White Earth Reservation, where he goes to the tribal collcge. Liam owns the House of Ink and Steel and is pursuing a name for himself in the UFC middleweight division," Josh explains.

"He's also the one who gave most of us our first tats and piercings."

"Have you told her about that year at the home?" Talon asks without looking up from the card table.

"A bit," Josh relays. "But not the story behind the tats."

As if on some invisible cue, all the guys stand up and begin stripping their shirts off.

Oh. My. "Are you boys planning on doing a calendar?"

They laugh good-naturedly.

Each of the guys is positioned with his left arm bent over his head to show off the left side of his ribcage. They each have the same exact tattoo, written in black script on the highest rib closest to the heart—*I am my brother's keeper.*

"What was the catalyst … that defining moment when you guys decided to do them?" I ask curiously. All of them look toward Liam.

Liam takes a pull of his beer. "Her name was Quinn."

They all readjust their shirts and take their seats.

"Quinn was Liam's girl," Josh tells me quietly.

"She was beautiful inside and out," Liam began. "She and I met and lived on the streets together. I kept her safe." A storm rolls over his expression, casting a shadow over his face and darkening his eyes. "We both ended up at North House, where she and all seven of us boys were living under Cade's roof, and all we did was fight."

"There were a lot of broken, bloody noses, cracked ribs and busted up faces." Reese grins.

"Fucking Cade had his hands full with us," Ryder adds.

"Quinn was the eternal peacekeeper." Liam looks like he's caught in a memory.

Josh says, "She was always scolding us and breaking up the skirmishes, telling us to get our acts together."

"She was like a sister to us," Talon puts in. "Except for when it came to Liam. We all knew they were together."

"But the leader of the Westhill Cartel had turned his attention to her," Josh explains.

"I'm sorry," I manage to say. "I never thought—"

"Please don't apologize. Quinn was very special to me, so it's not an easy discussion," Liam answers. "She was supposed to visit her mother, but it went bad fast. She walked to the nearest payphone and called Cade to come get her. But the cartel found her first."

The guys look as if they're there, in that time and place, again, and I'm scared of the outcome of the story. Liam is constantly referring to Quinn in the past tense.

Liam takes a sharp breath. "I need a real drink."

He drops his almost empty beer bottle hard onto the table, strides to the bar and grabs the Jack Daniels.

Josh takes over where Liam stopped, "The cops kept coming in and out that night, talking about what Vince, the leader here, along with his people had done, and the hospital findings. We all listened from upstairs. They hadn't meant to leave her alive." He shakes his head in disgust.

Liam tips his head back, downs a shot and says in a rough tone, "We dealt with them."

"And we've been fighting for each other ever since," Josh says resolutely.

Liam comes back and sits down. I can smell the whiskey that permeates the little bit of ice he put in the glass. "We vowed to be each other's keepers. I already had a homemade tattoo machine I'd been using on myself, so when we got back to the home, I gave each of us the tattoo."

"And Quinn?" I asked, holding my breath.

"She recovered." That's all Liam says.

"I'm glad." I wipe the tears as they streak down my face.

Josh passes me a napkin. "Cade walked by the room while Liam inked us. We were freaking busted up, but we stood together. We all thought Cade was going to come down on us hard. Instead, he stood in the doorway, watching us proudly. He said, 'You are now brothers of ink and steel.'"

"You're quiet," Josh observes.

He's parking in the private underground garage for hotel guests.

"Sophie, are you alright?" His brow furrows. "Please don't shut me out. You can tell me anything."

I stare at my knees, willing the right answer to show itself.

"Maybe I shouldn't have taken you," he contemplates.

Quickly, I assure him, "Don't second guess yourself or anything you've done, Josh. You really are the best man I've ever known, and now I …" I release a pained breath. "You know, I thought you'd just have your fun with me and move on. We could have been the greatest one-night stand ever, and then we could have gone back to the way it was, employer and employee, each in our own corners."

"You're not a one-night stand, Sophie. You're a forever."

"You don't know me, Josh. I have secrets. Secrets I haven't told anyone. If I told you, you could hurt Charlie and me so badly." I rub my forehead with my hand. "And, Josh, I'm scared. Honestly, I've been scared my entire life. But here with you, in your arms, it's the safest I've ever felt."

"I would never hurt you or Charlie. You're the only woman I want." Josh reaches over and takes my hands in his. "I love you, Sophie."

His eyes and voice are so serious, so sincere. "I love Charlie, too. I could adopt her."

His confessions and proposals are killing me inside.

"I want you both permanently in my life."

I shake my head; tears fill my eyes and spill over my cheeks.

"We can do anything we want," he reassures me.

"I can't," I whisper.

"Why?" Josh looks at me like he's ready to fix whatever the problem might be.

He can't fix this.

"I'm married."

CHAPTER EIGHTEEN

SOPHIE

FOUR YEARS EARLIER

"What did you call me?" Jim demands angrily.

The sudden shift in his mood and his strange question leave me confused.

"Bitch, I want an answer!" he growls.

"I don't understand what you're asking or why you're mad; we just—"

"You called me *Richard*!" he seethes. "I heard it come out of your fucking mouth. You've been fucking him behind my back?"

Richard? Richard is Jim's friend from the police academy. He's been sleeping on our couch over the Christmas holiday.

I'm sitting on the edge of our bed in our tiny one-bedroom apartment. Jim is up on his feet, pacing furiously. It's late Christmas night. We just watched a holiday movie together and made love. Everything was fine, except after he finished, he got really quiet. Dangerously, moody, quiet. I knew something bad was coming, but I wasn't expecting this. His question makes no sense.

I shake my head. My brain is trying to process the accusation. I hadn't said anything. There hadn't been any throes of passion; it was his quickie special.

My throat becomes bone dry as I swallow fearfully. "Why would I do that? I'm almost seven months pregnant. I look like a hippo. Besides, I don't care about him. I love you."

"You don't love me. You're a fucking slut. I knew you were a fucking slut, and still, I took your whore-ass in. I bet you that bastard baby isn't even mine." Jim contemplates me for a moment before he says in a low and sinister tone, "Whose baby is it?"

"Yours!" I can't believe he's even asking. I don't go anywhere or do anything except for work —he makes sure of that and even calls me throughout the day to check and make sure I'm there. How would she be anyone else's? "You're scaring me, Jim."

"WHAT EX-BOYFRIEND DID YOU WHORE AROUND WITH TO MAKE THAT BABY?"

"I never did!" I cry, holding my tummy. "She's yours! I promise!"

He stares at me with dark, ominous eyes. "I have a good mind to fucking shoot your lying ass," he says, and then he stalks out of the room.

I can't breathe. I can't move. I feel completely disoriented. I'm naked and exposed, and it's like I've turned into glass or stone. But the baby hasn't. She's circling and kicking wildly as the adrenaline pulses through my system. Silent tears cascade over my cheekbones and drip onto the sheet I've wrapped myself with.

Would he really kill me? A frightening chill rips through me. Dear God, I think he might.

How could he think I said Richard's name? *Did I say it? Why would I say it?* I didn't say it! I feel crazy as if I'm out of my body in some way.

My breathing is fast and shallow. My heart is pounding way too fast. I think I'm going to have a heart attack or pass out.

I can't do that. If I do that, I can't protect her.

I hear Jim in the other room. He's rambling to himself and cursing me. The familiar sound of bullets being loaded into one of his many guns sends a lightning bolt of terror shooting through my spine.

A moment later, I taste the salt of my own blood. Lifting my hand, I realize blood is pouring from my nose.

It's got to be from the adrenaline. Could this cause me to go into early labor?

I lift my heavy, pregnant body from the bed and quickly throw on some clothes.

"You're never going to fuck around on me again, bitch. You hear me?!" His voice is coming closer. He'll open the door in a second. "I'm going to make sure of it."

When the door busts open and hits the far wall, I jump fearfully and find myself staring into his double-barrel shotgun.

It's loaded! I'm dead. My baby's dead!

I can't think past the panic. How many times has he hit me, bit me and bruised me? Threatened me? He's threatened to kill me so many times I've lost track of the number. Now he's really going to do it.

Jim walks closer and shoves the gun in my face. "Blow you the fuck away, and you won't even be recognizable. Wouldn't be able to fuck nobody then, would you?"

I've never had a gun pointed at my head before.

A few minutes ago, I was naked in bed with him, and now I'm going to die by his hand. The baby is going to die.

"Jim, what the fuck are you doing?" Richard's voice says from behind him.

"Get the fuck out of here, asshole, before I

shoot you, too."

"Man, just give me the gun. Nobody needs to get hurt here."

"FUCK YOU, ASSHOLE! YOU FUCKED MY WIFE!"

"I've never even touched her!" Richard says. "What the fuck? Are you drunk?"

"Get out," Jim orders him in a frightening, low tone.

Richard backs up and disappears from view.

How do I protect her from this? How do I protect myself?

I'm on my own.

I've been on my own before. I've been scared and desperate before.

Something comes over me. My actions aren't thought out; they just happen.

I lift my hand in a gesture for him to stop. I say, "If you shoot me, you'll go straight to hell, and I'll go straight to heaven. And I'll never have to see you again."

He looks at me as if I've stunned him. A moment later, he lowers the gun. I have no idea what's going on in his head, but I realize this could be my only chance, and I begin backing up toward the door, my eyes never leaving his.

My boots are on a rug by the door. I scoop them into my arms.

"You don't get a coat, bitch," Jim says.

I'm wearing pajama shorts and a long t-shirt. My coat is right there by the boots, but I don't try to grab it. I'd rather take my chances with the New England winter night.

Once I'm out the door, I slip my bare feet into the boots and run.

SOPHIE
PRESENT

Josh says nothing for the rest of the ride back to the hotel. Nothing.

His face is stone, and he won't look at me. He's so angry that his hands stay balled into fists as we make our way up the elevator. A familiar pulse beats through my veins, making my head pound.

"I'm going to go to my room," I say, trying to sound resolute and strong.

"No, you're not. We need to talk."

Josh is not Jim. Josh is not Jim.

We enter his hotel room, and he closes the door behind him.

"What do you mean, *married?*" he says the word like a curse.

I swallow hard and realize this could easily be

mine and Charlie's undoing. My heart is beating so fast I feel faint. It takes everything I have to talk.

"I never meant to lie to you." My voice is quiet.

"No, but you did it anyway." Josh's voice rises. He swears and stalks into the bathroom. The door slams and makes me jump, sending adrenaline coursing through my body in waves. I hear him let loose a string of profanity.

I begin to tremble as a sense of panic threatens to overwhelm me. *What have I done?* I realize I'm standing next to the door. My hand is already poised to open it.

Josh comes back out and stands across from me, his face unreadable. "I want to hear what you have to tell me."

A vein stands out in his neck, and his tensed muscles strain against his shirt, reminding me of how lethal this man can be. My instinct is to run out the door, but this is Josh. Can he handle his anger?

"Josh, you're frightening me," I manage to get out between anxious breaths. I hear the pleading tone my voice takes on. This feels like a deadly test. "If you hit me, you could kill me." *My baby girl. What will happen to my baby girl?* "Just let me get back to Charlie, and I promise you'll never have to see me again."

"Hit you?" he says incredulously. "I would never, *never* hit you. I'd take my own fucking life before I *ever* laid a hand on you!"

I know that in my heart, it's true. *Josh is not Jim,* I remind myself.

But my body doesn't relax. I'm still shaking. "Yeah? You seem pretty mad."

"I'm fucking destroyed, Sophie!" He starts to pace, and the movement makes me flinch, but there's nothing threatening about his stance now. He just looks lost. *"You're fucking married!"*

"It's not how you think."

"I should have known something was wrong," Josh says. "You *never* opened up to me. You *never* told me *anything* about your past or Charlie's father."

"I couldn't … it's … just … when I got involved with you, I knew your reputation. I was sure you'd have your fun and let me go."

Josh stops pacing. He's turned away from me with his arms folded against his chest. His back looks as rigid and straight as iron. "Fine. If that's what you want, I'll give it to you."

I feel my heart shredding inside my chest. If I could find a way to tell him … a way to explain … even if it's only in half-truths to protect Charlie. But I don't know how.

"Please … leave." His tone is hard and solid.

I'm too scared to tell him the truth. I leave quietly.

I wish I had said no to his job offer, no to the sex, no to the intimacy. But I didn't. Foolishly, I embraced every part of it.

CHARLIE STIRS NEXT TO ME AS I WATCH THE sunlight peek through the window. I haven't slept all night. Seeing Josh at work today is going to be hell. Maybe this is my exit cue.

I flip my laptop open and wait for Expedia to load. Two plane tickets. Charlie and I can be out of here in no time.

No time for Josh to look at me with hate and disappointment in his eyes. No time for me to break down and tell him the truth. No time for Charlie to figure out what's really happening. We'll get back to the apartment in Williston, I'll pack up the car, and we'll be gone.

I leave the webpage open, and undecided, I take a hot shower. The water runs over my head and soothes my frazzled mind.

If I leave now, I will leave Josh without a massage therapist.

I'll go to work and give Silva my notice. If Josh doesn't want me there, which he won't, Silva can tally up the wages I've earned since my last paycheck and cut me a check.

And just like that, Charlie and I will disappear. Again.

I come into The Core with my head down.

"Sophie!" Liam shouts from across the room. I look over long enough to give a short wave. He's standing by the juice bar. Josh is sitting next to him, but his gaze stays on the counter.

Silva. Just find Silva.

I knock on the door to Silva's office.

"Come in."

"Good Morning, Mr. Silva," I greet him formally.

"Hey, Sophie. What's going on?" He smiles up from his papers.

"I'm giving my notice. I can leave immediately or stay on for the next two weeks until you find someone to replace me." I'm monotone.

His smile melts into an angry disbelief. "What the hell did Josh do?"

"He didn't do anything, I assure you. It's … family business I have to attend to." The words kill me.

"I don't believe it. I'm going to talk to him."

Silva pushes away from his desk and starts to stand.

"Please," I say, stopping him. "Not … not now." I rub my hands against my face. "You don't owe me anything, but I need to ask a favor just the same. Please, just let it go." I look at him with pleading eyes. "Soon, it'll be like I was never even here."

He leans against the desk, watching me. "I can only imagine what happened, and I'm sorry for it." He nods. "But I'll do what you ask."

"Thank you." I turn and flee from the office before I cry.

I'M A MESS. I'VE STAYED HIDDEN IN MY MASSAGE room the entire morning. I'm insane—I've gone over every possible scenario for what will happen when Josh comes through that door. I can't think anymore! My head is throbbing. I'd take Tylenol, but I feel like I deserve the extra agony of a stress headache.

I check the clock. It's going to be lunch soon.

He's not coming, I decide, and I leap up from the chair to grab my coat.

At that moment, a knock on the door startles me. "Yeah."

Josh opens the door and steps in. I take a deep breath, readying myself for whatever comes next.

"Liam says I need to let you explain."

"Do you do everything Liam tells you to?"

"Only when I know he's right," Josh says.

I pretend to busy myself. He wants me to explain, but I can't do that. I've spent the past three years running, and I can't stop now. I don't know how. "I really have nothing to say. If you're ready for your massage, we can—"

"My car's out front. I think you'll like the countryside, and everything is better during a long drive," he coaxes me.

"Long drives are for talking, and I already told you I have nothing to say," I repeat coldly, hoping to mask the pain in my voice.

"Good," he shoots back at me. "Then we can find a secluded place to pull off and make love."

I'm shocked into silence for a moment. "We're fighting!"

He's furious with me. The idea of making love somewhere in the winter countryside …

I bust up laughing. Only Josh.

He cracks a huge smile, and just like that, all my defenses crumble.

THE SUV HE RENTED IS SO HOT IT FEELS LIKE A sauna. We've driven quietly for almost an hour.

"It's really getting hot in here." I peel off my coat.

"That's the whole idea, scrapper," he says. "To make you naked."

"Josh …" I start.

He takes a right onto a dirt road. "You don't owe me anything, Sophie. I have no expectations. I just want to have as much time with you as I can get, whatever that means."

I don't know what to say.

He pulls into an old cornfield. The leftover stalks are painted with snow. When he feels confident we're secluded enough, he parks and turns off the engine but keeps the music on. He climbs out his door, opens the back and drops the seat.

He has it set up with a soft sheepskin blanket and a bottle of wine with two glasses on a small tray.

"Oh, Josh." I shouldn't be here. Why didn't I say no?

"No strings, scrapper." Josh moves over the blanket, leans back on his knees and slowly pulls his shirt over his head.

Seeing the flex of his muscle, the flash of his provocative, come-hither smile … yeah, I know I'm crawling back there.

"Come here, baby." He pulls me into his arms

while simultaneously removing my top. Then he sinks his long fingers into my hair and presses his mouth over mine. There's no hesitation. The kiss is hot and possessive, all tongue and teeth. He bites my bottom lip, pulling it into his mouth at the same time he sinks his hand into my panties and teases me with his fingers.

"Oh, God." I'm already burning for him. The heat of his touch silences my doubts for the moment and leaves no room for thinking. I can only *feel*.

He keeps licking and biting my lips while he unfastens my pants and pulls them down to my bent knees. This gives him the access he wants, and he slips a finger deep inside of me. His hands are rough and calloused from his work, and it adds an extra dimension to the sensations my body feels. It's incredible.

Josh unsnaps my bra and groans as my breasts pop free and are fully exposed. He kisses my chin and licks his way down the bend of my throat. My skin thrills at the feeling while the blood rushes between my legs. There's no doubt where his hot, soft mouth is heading. He loves my breasts.

Right before he gets to my nipple, he pulls his hand from my heat, making me whine for its return, and paints my wetness over my nipple before he sucks it between his lips.

I moan, ready and consumed by the flames that are burning inside of me.

"Mmm … I love the way you taste." His voice is sultry and deep and vibrates through me. "I have something I want to do for you."

Yes! Right now, I'd let him do anything. I need the sensation of his cock inside me, filling me completely, perfectly. He melts me every time he comes between my walls.

"I need you to lie on your belly and get comfortable," he instructs. "First, have some wine. I'm going to turn on the engine and get the heat going again."

Josh passes me the long-stemmed glass. I need the drink. I'm losing myself in his arms, and I know I want to disappear there. I drain more than half my glass.

"Okay." I'm not sure what he has in mind, but I lay down like he asked me to.

He's quiet. It makes me wonder what he's up to.

The sweet and musky scent of sandalwood fills the vehicle. I hear Josh rubbing his hands together, then feel the heat of his palms, slick with oil, caress the skin of my back.

"I should've done this for you a long time ago," Josh softly says as he strokes the muscles of my back with long, smooth strokes.

He's giving me a massage? Josh is giving me a massage!

"You've taken such good care of me. Thank you."

His words are an arrow that shoots straight through my heart. As his fingers sink into and knead my sore, tired and tense muscles, a hot, violent storm gathers behind my eyes.

I try to blink it away, but I can't.

The first sob rips through my chest. Josh feels it, and his hands halt.

"Are you alright?"

I can't breathe! *Dear God, it feels like my heart is shredding.*

"Sophie." Josh's warm, strong hand rests in the center of my shoulder blades.

I shake my head and bury my face further into the soft sheepskin. Nothing will be alright.

"No one has ever given me a real massage like this before. No one's ever planned something like this out—touched me this way purely out of love." My voice is muffled. I wonder if he even understood what I said.

"That can't be true," he replies.

"It's true. I swear, it's true."

"I'm so sorry, Soph." He hugs my shoulders in his firm grasp, and I'm thankful for the pressure because I feel like I'm going to shatter and fly apart.

Slowly, I lift myself until I'm sitting. Josh brings up the sides of the sheepskin and wraps it around me tenderly.

"Loving you and feeling loved back felt so good that I let myself pretend I could have you," I admit through furious tears. "That I could have a life with you—because even though I should have torn myself away from you, I couldn't leave. I wanted to be with you." I hitch in breath. "It's a long, ugly story that I didn't think you could understand. And then you confided in me, even when you thought I wouldn't accept you afterward … I want to trust you, Josh. I want to trust you!"

"Sophie," his voice is gentle, "I'm an asshole. All this time, I have been waiting for you to tell me about your life, and I knew it wasn't going to be easy for you, so I didn't push it. Then, the moment you finally felt secure enough to tell me, I acted like a fucking prick. I'm so sorry. Please forgive me."

Josh kisses the top of my head and breathes into my hair. "You said you were married. It threw me. But I love you, Sophie. You can trust in me. I will *never* hurt you; I swear it. Whatever it is, I'm on your side."

"I don't know where to start."

"Take your time. We have all day and night," he soothes.

I nod and close my eyes. "My eighteenth birthday was the first time I'd seen my mom since I was fourteen years old. She told me she never wanted to see me again unless … well, I don't know what made me want to see her. I guess it doesn't matter how old you are; you always crave your parents' acceptance or maybe approval." I take in a shuddering breath. Josh reaches into the glove compartment and comes back with a pouch of tissues.

"Thanks," I whisper and blow my nose.

"My mom belongs to a religious cult where her God is more important than her child, and it is righteous and godly to punish that child by isolating her—locking her in a room for days at a time—starving her, hitting her, telling her that because she was bad, God is going to destroy her for it."

I wipe my cheeks even though I'm still crying. He needs to know about Jim, but he needs to know about my mother first.

"Since I was little, she told me God was going to send birds to eat out my eyes and peck me to death or take his own hand and simply wipe me clean off the face of the earth. Those are some of my earliest memories, Josh."

Now that I've started, I can't stop weeping. "When I was fourteen, she told me I was of the devil. I ran away. I lived watching the skies, expecting God's wrath to pour from heaven at any moment and destroy me. In the meantime, I slept anywhere I could find safety for as long as I could —but places on the streets are anything but safe. After a seriously brutal year and almost being killed, I was picked up by authorities and put into the system. I went through foster homes, group homes, halfway houses, a detention center ..." I bury my face in my hands. "I had no dreams or goals or desires. I hated myself, I hated God, and I hated my life. I had become a homeless, unloved, unwanted street teenager. After I turned eighteen —old enough to be set free from social services—I got involved with a nice guy from Maine. I lived with him for a couple of months. He was good to me, and I began looking toward my future. I got a job and started taking community college courses.

"I was so stupid that day, driving six hours to see my mother and prove to her I was a good person, that God hadn't killed me. I mean, what the hell was I thinking? That she'd welcome me back with open arms? That she'd tell me that she loved me?"

I shake my head. "Anything good I'd achieved up to that point was obliterated once I met with her. In less than a half hour, I was psychologically reduced back to that frightened little girl. In the weeks that followed the visit, which had ended with her telling me she was never going to speak to me again and that God was just waiting for the right time to exact his vengeance on me, I reverted back to my old, self-destructive behavior. I didn't care what happened to me anymore. I thought that God hadn't killed me because it was more satisfying to watch me hurt and to torture me this way instead."

I glance toward Josh, wondering if he wants to give me up now. If he thought I had emotional baggage before, this is sure to rush him out the door.

Instead, he says, "Sophie, you never deserved any of it. You're the best mother and kindest person I know. I'm so sorry that was your upbringing."

I nod again. He hasn't heard the rest. "I left the good guy, quit my job, stopped going to school and started traveling around, homeless again. I'd have sex just to be held and pretend I was loved, even for a little while. I began drinking at the local party spots.

"Nothing mattered. I ended up in a small, nowhere town where everyone knew everyone else. One night, there was a big party at the boat ramp. The cops pulled up with blue lights blazing and busted in, but it was all a big joke; the cops were there to party, too. Remember, small town— it's a crucial detail. That's the night I met Officer Jim Murphy. He was excellent at psychological manipulation, and I was ripe to be manipulated. After a couple of weeks in the sack, I got pregnant."

The engine is still running, and the windows are all fogged from our breathing. I've gotten control over my emotions now. "Could you please pass me my clothes?"

"Of course." Josh's voice is hoarse. His eyes are bloodshot. He's tough, but he's tender.

I dress myself, knowing I'm coming to the serious obstacle in the story. I don't know if our relationship will make it over the hurdle.

CHAPTER NINETEEN
JOSH

*H*oly *fucking hell!* Sophie is so amazing, so sweet and loving, that never in a million years would I have guessed she was raised like that, abused and tortured.

"It'll be easier for me to talk, I think, if you're driving. Your eyes will have to stay on the road and not on me," she says.

"I can do that." I'll do whatever she needs. I maneuver up front, pass her back her boots and coat and open the back so she can walk easily to the passenger seat.

I wipe off the ice and condensation that's formed on the window, and soon, we're taking a ride on a long back road.

"A baby was a miracle to me," she says. I catch her smile and know she's thinking about

Charlie. "I would finally have someone to love who would love me back unconditionally. A baby, to me, was a gift from God. Maybe God didn't really loathe me after all."

Her smile fades into a grimace. "I married Jim at the justice of the peace a month later, and my existence became even more of a living hell. It was like I'd gotten everything my mother had promised me. Jim beat me physically. Psychologically, he crippled me."

She turns toward me. "I tried to leave him— several times. At first, he seemed so sorry that I believed him, so I went back to him. Then, once his apologies stopped working on me, he switched to a new tactic. He started threatening to kill me if I ever left him again."

Sophie's pained expression is killing me. "He'd hold his pistol to my head and tell me how he was going to kill me."

She's reliving it as she tells the story. She makes her hand into a pistol and holds it in her other hand. "He told me he'd keep me alive as a prisoner, but just barely, until the baby was developed enough to survive outside of my womb, then he'd cut her out of me and watch me die."

My breath catches in my throat. *Jesus Christ! What the fuck do you say to that? How the hell do you comfort someone who's experienced that?*

I have to look at her. I have to pull over. I *have*

to do something. My adrenaline is racing, but she doesn't look away from her hands.

She asked me to drive.

Just drive.

"When he let me out of the house, he reminded me that if I stepped out of line, he'd make good on his promise. He even drove by the local women's shelter to show me I wouldn't be safe there—of course, since he was a cop, he'd brought other women there to *protect* them. He made me go to work and would call me on the business phone every hour to make sure I was still there. He would take my paychecks—I never saw any of the money, and he never bought anything that the baby or I would need, including food. I was forced to steal cash from my work so I could eat. He used all our money for drinking, cocaine and women."

Her body is trembling, I can see it. I reach out and take her hand. She exhales as if she's been holding her breath.

I can't take it anymore. If I don't do something, I'll explode.

"I have to stop, Sophie." I turn the car into an empty parking lot, reach over and unfasten her seatbelt, and then pull her over onto my lap. "I have to hold you." I want to find the son-of-a-bitch and kill him. Hate and fury well up inside me, coiling my muscles, pumping me with fight instinct.

"I read news articles about women and children who are killed by their husbands or boyfriends and fathers all the time, and I know that could have been me." She begins to weep softly. "I'm lucky because Charlie and I are very much alive. When Charlie was born, she made me feel fearless. There was no way that man was going to hurt her. I got my own apartment behind his back and went straight to the courthouse, begging for someone to listen to me. I finally got the attention of a judge who'd been assigned to the district in transit to a position in the city. He wasn't friends with Jim, so he granted me a restraining order. He even sent transcripts and a letter to the police chief, strongly suggesting he suspend Jim from the force.

"Jim was furious. He caught me taking a walk with the baby in the stroller one day, pulled over the cruiser and told me he'd make me a paraplegic if I didn't come back. I was shaking, but I reminded him of the restraining order and his career. He left us alone for almost three months, but then the judge moved to the city, and none of the police would enforce the court order." She takes in a quivering breath. "To the point that, when he tried to break into my apartment after midnight, drunk off his ass, and when I called them for help, and even after they saw the weapon he held, they still let him in. They let him hold my baby, even after he told them he was going to kidnap her and kill me."

"They didn't arrest him?" I shake my head incredulously.

"They let him go." Sophie straightens. "That was it. I packed up everything I could stuff in the back of the car, and Charlie and I ran away that night."

Understanding floods me. I get it. Everything makes sense now. "Sophie—"

"Josh," Sophie pushes herself away from me and back into the passenger seat, "I could feasibly be a fugitive and a kidnapper. If he petitioned the court, and I never showed up for the hearing, I could be in a lot of trouble. And if he hasn't but is searching for us …"

"Sophie—"

"That's why I can't stay, Josh! I can't risk him finding us, finding Charlie. I never doubted his threats. I always thought it was just a matter of time, so I've moved from place to place every few months, changing our names. We don't own much more than a couple of backpacks stuffed with necessities." Suddenly, she opens the car door and gets out. Quickly, I jump out to stay with her.

"Sophie!"

"I'm sorry I've involved you in this, Josh. But,

so you know, I've never been in love with anyone but you. Charlie taught me about the true love between mother and child, but I didn't believe in love between a man and woman until you proved it could be real." She starts moving away from me, but I don't let her go.

"Sophie, please stop!"

She does.

"I love you. You love me." I take her by the shoulders. "Please, look at me. I love Charlie. I can protect you."

"There's nothing you can do," she cries.

"Wrong! There's nothing I *won't* do!"

She considers me a moment but replies, "You can't keep the authorities from throwing me into prison for kidnapping, and you can't guard me and Charlie every minute."

"Bet your ass I can," I guarantee. "My father and uncle have incredible pull—a couple of phone calls, and we can find out if that son-of-a-bitch has petitioned the court. We'll make sure your name is clear. And, Sophie, if it somehow isn't, I can afford the best lawyers. You shouldn't have to live like this. You deserve to be safe. You deserve to be free."

She drops her eyes. "I don't know if there's such thing as freedom for me."

"I will make and keep you safe. No one is going to get to you." My mind is racing. "We can stay here in Minneapolis until we find out what Jim's done, if anything, with the courts. While that's happening, we'll also find out exactly where he is and what he's doing and monitor him from now on."

I watch her tears fall, and I pray that I'm getting through to her.

"Let me protect you."

"If I did—let you protect me—what happens when you stop loving me?"

"I will never stop loving you, Sophie. That would be like me betraying my own life … like forsaking my very own soul." I lock my eyes with hers. "Please don't run. Give me a chance to make you safe—to make things right."

I can tell that she's struggling to agree, but finally, she gives me one solid nod.

I press my lips onto her forehead as a seal and a commitment before I bring her body into mine. I hold her there for a long time. I can barely believe she what she has survived. I feel more than ever that she is a gift to me.

"I thought it was a miracle—you coming to me and me finding you," I tell her. Now, I know you're the miracle. I'm so grateful you made your way to me." I have one more question. "Sophie?"

"Yes?"

"What is your name?" My eyes never leave her perfect face.

"Isabella Sofia Alise Estefanie Costa Bolen. I was named after each of my mother's grand-mothers and great-grandmothers. I didn't lie about my mother; she was born in Spain then immigrated to the U.S." She smiles, and the joy sparkles in her eyes.

"That's quite a name. It's beautiful, like you."

She blushes. "It's been … a very long time since I've told anyone my entire name. Charlie was born Emma-Jean Murphy. It was the name Jim chose. Everywhere she and I moved the first year, I always changed it up, but then she turned two and started talking. She needed to be able to have a name she identified with. Charlotte has a lot of nicknames, and Charlie can be for a boy or a girl. That's why I chose it."

"I knew you were a scrapper, *scrapper*. I just didn't realize how much." I touch her face to reassure her.

We're going to be okay.

We're going to be better than okay.

By the time we drive back and park at the hotel, it's become night.

Sophie says, "I'm too restless to go up to the room. I still feel saturated in everything we talked about. Would you like to take a walk?"

"Absolutely."

We exit the parking garage in front of the Hyatt and walk along the sidewalk on the snow-blown path.

"Everything is so beautiful," she exclaims, looking at the snow and the holiday lights that adorn the city. "I've always loved snow—the way it makes everything seem clean and new."

The lights sparkle in her eyes. They're still swollen from crying.

She believes in me, I realize and am overcome. She believes in me so much that she trusts me with her story, with her life. That was no small feat, what she accomplished tonight—having to relive that torment.

I take her gloved hand in mine. "Are you warm enough?"

"Yeah, I'm good," she says softly.

She's still back there in it, I know. That kind of trauma never goes away—only time and love can make it fade so it doesn't consume every bit of you.

The ultimate goal of my existence has just been solidified. Making Sophie and Charlie know they're loved, safe and forever happy is what I'm supposed to live for. I've done it all—the career, the titles and accolades, the awards—God, all I can think about is that three years ago, when I was training and working my way through the professional MMA circuit, Sophie was living through hell.

Never again, I think. *You'll never go through that again.* "I'm going to take care of you, Sophie. You know that, right?"

She squeezes my hand and nods.

Do I reiterate *forever*? Fuck, yeah!

"Until my dying breath."

She rests her weary head against my shoulder.

We stroll several blocks before coming to the city park. A winding path snakes around a center island of sorts, which is dotted with lit ice sculptures and colorful holiday décor.

"Do you want to go through the park?

"Sure."

We head down the path, and Sophie stops in front of the Charlie Brown Christmas display.

"I always love watching the animated specials every Christmas." She smiles, reminiscing. "Charlie always laughs when Snoopy licks Lucy, and then Lucy gags and runs screaming."

"I can totally see her laughing at that."

"Guess we're lucky they're still up."

"They'll pull them down in another week— end of January."

We cross a wooden bridge that brings us over a small, ornamental pond that's frozen over.

"Hey, do you ice skate?" I ask her.

"Not well." She laughs lightly. "But I'd be into trying. You?"

"I've spent a lot of time in Minnesota. There's an outdoor rink I know of. It's very family-friendly. They sell hot cocoa at the concession stand and have strands of lights that make the place really festive. We could rent skates, bring Charlie," I tell her.

"Sounds perfect." She stops all of a sudden, stands on tiptoe and kisses my cheek, lingering there. "I love you, Josh North."

I could absolutely melt through the snow.

"Alright, nice and slow, back away from each other," a man's demanding voice orders from behind us.

Sophie's expression goes from peace and love to horror in an instant.

"Okay, guy, no problem," I say. I lift my hands so he can see them but instead of stepping away from Sophie, I move behind her so my body is shielding hers. "What is it you need?"

The raucous laughter tells me there's more than one guy. I have to turn around to see what I'm facing.

"Your wallets and jewelry would be a good start," he commands.

"No problem. I've got to pull it out of my inner coat pocket, so I'm going to turn around so you can watch," I tell him.

"Then fucking get it done!" a different voice scorns.

I carefully face them. Four asshole thugs are making a semi-circle around us. The two guys who are closest to us have switchblades that glint in the light; the third guy brandishes a pistol, while number four seems like the leader.

"We're not wearing any jewelry, it's too fucking cold out here, but I have some cash." I pull the flap of my coat open. I'm not risking Sophie if all they're desperate for is some money. Unfolding my wallet, I remove my cash. "There's about three hundred here. Take it and go."

Without visible fear, the leader walks over and snatches the bills from my hand.

"Three hundred—fuck, yeah!" one of the guys crows. He doesn't even know how to hold a knife the right way.

"'Take it and go?' What the fuck, mother-fucker? I'm the one with the firepower, so you better give me some motherfucking respect!" The guy holding the cash shoves it into his pocket and considers us. "Get the girl. We could have fun with that bitch all fucking night."

Sophie makes a strangled sound behind me.

"That's not going to happen." My muscles coil, and I feel my gaze harden into steel.

They all laugh. "Oh, it is! Maybe we can let

him watch before we kill his ass," the leader says, all haughty.

Sophie's breathing is erratic, like she's going to hyperventilate.

I'm done. "You fucking douchebags picked the wrong night and the wrong couple to fuck with." I've wanted to hit someone since Sophie's story, and these four dickheads have Jim's name written all over them.

I lunge at guy number three, taking control of his gun hand, which I position to the left before I break his hand and wrist. When the pistol fires, it's aimed at the leader, sending a bullet into his leg.

They both scream. The leader's down, holding his leg.

Three's still standing, so I throw a hard right hook at the side of his head. He drops.

Guys one and two square off against me. With a roundhouse kick, my boot plants into two's face, throwing him backward, while a front kick to the sternum drives one to his knees. I take one's knife wrist in my grasp, twist and stretch his arm.

"Didn't your momma warn you not to play with knives?" I stomp my boot into his elbow. The break is audible.

I close the knife and throw it far into the surrounding shrubs and trees.

One's wailing and writhing when I turn to two.

His face is bloody from a broken nose the kick inflicted. He throws his own knife in the direction I threw one's, scrambles to his feet and runs like a bat out of hell.

I check Sophie. "You okay?"

She nods wide-eyed.

Smiling at her reassuringly, I reach for my cell and dial 911 to report the mugging and location and tell dispatch the perpetrators want to turn themselves in.

I swipe my cash back out of the leader's pocket. "You're lucky I don't kill you." Stepping hard, I grind the sole of my heavy work boot into the bloody bullet wound. I can see the sweat bead over his forehead as he screams, and then passes out.

First things first, I get Sophie out of the park and away from the scene to someplace safe—at least until the police show up. There's a CVS on the corner, from which we can still see the park. Leading her off into a side aisle, I check her head and body.

"Are you sure you're not hurt at all?"

"I'm telling you, I'm fine," she insists. "Shaken, but fine. Nobody even touched me."

I look into her irises—I don't see any sign of concussion. I'm satisfied.

"Are you hungry?" I ask.

She laughs. I take that as a yes and buy her a Snickers bar.

Sophie stays at the CVS while I talk to the police. When I'm finished, I meet back up with her.

"Let's get you back to the hotel. After we get cleaned up, I'll get you a proper dinner," I explain as we're walking away from the flashing lights of the squad cars. "And, Sophie, to finish our conversation—which was interrupted—I love you back."

CHAPTER TWENTY
SOPHIE

"Joshua …" my voice sing-songs through Josh's home workout room.

We've been back in Williston for over a week. Charlie and I have been staying at Josh's most nights—Charlie likes it that way.

So do I.

I step through the doorway and watch Josh go at the bag like an opponent. I know he's going to win the defending title fight. Spending so much time with him in training and knowing him and his past really makes me understand where he gets his strength and power and why a rough, blood-and-bones type of sport would be his passion— MMA is a fair fight of strength, endurance and courage. I've come to respect and admire the sport.

He can't hear me because his earbuds are in

place and his back is toward me, so I enjoy watching him without his knowing.

Holy. Hot. Damn! That man can melt me like butter.

Sweat soaks the back of his blue tank top; each muscle coils and springs on his demand; his legs are solid, and his ass is round and strong. I think of how it flexes hard when he's making love to me.

That gets me thinking about his dirty-talking mouth, and *that* gives me an idea.

I peel my clothes off, fully fantasizing what he's going to do to me—how he'll touch me, how he'll taste me, how he'll bring me, body and soul, into another dimension.

Leaving on only the pair of black high-heeled ankle boots he likes so much, I stroll over and lean up against the wall where he's sure to see me after this round of jabs.

Josh is breathing hard, and I can hardly wait. His black tribal ink comes alive with every taut motion of his arms.

He spots me out of the corner of his eye—I know because I watch the hungry smile spread across his glorious face. It makes me smile back.

After a couple of steps back from the bag, he pulls his earbuds from his ears.

"Oh, Josh, I love your ass." I make a show of running my hands up my body and into my hair.

"Not to mention each of your rock-hard muscles."

He's ready. He can't yank off his clothes fast enough.

I lie back against the luxurious, black suede sofa he has in the room and spread my legs provocatively. The fabric is soft and supple against my skin.

"You look like a goddess." His hard-on flexes and I feel my own insides squeeze at the thought of him.

He quickly strides over to his desk, and I know what he's after.

"No barriers. We've had enough barriers between us," I say. "I want to feel you and only you."

He turns and stares at me like he's been struck dumb. I can't help but laugh at him a little. "You okay, fighter?"

"You want to … not use a …?" he stammers.

"That's what I'm saying. I got fitted for a diaphragm," I confess. "I want to become one with you completely, wholly. Do you want that?"

His lungs empty of air like he just got punched. He nods. "Hell yeah, I want that."

I bite my lip in anticipation as he lays his perfectly sculpted body over mine. He searches my eyes and holds the sides of my face in his hands.

"I want you forever, Isabella Sofia Alise Estefanie." His eyes sparkle mischievously.

"I want you too," I whisper as I feel him working his shaft into my opening.

As he enters me, his cock fires off my every nerve. The sparks ignite a wildfire in my belly. I tilt my head back and moan. He overtakes me so I can think of nothing else—all that exists in the world is me and him.

Josh groans, "Oh my God, you're like velvet." He grips the flesh of my hips in his rough hands, pulls them up so I meet his hips, and pumps faster.

With each of his thrusts, my entire body is caught up. My inner walls quiver, and I orgasm, calling out his name. "Josh! You feel so good!"

"Holy fuck, baby!" His own head falls back in pleasure.

A moment later, he changes it up and pulls his divine, rigid cock out so slowly, to the farthest point, before pausing and then thrusting hard back inside of me.

The noises that rip from my mouth are animal.

"Oh, Christ!" he cries and does it again.

"Fuck!" I moan.

"Grab your tits," he orders me. "I want to watch you pinch your nipples." Josh drives his unyielding dick back in, forcing me to cry out in ecstasy.

I'll play his game. "I'll do anything for more."

I squeeze each of my nipples between my fingers as my eyes lock onto his, and he pounds inside of me with wild ferocity.

"Oh God, don't stop!" My eyes roll back, and I'm gone, lost in the sensations he's causing.

"Sophie, I can feel every ridge and curve of your perfect pussy."

"We're never using a condom again!"

"Christ," he grunts. "There's nothing else like you! You're so fucking hot and wet and tight."

I can't stop the staccato sounds escaping my chest with his every crash against me.

"I'm dying from how your pussy spasms and is milking my dick." Now he slowly grinds his hips against my thighs so his cock is stirring inside me. He's moaning and his eyes become hooded.

I love his dirty talk, and I know he likes it right back. I whine, "It's all you. You make me so wet."

He's so freaking amazing! He makes me feel so sexy.

"Tell me what you like …"

"I love how your long, hard cock feels as it's stroking me," I whimper. "Oh please … don't stop, Josh! Give it to me hard."

Effortlessly, he lifts my legs so they're locked onto his shoulders, and then he lies on top of me, pinning me with the heat and strength of his muscles. He pistons hard and fast with so much torque he's going to make me scream!

Holy hell! The man is so strong and can manipulate my body so fast. I LOVE being on the sexy end of Josh's MMA abilities.

"Oh my God, you're so deep!" I whimper as his cock fills me.

His pelvis is massaging my clit; he's crushing my breasts, and his sultry breath is playing hot against my ear. The rush of sensations coursing through my sex lights the fuse to my dynamite.

We're going over together. A guttural roar thunders from Josh's throat. His cock pulses, and his muscles seize—gooseflesh ripples across his skin.

When he releases my legs, we're both spent in the most euphoric way.

We hold each other and fall asleep, cuddled up on the couch until the sun rises.

He's the fist to stir awake, and I feel him laying kisses on my face, whispering how much he loves me.

There is nowhere on earth I'd rather be.

Josh makes a quick protein shake while I flip Charlie's mini whole-grain pancakes.

"Yummy!" Charlie opens Josh's fridge like she owns it and takes out the maple syrup. "Want some, Joshy?"

"Thank you, beautiful." He lifts his drink. You can see the egg yolk floating against the side of the glass. "But I have to have this breakfast today."

"Poor Joshy." Charlie shakes her head.

I smile. "Today's the big day with all the reporters. Are you excited?" I ask Josh as I pour us each a to-go tumbler of coffee.

He puts his mouth to my ear. "After being inside of you, skin on skin, *nothing* is going to excite me except for the prospect of getting in *there* again."

"With talk like that, you're going to be late," I say in a hushed tone.

He plants a kiss on my lips and smiles. "God, you're incredible."

He turns around, scoops Charlie into his arms and swings her once around.

"I love my girls!" he says, kissing the top of her head. "See you both later this afternoon." He grabs his gear bag and is out the door.

Charlie's lip pouts out like she's going to cry.

"After you're finished eating, would you like to shop for a Princess Elsa doll?" I bribe her to get a smile.

JOSH

REPORTERS FROM *SPORTS ILLUSTRATED*, *FIGHT Magazine* and the UFC, along with several newspapers, will be showing up in about three hours. That gives me the perfect amount of time to get in a morning run and maybe even a shower. The photographers like getting pictures of me sweating over the bags or sparring, so either way, it'll all work out.

I walk into the gym, and it's already cleaned spotless and somehow doesn't smell like sweat and gym socks. Silva, McGee and Caruso have the entire gym set up with seats for the guests and tables on the side walls with water pitchers and paper cups. I actually love getting interviewed before a fight; it pumps up my amperage that much more. Only two more weeks before I meet my opponent in the octagon, and this will certainly fuse adrenaline into my upcoming workouts.

After changing into my cold-weather running gear, I hit the pavement for a five-miler. All I think about is Sophie.

So, Sophie Bolen. I consider her true last name. *North.*

The thought pops into my head, and I realize it feels like a welcome friend.

"Sophie North," I speak it out loud. It sounds pretty damn good.

First things first, I have to get her free from the son-of-a-bitch that had ruined her life. And she needs time to really *feel* free—to savor that she's safe. She needs her power back.

I hear a text come in, and I check my phone. It's my dad.

He's already got calls in, using his chain of connections, to find out if the dickhead contacted the courts or reported Sophie and Charlie missing.

Josh, you need to see this.

The Boston Globe Newspaper headline reads:

When Trusted Cops Go Bad. Officer Jim Murphy, wanted in connection with several crimes …

I stop running, catch my breath and click the link. The article talks about how Murphy was a trusted police officer in a small town near Boston, but the county district attorney's office subpocnaed officials when reports and allegations went public about Murphy accepting bribes and torturing prisoners held in lock-up. He was also being charged with several counts of domestic violence and child endangerment.

Once I finish scanning the article, I call Sophie.

Voicemail. *Fuck!*

"Sophie, my dad sent a newspaper article about Murphy. I'm going to be going batshit crazy until I talk to you. Hurry and call."

I keep reading. When the town got a new police chief, Murphy was arrested for beating his girlfriend and her five-year-old son. After suspending him, the chief ordered a full investigation into all of Murphy's activities. He's now wanted in connection with drug trafficking, bribes, assault on prisoners, domestic violence …

Jesus Christ! He skipped bail six months ago, and there's a nationwide manhunt for him.

I dial her number again. "Sophie, he's a suspect in your disappearance. You were never wanted for kidnapping. Goddamn it, Sophie, answer your phone!"

Immediately, I head back to the gym.

ONE MILE DOWN, AND SHE HASN'T CALLED BACK.

I redial. Voicemail. *Shit!*

She's probably in the shower or taking a walk

with Charlie. I know she's fine; it's just reading all that has set me on edge.

Another mile closer to the gym, and I think of trying Ayana's cell. Maybe Sophie went home. But I get her voicemail, too. I check my watch. Yeah, she'd be at work by now.

I get to the gym, which is crawling with reporters. I go through the back door and remember that Sophie should have dropped Charlie off with Britt by now, so I call Britt.

"Hi, Sophie," Britt's voice rings out cheerfully.

"It's Josh. How long ago did Sophie drop off Charlie?" I ask.

"Hey, Josh. Actually, I thought she was with you. She was supposed to be here over a half hour ago. But you know, I was stuck in traffic from the construction on Route 2 this morning. It's a good half-hour wait."

That sounds about right. She never answers her phone in the car, either. "Thanks for reminding me. When you hear from her, tell her to call me right away. It's important."

"Of course." Britt hesitates. "Is everything okay?"

"Everything's great, actually. I just have some serious info she needs to hear."

I hang up and think about it. I definitely don't like the fact that Murphy's disappeared and there's a nationwide manhunt for him, but if he

347

has—or *had*—a girlfriend, it means he's moved on from Sophie. And the fact that Sophie isn't wanted is so fucking liberating, I can't wait to tell her!

After cleaning up and putting on the sponsor-labeled clothing and gear I'm to be photographed in, I go out to face the human circus. Reporters are everywhere. Immediately, the photo session starts—me throwing punches at the bag, me and McGee sparring in the ring, me lifting weights—it's an hour before we finally move on to the interview questions.

Another half hour later, I'm still answering questions into the thirty microphones positioned to catch my every word. I hold my phone in my hand—it's on vibrate. Although nothing has come in, I keep looking down to check it.

Caruso announces, "Ladies and gentlemen, we're going to take a ten-minute intermission."

Everyone disperses for the moment. I stay where I am and try Sophie *again*. I'm anxious and on edge and thinking I should beat it the fuck out of here to find her. Then I realize the sweet pain in the ass probably hasn't kept her phone charged, and it's dead now.

I leave another message that sounds like a

public service announcement to keep your phone *charged*!

My fingers go to my recent contacts, but before I hit Britt's number, McGee hands me a white envelope with my name on it in Sophie's handwriting.

When I throw a questioning look at Caruso, he says, "It was in the front mailbox."

But it was obviously personally delivered because the envelope is blank except for my name. I rip through the seal.

Josh,

I'm sorry I led you on. I can't stay here anymore. Please just forget about me. It'll be easier that way. Don't come after me. You know I know how to disappear.

Goodbye,
Isabella

CHAPTER TWENTY-ONE
JOSH

"Are you concerned about fighting Dalloway after having seen him put Whalen in the hospital?" the UFC interviewer asks.

Isabella?? Why the fuck did she sign her name Isabella??

I feel like I'm in a trance—or having an out-of-body experience. I lean in toward the microphone. "Honestly, he doesn't scare me. Whalen has serious weaknesses, and Dalloway found and exploited them. It's that simple."

What the fuck? How does she leave me a note like that? Even if she got scared again, I thought what we had was a hell of a lot fucking more than a four-sentence note!

"Josh, what are you eating during these two weeks before the fight?" the reporter from *Fighter* asks.

Why didn't she sign it Sophie? Was using the name

Isabella supposed to be some kind of reminder that she's not the Sophie I think I know?

"Um … low carbs and high protein to make weight," I say distractedly.

I'm sorry I led you on?? My brain is all fucked up. *Forget about me?* Is she fucking serious?! That's what the lateness was all about? She fucking left me!?

My mind races thinking about the last few days. Had she been acting nervous again, like she was ready to run? It sure as hell hadn't seemed like it. But she'd spent three years running, hiding from that bastard, and she'd admitted to me that it was hard for her to let go and stop looking over her shoulder all the time. Maybe she'd gotten skittish again and decided she just couldn't do it …

A guy from the Williston newspaper asks me about my motivation for this fight.

The answer is Sophie.

Every answer to every question is Sophie—her smile, her laughter, the beat of her heart, which races when we finish making love, the expression of love in her eyes when she looks at me. *It is real, goddamn it!* What we have is real!

"Mr. North?" A woman from *The Bismark Tribune* says my name. I hear it, but I don't reply. McGee's voice follows her question.

How am I going to find her? How am I going to get her back? I can't sit here anymore. I look down at my phone—no incoming calls, no texts. *How could she do this?*

My mind is going like a fucking runaway freight train. It still doesn't compute. What the fuck made her run? *After all of the confessions and promises?*

I'm not sure what I can do, but sitting here isn't it.

"Josh, we have Silva, Caruso and McGee here with us today, the valued members of your team," a reporter with *USA Today* is saying. "Where is the newest member, Ms. Garner?"

That got my attention. "What did you say?"

He's holding up a photograph of me and Sophie.

"Where did you get that?" I'm out of my chair.

The reporter's expression turns from the excitement of uncovering a juicy side story to looking very nervous, as if he's close to stepping on a landmine. "The photograph is all over the internet and social media. The articles surrounding it talk of a new member of your team, a massage therapist and *girlfriend,*" he says, and everyone wants to know more.

Silva quickly retrieves the photo and passes it to me. It's of me, Sophie and Charlie. Charlie is up on my shoulders, and Sophie and I are holding hands, shopping in downtown Williston.

Holy fuck! That's why she ran.

I look over at Silva and lean away from the mics. "I have to go find her."

Silva nods. "I got this." He holds his hands up to calm the crowd. "Let's settle it down, please. Josh has been called away on urgent family business, but we're here to answer any of your questions." I hear him talk about Sophie's part on the team and my recovery from the fire as I pull on my coat and slip outside the back to my car.

I'M BEGGING FOR A TICKET, GOING AS FAST AS I am, but I have to make up for lost time. There are only a few ways out of Williston. 94 is her best bet and because the photo and articles place her here in Williston, N.D., my guess is she's going to take the fastest way out of state possible, and that's the Montana line. She might even use Route 2.

Which do I take?

"Fuck!" I slam the steering wheel. "FUCK! FUCK! FUCK!"

The phone rings. I answer on speaker, "*SOPHIE?!*"

"No, Josh. It's Britt."

"Have you heard any—?"

"Get to Sophie's apartment as soon as you can." I think she's crying.

"What's wrong? Is she there?"

"No … but Ayana is … she's …" Britt's voice wavers.

"What is it?!" I'm aggravated as all hell.

"Ayana is dead!"

Ayana is dead. *Ayana is dead.* "What? *How* is she dead?"

"She's been shot, Josh!"

Dread consumes me. It starts at my heart and spreads through me like a fire.

"Is there any sign of Sophie or Charlie?" I press.

"They aren't here," she says, crying hysterically.

I spin the car around, fishtailing in the middle of the roadway. Drivers blare their horns at me and swerve to miss me. Righting the Vertigo, I tear across the road and accelerate in the opposite direction.

"Britt, have you called the police?"

"No, I just got here! The door was unlocked and partly opened. I thought maybe one of them was heading out, so I let myself in." Her voice is shaking, and it's nearly impossible to make out everything she's saying.

"Try to calm down," I tell her.

"Josh! Ayana was … shot in the head—I can see where the bullet went through … oh God … there is so much blood."

I careen through the next two red lights and dodge an oncoming semi.

"Look around for clues, Britt."

"I can't move," she answers, obviously panicking.

"Do NOT hang up on me!" I order.

"I can't move my legs." Her breathing is erratic. "I've never seen … a dead …"

"Britt, listen to me. You can do this. Close your eyes and think of Charlie," I say more gently. "Get a picture of her in your mind."

"Okay." she sobs.

"You have to get rid of your panic to help her." I take a hard right turn and almost graze a parked car. I'm only a mile away now.

"There's a gun … lying on the floor," Britt states.

"That a girl! Don't touch it," I tell her.

"It looks like it was thrown. It's over by the wall in the living room, near the window, but Ayana's …" She swallows hard. "She's on the couch."

I shudder. Britt's fear froze her before she could check the entire apartment.

Dear God, please … I beg. "Go check Sophie's room."

"I can't!" she says.

"You have to!" I shout. "You could save her life!"

"Okay …" A second later, she says, "She's not here."

"Is the room a mess, like a fight went on? Do you notice anything missing or off?"

"Like what? What's supposed to be missing?" I can hear the panic in her breath.

"I don't know … clothes? Toys? Sophie's personal things?" I try.

"Everything looks normal—clothes are in the closet; Charlie's toys are in the corner. I don't see Sophie's purse or Charlie's backpack."

"Okay, Britt, you need to call 911."

"Oh my God, I just found Sophie's cell phone!"

"You found her cell phone?" I bark.

"Yeah, it was on the floor, under the bed." She's completely hysterical again. "I've never seen this on a phone before. There's an S.O.S. text blinking on the main screen. It reads, 'Out of Zone' and … has the address for Red's Motor Inn."

"That's that abandoned hotel with the cabins a few miles out of the city," I think out loud.

"Josh! Oh my God! It says Amber Alert on the text, and there's a matching icon on her phone that's blinking!" she practically screams.

"Run the phone downstairs. I'm pulling onto the corner of Fourth now."

"Okay!" I hear her footfalls, and a moment

later, she's out the door and running toward the car.

I open the window. "Here, see." She shows me the text and icon.

I touch it, and a white and green app called Amber Alert GPS opens. "Amber Alert. Christ, it's Charlie's picture."

Britt gasps and throws her hands over her mouth.

It seems to be some sort of tracking app that Sophie has set up to track Charlie and warn her if Charlie leaves a set area. I tap the alert, and a Google map opens with a trail of red balloons leading to a green balloon over the hotel's address. *Please, God, let this be where they are.*

"Call 911! Tell them about the phone and send them to Red's. Give them the name of the known Massachusetts fugitive, Officer Jim Murphy. GO!" I can't waste time. Britt steps back, and I swerve around the corner.

I promised Sophie I would keep them safe. I fucking promised! She risked herself and Charlie for me.

Dear Christ, the time I wasted with the goddamn note! She didn't fucking run away and leave me!

Another instance when I wasted time flashes through my head … high school after football practice. Visions of Taylor's bloody body infiltrate my mind.

Terror and pain threaten to steal my strength. It's my fault. I was supposed to protect them.

Christ! It's not going to happen. Not again. Not on my watch!

Sophie and Charlie are my family!

I'm going to fucking kill him.

CHAPTER TWENTY-TWO

SOPHIE

M y head swims, and my stomach lurches with nausea. It's so cold. My eyes open slowly and painfully, taking time to focus. I'm in a small, decrepit structure, like an old cabin. It smells of mold and rotting wood, alcohol and urine. There's a kitchen space on the far side of the room, and an old sink under a window drips a steady stream. The window has been covered over with cardboard and duct taped. A half-full coffee pot with a cup beside it sits on the counter. Next to them are a box of Hefty black trash bags and a box of Ritz crackers. As I glance around me, I notice *all* of the windows in this room have been covered.

Charlie.

I try to move. My hands are taped behind my back, and my ankles are duct taped to the legs of the chair. He's stripped me of my boots, socks and winter coat. I'm barefoot and left only in my jeans and tank top. I want to scream, but I stop myself. The last time I did that, he killed my would-be rescuer, and the fact that my mouth *isn't* duct-taped tells me he's not too worried about me making noise.

Movement from an adjacent room gets my attention, and I can see the hallway entrance but no further down the hall.

A toilet flushes.

My heart quickens, and I have to force my breathing to be calm and steady. I can't pass out.

Hastily, I peer around the room to see if there's anything that can help me get loose.

A battered metal folding table stands against the side wall. I see my bag and Charlie's back-pack. Both are overturned, and their contents are strewn across the table.

Fuck! Did he find the secret compartment? *I've got to get to that bag!*

"Look here. The whore is awake." Jim strolls slowly from the hallway, wiping his hands and face on a ratty towel that he throws over his shoulder when he's finished.

I think about how he caught us.

A KNOCK ON THE DOOR.

"Fed Ex," he said.

Charlie and I were already about to walk out, and I didn't even check through the peephole. When I opened the door, Jim grabbed me. I screamed, twisted in his arms and slammed my head into his face. When he let go, I tried to kick him in the groin, but he was ready for it. He got hold of my leg and forced me to the floor.

That was when Ayana walked in.

Jim drew his gun and shot her right in the forehead. He had a silencer on the pistol, so there was only the sound of a muffled shot, then the thud of her body hitting the floor.

"Mommy?" Charlie ran into the room, her coat zipped, and her backpack strapped to her.

"RUN!" I screamed and kicked Jim square in the kneecap.

"FUCKING BITCH!" He went down, but even though I quickly scrambled to get back on my feet, he got hold of me.

Jim cupped my chin and forced my head back while he stuck the gun in my face.

"Emma-Jean?"

"Let go of my mommy!" she screamed.

"Your mommy has been very bad," he told her.

"You're bad!"

"Do you see the gun? You don't want me to hurt her, do you?"

Charlie shook her head.

"Then you have to be quiet. You can't yell," Jim warned before turning his attention back to me. "Get up."

He held my arm like a vice as I stood. For just a second, he scanned the room.

I slammed against him, jarring the gun from his grasp. It flew across the living room. We wrestled for a moment before he pulled a syringe out of his jacket pocket and lunged at Charlie.

"What are you going to do now?" The needle tip poked threateningly against the soft skin of Charlie's neck.

"No, please. Don't use that. I'll be quiet. I'll even help you," I tried to persuade him.

"Don't do any fucking fancy shit like that again, and I want to see your hands at all times."

"Okay. Anything you want," I assured him.

"You're going to write a note to your fuck buddy, breaking up with him."

"There's a pad and envelopes over at the desk." My eyes glanced at the piece of furniture by the window.

"Go ahead. I know you'll be good," he said and looked down at Charlie.

I stepped over Ayana's bloody body. "I'm sorry. I'm so, so sorry," I breathed.

I wrote the note fast and stuck it in the envelope. I signed it Isabella, hoping it would alert Josh that something was wrong.

Moving slowly and non-threateningly, I went back over to the foyer, where he was waiting.

"I should've known when I found you, you'd be whoring around."

He looked over at the table where we threw our keys and stuff by the door. I saw the newspaper photo he must have put there. It was a picture of me, Josh and Charlie with a caption that read, Has the Williston fighter playboy found his true love?

"Over two years ... I searched for your fucking ass. I'd about given up on finding you when I saw this."

Charlie was crying as he held her out of my reach.

Jim had my purse slung over his shoulder. "Nice and slow. We're going to go down to my car," he instructed.

I knew if we got in that car, we were as good as dead.

For the first time, I noticed the blood running from his nose. I wondered if I broke it when I slammed into him with the back of my head. I thought about diving to strike it again, but the needle still at Charlie's neck stopped me.

"You first, Bella," he ordered me.

I didn't move.

"Turn and walk toward the door," he grated forcefully.

I obeyed. As I closed my hand over the doorknob, I felt the sting of the needle pierce my flesh and press into my muscle.

A moment of panic coursed through me as I felt myself blacking out. I got one last glimpse of Charlie crying, "Mommy!"

"Where's Charlie?" I seeth.

"You're in no position to be demanding anything, bitch." He comes over and backhands me across the face.

It's so hard that my already compromised vision goes in and out of focus.

"Tell me you haven't hurt her." I know better than to beg or cry; it only fuels his violence and dehumanizes me, so I keep my voice steady and polite.

"She's in a ketamine induced sleep in the other room."

Ketamine … Ketamine? What the hell is that?

"I haven't hurt her yet." He drags out the word *yet*. "That will depend on how I feel when I'm done hurting *you*."

"Do you want us to go back home with you? We could be a family again." This is psychological warfare. If I can just keep him thinking, throw him off … maybe I can keep us alive.

"LYING SLUT! You gave yourself away and spread your legs to that fighter, and who knows who else! You're all used up, bitch." He spits at me disgustedly and takes a hunting knife from his back pocket, opening it to reveal the long, jagged blade.

My breath hitches, and my heart slams in my chest. I bite the inside of my lip as my body begins to produce tears without my permission. I push them back.

"No, you had your chance for that," he says.

It's so cold in here. He's wearing a coat, and I can see his breath. Icy wind blows outside and through the walls.

There's no heat, I realize.

He walks a slow circle around me. "No, this time, I'm going to make good on my promise to you." Jim slides the flat of the knife blade down my arm. "I'm going to cut you into such little pieces that no one will ever be able to put you back together again." He sneers. "Small enough to fit you in those garbage bags over there." He points the knife tip toward the box of bags I saw earlier on the counter. "You are, after all, nothing but worthless trash."

My wrists strain against the duct tape, but I'm wrapped tight. There's a method to tearing duct tape; Josh showed me. *How do you do it? I can't remember!*

"Always trying to run away." He shakes his head. "We could have had a good thing, me and you." Jim runs the knife point down the leg of my jeans from thigh to knee. Painfully, it slices through the denim. Blood colors my jeans.

I groan through it. He lifts the knife and wipes the blade with the towel.

"What are you going to do to our little girl?" I grit out through my teeth.

"*If* she's mine, I'll let her live. If she's not, she'll share your fate."

"She's yours, Jim. I promise."

"Your promises are lies!" he screams into my face. I taste his acrid breath. "I've wasted so much time on you! I've searched fucking everywhere. How the fuck could you stay hidden from me for so long!?" Jim paces back and forth in front of me, brandishing the knife.

"I'm sorry. You were a good man. I should never have left," I say as my body trembles due to its plunging temperature.

"DON'T PATRONIZE ME!" He punches me across the jaw with the hand holding the knife.

When I wake up, I'm soaked to the bone. My face and leg hurt.

"Open your fucking eyes!" Jim stands over me with a filthy soup pot.

I'm confused. I remember him hitting me, and I must have passed out.

My clothes are drenched with ice-cold water. I'm going to freeze to death.

"We can talk this out." I feel vulnerable and helpless. I'm tied up with duct tape, my baby's in the next room asleep in a drug-induced coma, and Jim intends on murdering me.

My teeth start chattering uncontrollably as I begin to shiver.

"You had a sweet cunt until you got fat and loose from the baby."

I cringe—I hate that word. He's called me that so many times.

"In fact, it was so sweet that I'm thinking about having a go with you one more time." He runs the knife up my leg now and positions the tip of it at my inner thigh.

Terror strangles me. The thought of the agony he can inflict engulfs and blankets me like a nightmare.

I check my breath. "You can't have real good sex unless you untie me from this chair."

It's a deadly game of cat and mouse, but I would do anything to have him untie me because that's my only hope.

"No one is coming for you," he reminds me.

I know.

The Amber Alert GPS tracker is disguised in Charlie's wristband, but it only works with my phone. I don't even know where my phone is. I never thought Jim would take me. *Why didn't I tell Josh about the GPS? I could have added his phone to it, too.* I wasn't thinking— things had been going so well that I'd let my guard down. *Deadly mistake. Don't dwell on it — think!*

"Then that gives us more time," I say.

Jim glides the knife now to my throat. I feel it prick my skin, and a bead of blood rolls down my neck.

"How can I trust you?" he sneers.

I imagine Charlie alone with him after I'm gone. I can taste her fear.

"I guess you can't, Jim. But isn't that what makes it more interesting? The gamble?" I lean into the knife, cutting myself deeper, and it startles him enough that he takes a step back.

If he's going to kill me, it will be on my terms. I will do everything I can to cooperate and get my little girl safe.

"Do you know where we are?" he asks like he's holding all the cards.

"I don't know, but I've been in better. Couldn't you afford the room with the mini-bar?" I chide, my body shaking violently from the cold and my own dread.

"Scream," he commands.

"I don't want to wake up the baby."

"Oh, you won't wake her. I injected her with the same shit doctors give patients before surgery." He's so pleased with himself. "Now scream!"

He forces the knife into the muscle of my leg and twists it.

I scream. It's guttural and bone-chilling, like a wild animal caught in a hunter's trap.

Jim smiles menacingly as he rips out the blade. "There now. No one within miles—no houses, no nothing. We aren't even on a main route, so if you're thinking about running, you'd freeze to death before you got to someone who'd help you." He walks around me again, sometimes touching me with his knife, just so I remember. "And who would help you? Your own mama didn't want you. You've got no daddy. You got no one, no friends, no relatives—the only person you ever belonged to was me. No one even looked for you after you left. Unloved, unwanted piece of trash." He laughs. "All I'll be doing is taking out the garbage."

"Fuck you! I know love. You pathetic excuse for a man—kidnapping a little girl and your ex-wife—"

"WIFE!" Jim shouts. "NOT EX! You are STILL my wife!"

"And look at you, cutting me up while my hands are tied behind my back." I'm seething. The cold isn't even bothering me anymore. Maybe I'm not here anymore. Maybe my soul is already gone, and my body's been left to fight because I don't feel real. "Tying up a girl and acting all big and bad. You're not a man, you're a pussy."

Jim slaps me across the face. "Bitch!"

But I won't stop. I can't. "If you were a real man, you'd let me loose and take your chances on a real fight."

I see the confusion behind his eyes. That's what I want.

"You know, I could just keep you here!" he rages. "And do what I want to you for as long as I want."

I might not like the prospect, but I'm not dead yet, so every moment is a moment closer to freedom.

A cell phone rings from his pocket. "We're not finished." He points the knife at me.

He turns and walks into the hallway for privacy, but I can hear everything. Whoever is on the phone is in on the plan with him.

"Yeah," he says. "Got them both. It was fucking easy. I even got a third bitch in the process."

Ayana. I wince. *Third bitch?*

An extra dose of fright surges through my veins. He doesn't mean to keep Charlie alive. He's going to kill her too.

"How much longer before you get here?"

He's bringing in someone else? To help him? Any hope I've conjured deflates.

"Awesome, man. Yeah, we should be done in time for dinner." He laughs.

We.

There is nothing within my reach! I'm in the middle of the fucking floor! I don't have nails long or sharp enough to break through the tape.

Then I remember. I work the tape by twisting the wrists side to side.

I start twisting fast.

I listen to Jim take another piss.

As he does, I hear his friend's car pull up outside.

I can't stop fucking shaking!

Suddenly, the duct tape gives way, and a second later, it snaps.

I broke the tape!

Another moment passes, and Jim's footfalls are advancing down the hallway.

God, he's coming back!

Quickly, I bend and rip the tape from one ankle. I'm about to start on the other one, but I'm startled when his buddy bangs on the door.

I know the door is locked right now, and I know my chances of survival are zero if I have to contend with two of them.

Jim comes out from the hallway with his eyes on the door.

Josh told me to always hit first.

As he comes through the main room to get to the door, I don't waste time. With the element of surprise, I leap to my free foot, position my weight for balance, and power-kick with my foot that's still attached to the chair. It's a high kick, causing the metal folding chair to strike him in the head.

There's such force, and the speed of the chair creates so much momentum that as Jim buckles to the floor, I'm thrown with the chair into the kitchen counter.

"FUCKING WHORE!" he yells. "You're going to pay heavily for that!"

I don't have time. I've got to get this fucking chair *off* of me! The tape is already half ripped. I tear it the rest of the way, spin myself to my feet and wield the chair in front of me as a weapon. Unfortunately, I know he's a lot stronger than me.

Getting a good look at Jim, who is now back to standing, I see that the chair did some damage. His nose is gushing blood again, and the side of his face is scraped and inflamed. He's poised to charge at me.

I blank out my mind, ignoring the killer who's smashing through the door.

Strategy—battle consciously, not emotionally, Josh would say. *Turn your hip—elbows move with knees—use your every muscle to feed torque into the blow.*

I pivot away from Jim's rush and crack the chair over his back with all my might.

Jim drops while the chair breaks free from my hold.

I race to my bag, and my fingers catch hold of the fabric.

Jim's arms lock around my waist, and as he throws me onto the floor, the bag falls with me. The air knocks out of my lungs, and now he has the advantage as his full weight crushes my stomach. I can't breathe.

"Fuck it, bitch. We can do it this way instead." He smiles. Blood cakes his teeth and mingles with his spit, dripping to my face.

He slides my bag out of my reach. My hope goes with it.

The front door splinters and crashes open.

"What the fuck!" Jim looks up angrily and shouts.

A boot sails over my head and catches Jim under his chin, sending him vaulting away from me.

I don't know what kind of altercation he and his partner had or what is going on. I have to move, but the edges of my vision blur, maybe from a lack of oxygen. I ignore it and crawl behind the overturned table. *I have to get my bag!*

Looking up to see where the two men are, I see Josh. He's fighting Jim.

Josh?! I blink. *Am I hallucinating?*

I shake my head to try to bring myself to my senses and crawl madly toward my bag. There's so much blood coming from my leg, and I keep slipping.

"SOPHIE!" It's Josh's voice.

I look up. In a matter of seconds, Jim has his knife in front of him, ready to cut Josh. Josh backs away just enough to get out of range but still close enough to get control of Jim's knife arm. The knife clanks to the floor, and Josh punches Jim ferociously.

I don't know how it's Josh, but it is.

I stand and move shakily into the tiny hallway, where I see the bathroom on one side and a room on the other. There's my baby. Charlie is laid out over the top of a bare mattress with only the clothes she was captured in—her pink coat and pants.

She looks lifeless. I can't tell if she's breathing!

"SOPHIE?!" Josh shouts.

"Back here!" My hoarse voice shakes and cracks.

Josh races into the room.

"We got to get her warm," I cry.

He takes a quick look at me, pulls off his coat and wraps it around my shoulders before picking Charlie up from the bed. In one arm he holds Charlie, in the other he holds all of my body weight as he gets the two of us out of the bedroom and to the front door.

To the right, I see Jim sprawled over the floor, knocked out in a bloody heap.

Josh stoops and throws me over his shoulder before carrying us to the car. "We have to get you two to the hospital." He sets me in the bucket seat of his Vertigo first, then lays Charlie over my lap before closing the door.

Relief floods through me at our rescue. I hold Charlie's little body against me; reaching my hand under her coat, I can feel the weak rising and falling of her chest. She's breathing, but only barely.

Before Josh gets to the open driver's side, a silver sedan tears into the parking lot, kicking up snow and gravel.

"Jim has a partner!" I say as loud as I can between the brutal grinding of my teeth.

The car stops, and a man leaps out and shouts, "Who the fuck are you?"

"Get back in your car before I rip you to pieces," Josh threatens.

The guy throws him a sideways glance, and then he sees me in the front seat.

"What are they doing in there?" he barks.

It's then that Charlie starts to cough. Immediately, it becomes choking and sputtering. *She could be drowning in her own vomit!* I flip her over onto her side between the two front seats, and she immediately throws up.

When I face forward, Jim—broken and bloodied—is out of the cabin and pointing a shotgun at Josh.

"Motherfucker thinks he can come in here and FUCK UP MY LIFE!" Jim's voice cracks.

My bag is at my feet. I must have clutched onto it as Josh moved me out here.

When the gun goes off, the sound of it reverberates through the empty, snow-encrusted landscape.

Out of my peripheral, I see Josh turn his head toward me, but my focus is on Jim as he falls face-first into the dirty snow.

Police sirens scream in the background of my haze-filled mind. Jim's partner runs toward his car. Josh runs to me.

I'm almost surprised my numb fingers were able to pull the trigger.

CHAPTER TWENTY-THREE

SOPHIE

"Come on, scrapper, come back to me." Josh's voice is pained and choked.

Where's Charlie? I think I form the words, but I don't hear them come out of my mouth.

"Nurse! She's opening her eyes!"

I swallow. "Josh." It barely comes out.

"Oh God, Sophie! I'm right here." His warm hand squeezes mine gently.

"Charlie …"

"She's fine. She's safe at home with my mom," he says quickly.

I'm confused.

Josh continues. "The doctor kept her here for 24-hour observation. Once the ketamine was expelled from her body, she was fine."

Ketamine—Jim.

"She's okay," I say. Emotion overtakes me; weakly, I begin to cry.

"You're my scrapper." Josh leans over, buries his face in the crook of my neck and holds me. His tears fall, warm and wet, down my neck. "The doctors weren't so sure about you, though. You've been out three days." He sits up to look at me again and swipes the tears away from his face before he whispers huskily, "You fought real good, scrapper."

A nurse comes rushing to the bed. "The doctor is on his way," she tells Josh, then holds a small pen light up to my eyes. "Hello, Sophie. Can you follow the light with your eyes?" She checks my eye movement, then shoots a barrage of questions at me, like what my name is, when and where was I born, what year we're in and my profession.

The doctor comes in next with more nurses and machines.

After talking to me and giving me some physical tests—they check my reflexes, and test whether or not I can feel my feet, toes, fingers and hands—he seems satisfied and smiles at me and Josh, "I think Sophie is going to be just fine."

Josh moves his face close to mine. "Do you remember that you love me?"

A strained laugh wheezes through my lungs. "That I remember the best."

DALLOWAY TAPS OUT.

The referee comes over and hands the coveted golden belt to Josh "The Jackhammer" North, who then lifts his arms victoriously into the air.

I'm so proud of him!

The audience goes insane, and the Jumbotron shows a close-up as the ref saunters over with the microphone and asks Josh about his motivation for the fight.

"One word," he says. "Sophie."

The crowd cheers and Josh shouts into the mic over them, "Sophie, I need you to come up here for a minute. I have a question to ask you."

Phillip Phillips' song "Unpack Your Heart" plays through the sound system. Caruso, who's standing on the side of the cage, reaches down for my hand. He wears a big, knowing smile as he, Silva and McGee pull me up and into the octagon.

I'm more than a little disoriented as I walk tentatively to the middle of the mat. Josh's beautiful, albeit bruised, smile puts me completely at ease in front of the thousands of people yelling in the stands and the millions watching on the television. I walk right into his chest, and he closes me in with his perfect, muscled arms, where I feel so safe and secure.

The music is turned down and plays softly in the background as Josh speaks through the microphone.

"Sophie Garner …
I'm going to make you forget every man
    you ever knew
I'm going to heal your heart from every
    broken I love you
I'm going to take on your old demons,
    chase the shadows until day;
I'll cherish you forever and never go
    away.
I'm going to love you like you've
    never seen
Darlin', I'm the only man that you're ever
    going to need."

The words sink in. I pull back, and our eyes meet. He moves his finger and, from the title belt, drops a string with a gorgeous platinum and diamond ring hanging at the end of it.

"You're everything to me … let me be everything to you."

"You already are," I say, crying as if it's just the two of us.

"Say yes, Mommy," Charlie's sweet little voice

tells me. I look beside me, and there she is, tugging on my long blouse.

The entire North family clan, along with the Ink and Steel clan, are now standing ringside next to Silva, McGee and Caruso. They're all smiling. I guess they were all in on the big secret.

"Mommy?"

I lift Charlie onto my hip—we are a package deal, after all.

"What do you say, scrapper?" Josh touches his forehead to mine affectionately.

I tumble into the depths of his warm, brown eyes. Lifting a soft palm, I rest it over his jaw, which clenches sexily with the action.

"Yes."

EPILOGUE

SOPHIE

I wake up to the obnoxious noise of a hammer. *What in the world?*

Wrapping myself in my robe I take a quick peek at the clock—six a.m.—*Josh!* I move into the hallway and in the direction of the offense.

Charlie is giggling.

Josh says, "I told you I was going to do something special with it."

"What is going on?" My voice is still sluggish with sleep.

"Sorry for waking you, but I had to do this before I left," Josh apologizes. He doesn't look the least bit sorry as he smiles proudly at his handiwork.

Charlie jumps up and down in excitement, then squeezes Josh's leg for all she's worth.

My eyes follow his. There on the wall, next to

the black frames I got him for Christmas, is a big pink frame showcasing Charlie's pink hand-printed wrapping paper.

"You framed it." The loving sentiment fills me. "Oh, Josh, it's beautiful!"

When I left the hospital, Josh told me he was "bringing me home'—that meant to his place. Charlie and I have been "home" ever since. And even though I like his style, he wanted to give me the gift of putting my own home together. We shopped together, and I got to pick out all new furnishings, linens and décor. Charlie now has her very own room, just the way she's always wanted.

Now Josh has hung the frames I gave him in the living room and added—as a surprise—Charlie's art right next to them.

"These totally belong here," he says, still admiring the wall. "Especially that one." He points to the fifth frame with the hammer.

The fifth frame is the one I'd left empty, telling him that he'd have to fill it with a picture of the next thing he achieved, even if he had to go through fear to do it.

Tears well into my eyes. "Josh." I pull my quivering lip into my teeth to still it. Tears spill down my face.

"Our first family photo," he says as he picks Charlie up and settles her on his hip. "What do you think, scrapper?" Josh tosses the hammer to the couch, gets his arm around my shoulders and yanks me to him.

It's a photograph of me, Charlie and Josh. It was an impromptu picture taken by his mom. When I gave him the frames, I never thought for a second that there would be a picture of us in any of them.

I cry happy tears.

Peaceful tears.

We're finally at home tears.

The End

A FINAL NOTE FROM THE AUTHOR

Dear Reader,

Your voice and opinion are very important to me.

If you enjoyed DARE, please consider leaving a review.

Even just a few words mean a lot <3

Now that you've finished DARE, jump right into Liam and Quinn's story in

BURN (Brothers of Ink and Steel Book 2)
https://amzn.to/44vucc2

ABOUT THE AUTHOR

Aurora Wilding is a *USA Today* and Top 100 Amazon bestselling author.

From gritty angst and dark romance to suspense, romantic comedy, and everything in between, Aurora crafts heart-racing stories with intense chemistry, steamy passion, irresistible swoon, and always a Happily-Ever-After.

She can often be found traveling and adventuring in her van, whether on the beach or in the mountains, daydreaming and weaving tales about heroic alpha males and strong-willed heroines, all while plotting the perfect ways to make them fall in love!

Follow Aurora Wilding

Website:
www.aurorawilding.com

Goodreads
Become a fan and friend:

https://www.goodreads.com/author/show/
49928567.Aurora_Wilding

facebook.com/aurorawildingromance

tiktok.com/@aurora.wilding.romance

amazon.com/author/aurorawilding

bookbub.com/authors/aurora-wildin

youtube.com/@AuroraWildingRomance

ALSO BY AURORA WILDING

True North and Brothers of Ink and Steel are an Interconnected Series. DARE is the "bridge book" to both.

All books in each series can be read as standalones.

TRUE NORTH SERIES

Finding Home (True North Book 1):

A Second Chance, Military, Brother's Best Friend Romance

https://amzn.to/3VMFLJ6

Finding Us (True North Book 2):

A Small Town, Friends to Lovers, Boss's Daughter Romance

https://amzn.to/3xk1ChU

Finding Now (True North Book 3):

A Reverse Age Gap, Professor/Student, Rockstar Romance

https://amzn.to/3yYDVMn

BROTHERS OF INK AND STEEL SERIES

Dare (Brothers of Ink and Steel Book 1)

https://amzn.to/3UMTm2G

Burn (Brothers of Ink and Steel Book 2)

https://amzn.to/44vucc2

Dare You Forever (Brothers of Ink and Steel Novella 2.5)

https://amzn.to/4ag7DcK

Defy (Brothers of Ink and Steel Book 3)

https://amzn.to/3WxM44e

Risk (Brothers of Ink and Steel Book 4)

https://amzn.to/4bs2D5J

STANDALONE NOVELS

Stripped (A Romantic Comedy)

My Book

amazon.com/dp/B01DKVAE2Y

Orion (A Constellations Novel) A Military Thriller Romance

My Book

amazon.com/dp/B0777MKM9T